YAMADA MONOGATARI:
TO BREAK THE DEMON GATE

BOOKS BY RICHARD PARKS

YAMADA MONOGATARI:
TO BREAK THE DEMON GATE

RICHARD PARKS

PRIME BOOKS

Parks

YAMADA MONOGATARI:
TO BREAK THE DEMON GATE

Prime Books
www.prime-books.com

For more information, contact Prime Books:
prime@prime-books.com

ISBN: 978-1-60701-435-5 (print)
ISBN: 978-1-60701-441-6 (ebook)

For Fritz Leiber,
who proved not only that genre wasn't a cage,
but that there was no cage.

PART ONE

No mountain stands aside,
Nor seas grow calm at our word.
The World is a Dream,
But not of our dreaming.
All must weep, but who will dance?

In the early evening a tiny moth-demon was trying to batter its way into my room through a tear in the paper screen, no doubt attracted by the scent of poverty. I was debating whether to frighten the silly thing away or simply crush it, when the Widow Tamahara's delightful voice sent the poor creature fluttering away as fast as its little wings could carry it.

"Yamada-san, you have a visitor!"

Tamahara kneeled by the shoji screen that was the only door to my rooms. Besides the volume, there was an edge of excitement in the formidable old woman's voice that worried me just a little. The fact that aristocracy impressed her had worked to my advantage more than once when the rent was late, but her deference meant that just about anyone could get closer to me than might be healthy; that is, if they were of the right station in life. Anyone else giving a hint of trouble in her establishment she would throw out on their ear, if they were lucky.

"Who is it, Tamahara-san?"

"A messenger and that is all I know. She's waiting in the courtyard with her escort."

She?

Well, that explained why Widow Tamahara had not simply brought the person to my rooms. That would not have been proper, and the Widow Tamahara always did the right thing, to the degree that she understood what "the right thing" was.

"Just a moment," I said.

After some thought I tucked a long dagger into my sleeve but left my *tachi* where it was. I wasn't wearing my best clothes, but my best would have been equally unimpressive. At least everything was clean. I followed Tamahara out into the courtyard. The sun had set, but there was light enough still.

The woman kneeled near a small pine tree, flanked on either side by her escorts. No rough provincial warriors these; the two men were polite, impassive, well-dressed and well-armed. The younger man wore the red and black clothing and bore the butterfly *mon* of the Taira Clan, the other wore plain black and bore no family crest or identification at all. I judged them as best I could. The escort wearing Taira livery I think I could have bested, if absolutely necessary and with a bit of luck. But the other . . . well, let's just say I didn't want any trouble. I also could not escape the feeling that we had met before.

I bowed formally and then kneeled in front of the woman. I noted the rightmost warrior's quick glance at my sleeve and how he inched almost imperceptibly closer, all the while not appearing to have noticed or moved at all. The man was even more formidable than I had suspected, but now my attention was on the woman.

Her *kimono* was very simple, as befitted a servant. Two shades of blue at most, though impeccably appropriate for the time of year. She wore a *boshi* with a long veil that circled the brim and hid her features. Naturally, she did not remove it. She merely bowed again from her seated position and held out a scroll resting on the palms of her small hands.

I took the offered scroll, all the while careful to make no sudden movements, and unrolled it to read:

> *The Peony bows*
> *to no avail; the March wind*
> *is fierce, unceasing.*

So there I was, caught like a rabbit in a snare. Not that my heart had ever left the Imperial Compound, but I don't think I'd truly understood how easy it would be to pull back the rest of me as well. Just the first three lines of a *tanka*, the *kami-no-ku*, was all she needed. The poem was not yet complete, of course; the part of the poem known as the *shimo-no-ku*, the lower phrase, was missing. That part was up to me.

I looked at the shadow of the woman's face, hidden behind the veil. "Are you instructed to await my reply?"

Again she bowed without speaking. The escort on her right produced a pen case and ink. I considered for a few moments, then added the following two lines:

> *The donkey kneels down to rest.*
> *In his shadow, flowers grow.*

My poetic skills—never more than adequate—were more than a little rusty, and the result was no better than passable. Yet the form was correct and the meaning, like that of the first segment, more than clear to the one who would read it. The woman took the message from me, bowed again, then rose as one with her escorts and withdrew quickly without further ceremony.

The Widow Tamahara watched all this from the discreet distance of the veranda encircling the courtyard.

"Is this work?" she asked when I passed her on the way back to my room. "Will you be paid?"

" 'Yes' seems the likely answer to both," I said, though that was mostly to placate the old woman. I was fairly certain that I would be the one paying, one way or the other.

Later that evening I didn't bother to prepare my bedding. I waited, fully clothed and in the darkness of my room, for my inevitable visitor. The summons was clear and urgent, but I couldn't simply answer it. The matter was much more complicated than that.

The full moon cast the man's shadow across the thin screen that was my doorway. It wasn't a mistake; he wanted me to know he was there. I pulled the screen aside, but I was pretty sure I knew who would be waiting.

He kneeled on the veranda, the hilt of his sword clearly visible. "Lord Yamada? My name is Kanemore."

"Lord" was technically correct but a little jarring to hear applied to me again, especially coming from a man who was the son of an emperor. I finally realized who he was.

"Prince Kanemore. You were named after the poet, Taira no Kanemore, weren't you?" I asked.

He smiled then, or perhaps it was a trick of the moonlight.

"My mother thought that having a famous poet for a namesake might gentle my nature. In that I fear she was mistaken. So, you remember me?"

"I do. Even when you were not at Court, your sister Princess Teiko always spoke highly of you."

He smiled faintly. "And so back to the matter at hand: Lord Yamada, I am charged to bring you safely to the Imperial Compound."

The light was poor, but I used what there was to study the man a little more closely than I'd had time to do at our meeting earlier in the day when he'd formed part of the veiled woman's escort. He was somewhat younger than I, perhaps thirty or so, and quite handsome except for a fresh scar that began on his left cheek and reached his jaw line.

He studied me just as intently; I didn't want to speculate on what his conclusions might be. Whether caused by my involvement or the situation itself—and I still didn't have any idea what that was—Kanemore was not happy. His face betrayed nothing, but his entire being was as tense as a bow at full draw.

"I am ready, Prince Kanemore."

"Just Kanemore, please. With the Emperor's permission, I will renounce my title and start a new clan, since it is neither my destiny nor wish to ascend the throne."

"I am Goji. Lead on then."

The streets were dark and poorly lit. I saw the flare of an *onibi* down an alleyway and knew the ghosts were about. At this time of evening demons were a possibility too, but one of the beauties of Kyoto was that the multitude of temples and shrines tended to make the atmosphere uncomfortable for most of the fiercer demons and monsters. The rest, like the moth-demon, were used to skulking about the niches and small spaces of the city, unnoticed and deliberately so—being vulnerable to both exorcism and common steel.

We reached the thoroughfare known as Shijo without incident and turned west. The full moon was high now, and I wished there had been time to turn east to Shijo Bridge, where the view would be so much better with the moonlight reflecting off the water. However, we did pass a small fountain, and Kanemore's attention was focused on the moon's reflection as he paused for a second or two to admire it. I found this oddly reassuring; a man who did not pause to view a full moon at opportunity had no soul, but the fact that his moon-viewing amounted to little more than a hesitation on the way to the Imperial Compound showed his attention to duty. I already knew I did not want Kanemore as my enemy. Now I wondered if we could be friends.

"Do you know what this is about?" I asked.

"Explanations are best left to my sister," he said. "My understanding is far from complete."

"At this point I would be glad of scraps. I only know that Princess Teiko is in difficulty—"

He corrected me instantly. "It is her son Takahito that concerns my sister most. She always thinks of him first."

I didn't like the direction this conversation was taking. "Is Takahito unwell?"

"He is healthy," Kanemore said, "and still his half-brother's heir, at present."

That was far too ominous. "Kanemore-san, it was my understanding that the late Emperor only allowed the current

Emperor to ascend on the condition that Takahito be named heir after him, and that Takahito would in turn inhabit the Sanjo Palace and take his royal grandfather's nickname upon his eventual ascent. Is Emperor Reizei thinking of defying his father's wishes?"

Kanemore looked uncomfortable. "There have been . . . complications. Plus, the Fujiwara favor another candidate, Prince Norihira. He is considered more agreeable. I can say no more for now." More agreeable because, unlike Princess Teiko, Norihira's mother was Fujiwara.

I considered this. If the Fujiwara Clan supported another candidate, then this was bad news for Takahito. As the Taira and Minamoto and other military families were the might of the Emperor, so were the Fujiwara his administration. Court ministers and minor officials alike were drawn primarily from their ranks. All power was the Emperor's in theory, but in practice his role was mostly ceremonial. It was the Fujiwara, especially Chancellor Yorimichi, who kept the government in motion.

Still, the politics of the Imperial Court and the machinations of the Fujiwara were both subjects I had happily abandoned years ago. Now it appeared that I needed to renew my understanding and quickly. Despite my desire to question him further, I knew that Kanemore had said all he was going to say on the matter for now. I changed the subject.

"Did you see much fighting while you were in the north?"

"A bit," he admitted. "The Abe Clan is contained, but not yet pacified. I fear more trouble . . . " he trailed off, then stopped and turned toward me. "Lord Yamada, are you a seer in addition to your other rumored talents? How did you know I had been in the north?"

I tried to keep from smiling. "That scar on your jaw is from a blade and fairly new. Even if you were inclined to brawling—which I seriously doubt—I don't believe the average drunken *bushi* could so much as touch you. That leaves the northern campaigns as the only reasonable conclusion. It was an educated guess, no more."

He rubbed his scar thoughtfully. "Impressive, even so. But the hour grows late, and I think we should be on our way."

We had taken no more than a few steps when two *bushi* staggered out of a nearby drinking establishment. One collided with me and muttered a slurred curse and reached for his sword. I didn't give the fool time to draw it. I struck him with my open palm square on the chin and his head snapped back and collided with a very hard lintel post. This was fortunate for him, since Kanemore's *tachi* was already clear of its scabbard and poised for the blow swordsmen liked to call "the pear splitter", because a split pear is precisely what the victim's bisected head resembled once the blow was completed. I have no doubt that Kanemore would have demonstrated this classic technique on that drunken lout had I not been in the path of his sword. The drunk's equally inebriated companion had his own sword half-drawn, but took a long look at Kanemore and thought better of it. He sheathed his sword, bowed in a rather grudging apology, and helped his addled friend to his feet. Together they staggered off into the night.

Kanemore watched them disappear before he put his sword away. "That, too, was impressive. But pointless. You should have let me kill him. One less provincial thug swaggering about the city. Who would miss him?"

I sighed. "His lord, for a start, who would demand an explanation. The man's companion would say one thing and we

14

would say another, and justice ministers would become involved and there would be time spent away from the matter at hand that I don't think we can afford. Or am I mistaken?"

Kanemore smiled. "I must again concede that you are not. I'm beginning to see why my honored sister has summoned you. May your lack of error continue, for all our sakes."

⛩

The South Gate to the Imperial Compound was closest, but Kanemore led me to the East Gate, which was guarded by *bushi* in the red and black Taira colors, one of whom I recognized as the messenger's other escort. They stood aside for Kanemore and no questions were asked.

We weren't going to the Palace proper. The Imperial Compound covered a large area in the city, and there were many smaller buildings of various function spread out through the grounds, including houses for government officials and some minor palaces. Other palaces and mansions such as the Sanjo Palace, which had given Teiko's father his nickname, were scattered throughout the city itself.

Considering our destination, it was clear we needed to attract as little attention as possible; Kanemore led me through some of the more obscure garden paths. At least, they were obscure to other people. I remembered most of them from my time at Court. Losing access to the gardens was one of two regrets I had about leaving the Court.

Princess Teiko was the other.

Kanemore escorted me to a fine, large house; a small palace

actually, and quite suitable for the widow of an Emperor. A group of very well-dressed and important-looking visitors were leaving as we arrived, and we stepped aside on the walkway to let them pass. There was only one I recognized in the lamplight before I kneeled as courtesy demanded: Fujiwara no Sentaro, Deputy Minister of the Right and current Minister of Justice. It seemed only fitting—my one visit to the Compound in close to fifteen years and I *would* encounter my least-favorite person at the Imperial Court or probably anywhere else, now that I considered the matter. The coldness of Kanemore's demeanor as they walked by wasn't exactly lost on me either. If Sentaro recognized me, he gave no sign. Possibly he'd have forgotten me by now, but then a good politician did not forget an enemy while the enemy still drew breath.

"I gather Lord Sentaro is not in your favor?" I asked after they had gone.

"To call him a pig would be an insult to pigs," Kanemore said bluntly. "But he is the Minister of Justice, a skilled administrator, and has our Emperor's confidence. The gods may decree that he becomes Chancellor after Lord Yorimichi, as both his birth and luck seem to favor the man. My sister, for some reason I cannot fathom, bears his company from time to time."

I started to say something about the realities of court life but reconsidered. While the saints teach us that life is an illusion, Sentaro's presence indicated that, sadly, some aspects of life did not change, illusion or not. We climbed the steps to the veranda.

"Teiko-hime is expecting us," Kanemore said to the *bushi* flanking the doorway, but clearly they already knew that and stepped back as we approached. A servant girl pulled the screen aside, and we stepped into a large open room, impeccably furnished with bright silk cushions and flowers in artful arrangements, and lit by several paper lanterns. There was a dais on the far wall, curtained-off, and doubtless a sliding screen behind it that would allow someone to enter the room without being seen.

I had hoped to at least get a glimpse of Teiko, but of course that wasn't proper. I knew the rules, even if I didn't always follow them. Kanemore kneeled on a cushion near the dais, and I followed his example.

"My sister has been informed—" he started to say but didn't get to finish.

"Your older sister is here, Kanemore-kun."

Two more maids impeccably dressed in layered yellow and blue *kimonos* entered the room and pulled back the curtain. A translucent veil remained in front of the dais. I could see the ghostly form of a woman kneeling there, her long black hair down loose and flowing over her shoulders. I didn't need to see her clearly to know it was the same woman who had brought the message to me in the courtyard, whose face I had not seen then, either. No need—the way she moved and the elegance of a gesture, both betrayed her. Now I heard Princess Teiko's voice again, and that was more than enough.

Kanemore and I both bowed low.

There was silence, and then that beautiful voice again, chiding me. "A *donkey*, Lord Yamada? Honestly . . . "

I tried not to smile, but it was hard. "My poetry is somewhat . . . unpracticed, Teiko-hime."

"Teiko, please. We are old friends."

At this Kanemore gave me a hard glance, but I ignored

him. Formidable as he was, Kanemore was no longer the most dangerous person in my vicinity, and I needed all my attention for the one who was.

"I think there is something you wish to discuss with me," I said. "Is this possible?" It was the most polite way I knew to phrase the question, but Teiko waved it aside.

"There is no one within hearing," she said, "who has not already heard. You may speak plainly, Lord Yamada. I will do the same—I need your help."

"You have read my answer," I said.

"True, but you have not heard my trouble," Teiko said softly. "Listen and then tell me what you will or will not do. Now then— do you remember a young Fujiwara named Kiyoshi?"

That was a name I had not heard in a long time. Kiyoshi was about my age when I came to the Court as a very minor official of the household. Since he was handsome, bright, and a Fujiwara, his destiny seemed fixed. Like Kanemore, he chose the somewhat disreputable *bushi* path instead, and died fighting the northern barbarians. He was one of the few of that clan I could tolerate, and I sincerely mourned his death.

"I do remember him," I said.

"There is a rumor going around the Court that Kiyoshi was my lover and that my son Takahito is his issue, not my late husband's."

For a moment I could not speak. This matter was beyond serious. Gossip was close to the rule of law at Court. If this particular gossip was not silenced, both Takahito's and Teiko's positions at Court were in peril, and that was just for a start.

"Do you know who is responsible for the slander?"

"No. While it's true that Kiyoshi was very dear to me, we grew up together at Court and our affections to each other were as brother and sister, as was well understood at the time. You know this to be true."

I did, if I knew anything. "And you wish for me to discover the culprit? That will be . . . difficult."

She laughed softly then, decorously covering her face with her fan even though the veil prevented me from seeing her face clearly. "Lord Yamada, even if I knew who started the rumors, it would do little good. People repeat the gossip now without even knowing from whom they heard it. What I require now is tangible and very public proof that the rumors are false."

I considered. "I think that will be difficult as well. The only one who could swear to your innocence died fifteen years ago. Or am I to pursue his ghost?"

She laughed again. The sound was enchanting, but then everything about her was enchanting to me; there was a reason Princess Teiko was the most dangerous person in that room. I found myself feeling grateful the screen was in place as I forced myself to concentrate on the business at hand.

"Nothing so distasteful," she said. "Besides, Kiyoshi died in loving service to my husband, the late Emperor, and on the path he himself chose. If he left a ghost behind, I would be quite surprised. No, Lord Yamada, Kiyoshi left something far more reliable—a letter. He sent it to me when he was in the north, just before . . . his final battle. It was intended for his favorite and was accompanied by a second letter for me."

I frowned. "Why didn't he send this letter to the lady directly?"

She sighed then. "Lord Yamada, are you a donkey after all? He couldn't very well do so without compromising her. My friendship with Kiyoshi was well known; no one would think twice if I received a letter from him in those days. In his favorite's case, the situation was quite different. You know the penalty for a Lady of the Court who takes a lover openly."

I bowed again. I did know, and vividly: banishment or worse; yet, for someone born for the Court and knowing no other life, there probably *was* nothing worse. "Then clearly we need to acquire this letter. If it still exists, I imagine the lady in question will be reluctant to part with it. Who is she, if it is not indiscreet to ask?"

"Her name was Taira no Hoshiko, not that this is of consequence now. The letter was never delivered to her." Teiko raised her hand to silence me before I even began. "Do not think so ill of me, Lord Yamada. News of Kiyoshi's death reached us months before his letter did. By then my husband had given the wretched girl in marriage to the Lord of Hizen province as reward for some service or other, and I did not wish to risk complicating her new position. Since Kiyoshi's letter was not intended for me, I never opened it. I should have destroyed it, I know, but I could not."

"That decision was perhaps foolish but potentially fortunate. Though I presume there is a problem, or I would not be here?"

"The letter has been stolen, Lord Yamada. Without it I have no hope of saving my reputation and my son's future from the crush of gossip."

I let out a breath. "When did you notice the letter was missing?"

"Lord Sentaro says it disappeared three days ago."

Now I really didn't understand, and judging from the grunt to my immediate right, neither did Kanemore. "What has Lord Sentaro to do with this?"

"He is the Emperor's Minister of Justice. In order to clear my reputation I had to let him know of the letter's existence, and arrange a time for the letter to be read and witnessed. He asked that it be given to him for safekeeping. Since he was also Kiyoshi's uncle, I couldn't very well refuse."

She said it so calmly, and yet she had just admitted cutting her own throat. "Teiko-hime, as much as this pains me to say, the letter has surely been destroyed."

There was nothing but silence on the other side of the veil for several seconds, then she simply asked, "Oh? What makes you think so?"

I glanced at Kanemore, but there was no help from that direction. He looked as confused as I felt.

"Your pardon, Highness, but it's my understanding that the Fujiwara have their own candidate for the throne. As a member of that family, it is in Lord Sentaro's interest that the letter never resurface."

"Lord Sentaro is perhaps overly ambitious," Teiko said, and there was more than a hint of winter ice in her voice. "But he is also an honorable man. He was just here to acquaint me with the progress of the search. I believe him when he says the letter was stolen; I have less confidence in his ability to recover it. Lord Yamada, will you help me or not?"

I bowed again and made the only answer I could. "If it lies within my power, I will find that letter for you."

⛩

Kanemore and I did not speak again until we had taken our leave of Princess Teiko. Kanemore was the first to break the silence.

"That," he said after we had passed through the eastern gate, "was very strange." The man had, besides his martial prowess, quite a gift for understatement.

"You didn't know about the letter?"

"Teiko never mentioned it before, though it doesn't surprise me. Yet . . . "

"The business with the Minister of Justice does surprise you, yes?"

He looked at me. "Since my sister trusts you, I will speak plainly—Lord Sentaro is Chancellor Yorimichi's primary agent in the Fujiwara opposition to Takahito. If I had been in Lord Sentaro's place, I would have destroyed that letter the moment it fell into my hands and danced a tribute to the Gods of luck while it burned."

I rubbed my chin. "Yet Teiko-hime is convinced the letter was not destroyed."

Kanemore grunted again. "Over the years I've gone where my Emperor and his government have required. My sister, on the other hand, knows no world other than the Imperial Court. If Teiko were a *koi*, the Court would be her pond, if you take my meaning. So why would something that is immediately obvious to us both be so unclear to her?"

"Perhaps we're the ones who aren't clear," I said. "Highness, let's assume for that moment that your sister is right and that the letter was simply stolen. That would mean that Lord Sentaro had a good reason for not destroying it in the first place."

"That makes sense. Yet I'm having some difficulty imagining that reason," Kanemore admitted.

"As am I."

I looked around. Our path paralleled the river Kamo for a time, then turned southwest. Despite the lateness of the hour, there were a few people on the road, apparently all in a rush to reach their destinations. Demons were about at this time of night, and everyone's hurry and wariness was understandable. Kanemore and I were the only ones walking at a normal pace by the light of the setting moon.

"Your escort duties must be over by now and, as I'm sure you know, I'm used to moving about the city on my own," I said.

Kanemore looked a little uncomfortable. "It was Teiko's request. I know you can take care of yourself under most circumstances," Kanemore said, and it almost sounded like a compliment, "but if someone *did* steal the letter, they obviously would not want it found, and your audience with my sister will not be a secret. Sentaro himself saw you, for one."

"I didn't think he recognized me."

"I would not depend on that," Kanemore said drily. "The man forgets nothing. His enemies, doubly so."

"You flatter me. I was no threat to him, no matter how I might have wished otherwise."

"If I may be so impolite as to ask, why did you resign your position and leave the Court? It could not have been easy to secure the appointment in the first place."

Not easy at all, considering the stain on my family's honor, though of course Prince Kanemore was too polite to mention it. While I had little doubt that he had already heard the story from Teiko, I didn't mind repeating events as I remembered them.

"Your sister was kind to me, in those early days. Of course there

23

would be those at Court who chose to misinterpret her interest, especially after the late Emperor chose her as a secondary wife. I had become a potential embarrassment to Princess Teiko, as Lord Sentaro delighted in making known to me."

"Meaning he would have made certain of it," Kanemore said. "I wondered."

I shrugged. "I made my choice. Destiny is neither cruel nor kind. So, Kanemore-san, I've answered a personal question of yours, now I must ask one of you: what are you afraid of?"

"Death," he said immediately. "I've never let that fear prevent me from doing what I must, but the fear remains."

"That just means you're not a fool, which I already knew. So, you fear death. Do you fear things that are already dead?"

"No . . . well, not especially," he said, though he didn't sound completely convincing or convinced. "Why do you ask?"

"I ask because I'm going to need help. If the letter is in the Imperial Compound, it's beyond even your reach. Searching would be both dangerous and time-consuming."

"Certainly," Kanemore agreed. "Yet what's the alternative?"

"The 'help' I spoke of. We're going to need several measures of uncooked rice."

He frowned. "I know where such can be had. Are you hungry?"

"No. But I can assure you that my informant is."

About an hour later we passed through Rashamon, the southwest gate. There was no one about at this hour. The southwest exit of the city, like the northeast, was not a fortunate direction as the priests often said these were the directions from which both demons and trouble in general could enter the city. I sometimes wondered why anyone bothered to build gates at such places, since it seemed to be asking for trouble, yet I supposed the demands of roads and travelers outweighed the risks. Even so, unlike the Demon Gate to the northeast, the area around Rashamon was mostly deserted. Even the most loyal and hardened *bushi* would not accept a night watch at the Rasha Gate, and it was pretty much left open to the demons and ghosts, and anyone else who cared to use it.

The bridge I sought was part of a ruined family compound just outside the city proper, now marked by a brokendown wall and the remnants of a garden. In another place I would have thought this the aftermath of a war, but not here. Still, death often led to the abandonment of a home; no doubt this family had transferred their fortunes elsewhere and allowed this place to go to ruin. It was wasteful, but not unusual.

The compound was still in darkness, but there was a glow in the east; dawn was coming. I hurried through the ruins while Kanemore kept pace with me, his hand on his sword. There were vines growing on the stone bridge on the far side of the garden, but it was still intact and passable, giving an easy path over the wide stream beneath it. Not that crossing the stream was the issue. I pulled out one of the small bags of uncooked rice that Kanemore had supplied and opened it to let the scent drift freely on the night breezes.

The red lantern appeared almost instantly. It floated over the curve of the bridge as if carried by someone invisible, but that wasn't really the case—the lantern carried itself. Its one glowing eye opened, and then its mouth.

I hadn't spoken to the ghost in some time, and perhaps I was misremembering, but it seemed much bigger than it had been on our last meeting. Still, that wasn't what caught my immediate attention—it was the creature's long, pointed teeth.

Seita did not have teeth . . .

"Lord Yamada, drop!"

I didn't question or hesitate but threw myself flat on the ground, just as the lantern surged forward and its mouth changed into a gaping maw. A shadow loomed over me, and then there was a flash of silver in the poor light. The lantern shrieked and then dissolved in a flare of light as if burning to ashes from within. I looked up to see the neatly sliced-open corpse of a *youkai* lying a few feet away from me. The thing was ugly, even for a monster, and a full eight feet tall, most of that consisting of mouth. The creature already stank like a cesspit, and in another moment it dissolved into black sludge and then vanished. I saw what looked like a scrap of paper fluttering on a weed before it blew away into the darkness.

Where did the thing go?

I didn't have time to ponder; another lantern appeared on the bridge, and Kanemore made ready, but I got to my feet quickly.

"Stop. It's all right."

And so it was. Seita came gliding over the bridge, with his one eye cautiously watching the pair of us. Now I recognized the tear in the paper near his base and his generally tatty appearance; things that had been missing from the imposter's disguise.

"Thank you for ridding me of that unpleasant fellow," he said, "but don't think for a moment that will warrant a reduction in my fee."

Kanemore just stared at the ghost for a moment, then glanced at me, but I indicated silence. "Seita-san, you at least owe me an explanation for allowing your patron to walk into an ambush. How long has that thing been here?"

I think Seita tried to shrug, but that's hard to do when your usual manifestation is a red paper lantern with one eye, one mouth and no arms, legs, or shoulders.

"A day or so. Damned impertinent of it to usurp my bridge, but it was strong and I couldn't make it leave. I think it was waiting on someone. You, perhaps?"

"Perhaps? Almost certainly, yet that doesn't concern me now. I need your services."

"So I assumed," said the lantern. "What do you want to know?"

"A letter was stolen from the Imperial Compound three days ago. I need to know who took it and where that letter is now. It bears the scent of Fujiwara no Kiyoshi, among others."

Kanemore could remain silent no more. He leaned close and whispered, "Can this thing be trusted?"

"That 'thing' remark raises the price," Seita said. "Four bowls."

"I apologize on behalf of my companion. Two now," I countered, "two more when the information is delivered. Bring the answer by tomorrow night, and I'll add an extra bowl."

The lantern grinned very broadly. "Then you can produce five bowls of uncooked rice right now. I have your answer."

That surprised me. I'd expected at least a day's delay. "Seita-san, I know you're very skilled or I wouldn't have come to you first, but how could you possibly know about the letter already? Were the *rei* involved?"

He looked a little insulted. "Lord Yamada, we ghosts have higher concerns than petty theft. This was the work of *shikigami.*

The fact that they were about in the first place caught my attention, but I do not know who sent them. That is a separate question and won't be answered so quickly or easily."

"Time is short. I'll settle for the location of the letter."

Seita gave us directions to where the letter was hidden. We left the rice in small bags, with chopsticks thrust upright through the openings as proper for an offering to the dead. I offered a quick prayer for Seita's soul, but we didn't stay to watch; I'd seen the ghost consume an offering before, and it was . . . unsettling.

"Can that thing be trusted?" Kanemore repeated when we were out of earshot of the bridge, "and what is this *shikigami* it was referring to?"

"As for trusting Seita, we shall soon know. That thing you killed at the bridge was a *shikigami*, and it's very strange to encounter one here. Thank you, by the way. I owe you my life."

Kanemore grunted. "My duty served, though you are quite welcome. Still, you make deals with ghosts, and encountering a simple monster is strange?"

"A *shikigami* is not a monster, simple or otherwise. A *youkai* is its own creature and has its own volition, nasty and evil though that may be. A *shikigami* is a created thing; it has no will of its own, only that of the one who created it."

He frowned. "Are you speaking of sorcery?"

"Yes," I said, "and of a high order. I should have realized when the thing disappeared. A monster or demon is a physical creature and, when slain, leaves a corpse like you or I would. A *shikigami* almost literally has no separate existence. When its purpose is served or its physical form too badly damaged, it simply disappears. At most it might leave a scrap of paper or some element of what was used to create it."

"So one of these artificial servants acquired the letter and hid it in the Rasha Gate. Fortunate, since that's on our way back into the city."

"Very fortunate."

Kanemore glanced at me. "You seem troubled. Do you doubt the ghost's information?"

"Say rather I'm pondering something I don't understand. There were rumors that Lord Sentaro dabbled in Chinese magic, even when I was at Court. Yet, even if that were true, why would he choose *shikigami* to spirit the letter away? It was in his possession to begin with; removing it and making that removal seem like theft would be simple enough to arrange without resorting to such means."

Kanemore shrugged. "I've heard these rumors as well, but I gave them no credence. Even so, it is the letter that concerns me, not the workings of Lord Sentaro's twisted mind."

Concentrating on the matter at hand seemed a very sensible suggestion, and I abandoned my musings as we approached the deserted Rasha Gate. At least, it had seemed deserted when we passed through it earlier that evening; I was not so certain of that now. I regretted having to leave my sword behind for my audience with Teiko-hime, but I still had my dagger, and I made certain it was loose in its sheath.

The gate structure loomed above us. We checked around the base as far as we could but found no obvious hiding places. Now and then I heard a faint rustle, like someone winding and unwinding a scroll. Kanemore was testing the looseness of a stone on the west side of the gate. I motioned him to be still and listened more closely. After a few moments the sound came again, from above.

This time Kanemore heard it, too. He put his sword aside in favor of his own long dagger, which he clenched in his teeth like a Chinese pirate as he climbed the wooden beams and crossbars that supported the gate. I quickly followed his example, or as quickly as I could manage. Kanemore climbed like a monkey, whereas I was not quite so nimble. Still, I was only a few seconds behind him when he reached the gap between the gate frame and the elaborate roof.

"Yamada-san, they are here!"

I didn't have to ask who "they" were. The first of the *shikigami* plummeted past, missing me by inches before it dissolved. If the body survived long enough to strike the flagstones, I never heard it, but then I wasn't listening. I hauled myself over the top beam and landed in a crouch.

I needn't have bothered; the gap under the roof was quite tall enough for me to stand. Kanemore had two other lumbering *shikigami* at bay, but a third moved to attack him from the rear. It was different from the other two. Snakelike, it slithered across the floor, fangs bared and its one yellow eye fixed on Kanemore's naked heel.

I was too far away.

"Behind you!"

I threw myself forward and buried my dagger in the creature near the tip of its tail, which was all I could reach. Even there the thing was as thick as my arm, but I felt the dagger pierce the tail completely and bury its tip in the wood beneath it. My attack barely slowed the creature; there was a sound like the tearing of paper as it ripped itself loose from my blade to get at Kanemore.

Kanemore glanced behind him and to my surprise took one step backward. Just as the thing's fangs reached for him, he very swiftly lifted his left foot, pointed the heel, and thrust it down on the creature's neck just behind the head. There was a snap like the breaking of a green twig, and the serpent began to dissolve. In that instant the other two *shikigami* seized the chance and attacked, like their companion, in utter silence.

"Look out!"

I could have saved my breath. Kanemore's dagger blade was already a blur of motion, criss-crossing the space in front of him like a swarm of wasps. Even if the other two creatures intended to scream, they had no time before they, too, dissolved into the oblivion from whence they came. Kanemore was barely breathing hard.

"Remind me to never fight on any side of a battle opposite you," I said as I got back off the floor.

"One doesn't always get to choose one's battles," Kanemore said dryly. "In any case it seems you've returned the favor for my earlier rescue, so we may call our accounts settled in that regard."

I picked up a ragged bit of mulberry paper, apparently all that remained of our recent foes. There were a few carefully printed *kanji*, but they were faded and impossible to read. "Fine quality. These servitors were expensive."

"And futile, if we assume they were guarding something of value."

It didn't take long to find what we were searching for; I located a small pottery jar hidden in a mortise on one of the beams and broke it open with my dagger hilt. A scroll lay within. It was tied with silk strings, and the strings' ends were pressed together and sealed with beeswax embossed with the Fujiwara *mon*. I examined it closely as Kanemore looked on.

"Your sister will have to confirm this," I said at last, "but this does appear to be the missing letter."

The relief on the man's face was almost painful to see. "And now I am in your debt again, Lord Yamada. It has been a long night and we are both weary, yet I do not think that this can wait. Let us return to the Palace now; it will be stirring by the time we arrive."

The lack of sleep plus the sudden stress of the fight, now relieved, left me feeling as wrung out as a washerwoman's towel. I knew Kanemore must have felt nearly as bad, even though from his stoic demeanor I'd have thought he could take on another half-dozen *shikigami* without breaking a sweat.

"We'll go directly," I said, "but I'm going to need a breath or two before I try that climb again. You could do with some rest yourself."

Prince Kanemore finally allowed himself to sit down in that now empty place. "I am too tired to argue, so you must be right."

We greeted the dawn like two roof-dragons from the top of the Rasha Gate, and then made our way back into the city. The Imperial Compound was already alive with activity by then, but Kanemore didn't bother with circuitous routes. We proceeded directly to Teiko-hime's manor and at the fastest speed decorum allowed. We probably attracted more attention than we wanted to, but Kanemore was in no mood for more delays.

Neither was I, truth to tell, but Teiko-hime had not yet risen, and I had to wait on the veranda while Kanemore acquainted his sister with the news. I waited, and I waited. I was starting to feel a little insulted by the time Kanemore finally reappeared, but he did not come from the house; he came hurrying through the garden path, and his face . . . well, I hope I never see that expression again on a human being.

"I am truly sorry . . . to have kept you waiting, Lord Yamada. This . . . I was to give you this . . . "

"This" was a heavy pouch of quilted silk. Inside were half a dozen small cylinders of pure gold. I take pride in the fact that I stared at them for only a moment or two.

"Kanemore-san, what has happened?"

"I cannot . . . "

"I think you can. I think I will have to insist."

His eyes did recover a little of their old fire then, but it quickly died away. "My sister was adamant that we deal with the matter at once. I escorted her to the Ministry of Justice as she insisted. I guess the burden of waiting had been too much; she did not even give me time to fetch you . . . oh, how could she be so reckless?"

I felt my spirit grow cold, and my own voice sounded lifeless in my ears. "The letter was read at the Ministry? Without knowing its contents?"

"Normally these matters take weeks, but considering what had happened to the letter under his care, Lord Sentaro couldn't very well refuse Teiko's demand for an audience. I must say in his favor that he tried to dissuade her, but she insisted he read it before the court. We all heard, we all saw . . . "

I put my hands on his shoulders, but I'm not even sure he noticed. "Kanemore?"

He did look at me then, and he recited a poem: "The Wisteria pines alone in desolation, without the bright Peony."

I could hardly believe what I was hearing. Three lines of an incomplete *tanka*, like the three that Teiko had used to draw me back to Court, in turn had damned her. Wisteria was of course a reference to the Fujiwara family crest, and "Peony" had been Teiko's nickname at Court since the age of seven. Clearly the poem had been hers to complete and return to Kiyoshi. The imagery and tone were clear, too. There was no one who could hear those words and doubt that Kiyoshi and Teiko had been lovers. For any woman at Court it would have been indiscreet; for an Imperial Wife it amounted to treason.

"What is to be done?" I asked.

"My sister is stripped of her titles and all Court honors. She will be confined and then banished . . . " Here Kanemore's strength failed him, and it was several heartbeats before he could finish. "Exiled, to the northern coast at Suma."

Say, rather, to the ends of the earth. It was little short of an execution.

"Surely there is . . . "

"Nothing, Lord Yamada. In our ignorance we have done more than enough. The writ is sealed."

He left me there to find my own way out of the compound. It was a long time before I bothered to try.

⛩

It took longer to settle my affairs in Kyoto than I'd hoped, but the gold meant the matter would be merely difficult, not impossible. The Widow Tamahara was, perhaps, one of the very few people genuinely sorry to see me leave. I sold most of my belongings and kept only what personal items I could carry, along with my new traveling clothes, my sword, and the balance of the gold, which was still quite substantial.

On the appointed day, I was ready. Teiko's party emerged from the eastern gate of the compound through the entrance still guarded by the Taira. Yet *bushi* of the Minamoto Clan formed the bulk of her escort. Kanemore was with them, as I knew he would be. His eyes were sad but he held his head high.

Normally a lady of Teiko's birth would have traveled in a covered oxcart, hidden from curious eyes, but now she walked, wearing the plain traveling clothes she'd used to bring that first message in disguise, completing her disgrace. Still, I'd recognized her then as I did now. When the somber procession had moved a discreet distance down the road, I fell in behind, just another traveler on the northern road.

I was a little surprised when the party took the northeast road toward Lake Biwa, but I was able to learn from an attendant that Teiko wished to make a pilgrimage to the sacred lake before beginning her new life at Suma. Since it was only slightly out of the way, her escort had seen no reason to object. Neither did I, for that matter, since I was determined to follow regardless. The mountains surrounding the lake slowed the procession's progress, and it took three days to get there. When the party made camp on the evening of the third day, I did the same nearby.

I wasn't terribly surprised to find Kanemore looming over me and my small fire within a very short time.

"I was just making tea, Kanemore-san. Would you care for some?"

He didn't meet my gaze. "My sister has instructed me to tell you to go home."

"I have no home."

"In which case I am instructed to tell you to go someplace else. I should warn you that should you reply that where you are now *is* 'someplace else,' she has requested that I beat you senseless, but with affection."

I smiled. "She anticipated my response. That's the Teiko I always knew. So, are you also instructed to kill me if I refuse your sister's order?"

Now he did look me squarely in the eye. "If killing you would atone for my own foolishness," Kanemore said, "I'd do it in a heartbeat. Yet I cannot blame you for what happened, try as I might. You only did as my sister bid—"

"As did you," I pointed out.

He managed a weak smile. "Even so, we still share some of the responsibility for what happened. I could not prevent her disgrace, so I am determined to share it."

"That is my wish as well," I said.

"You have no—" he began but did not finish.

"Exactly. My failure gives me that right, if nothing else does. Now consider: what about Prince Takahito? Your nephew? Where is he?"

"At Court. Takahito of course asked to accompany his mother, but permission was refused."

"Indeed, and now he remains at Court surrounded by his enemies. Who will look after him?"

"Do not lecture me on my duties! Who then will look after my sister? These men are to escort her to Suma. They will not remain and protect her afterward."

I waved that aside. "I well understand the burden of conflicting obligations. Your instinct for love and loyalty is to protect both your sister and her son. How will you accomplish this when they are practically on opposite ends of the earth? Which path would Teiko choose for you?"

His face reddened slightly; I could tell that the subject had already come up—repeatedly, if I knew Teiko.

"We've spoken our minds plainly to each other in the past, Kanemore-san, and I will do the same now: your sister is going to a place where life is harsh and she will be forced to make her own way. Despite her great gifts, neither she nor her two charming and loyal attendants have the vaguest idea of how to survive outside the shelter of the Imperial Court. I do."

Kanemore didn't say anything for several long moments. "My sister is the daughter of an Emperor. She was born to be the mother of an Emperor," he said finally.

"If that were the case, then it would still be so," I said. "Life does not always meet our expectations, but that should not prevent us from seeking what happiness we can."

"You are unworthy of Princess Teiko," Kanemore said, expressionless, "and I say that as someone who holds you in high regard. Yet you are also right. For what little it may be worth, I will speak to my sister."

"When I finish my tea," I said, "and with your sister's permission, so will I."

⛩

Teiko agreed to see me, perhaps because she saw no good way to prevent it. After fifteen years I did not care what her reasons might be. The fact that she did agree was enough.

I found her sitting by herself in a small clearing. She gazed out at a lovely view of Lake Biwa beyond her. The sun had dipped just below the mountains ringing the lake, and the water had turned a deep azure. Teiko's escort was present but out of earshot, as were both of her attendants. She held an empty teacup; the rice cakes beside her looked hardly touched. She still wore her *boshi*, but the veil was pulled back now to reveal her face. It was a gift, I knew, and I was grateful.

I can't say that she hadn't changed at all in fifteen years: there might have been one or two gray strands among the glossy black of her hair, perhaps a line or two on her face. I can say the changes didn't matter. She was and still remained beautiful. She looked up and smiled at me a little wistfully as I kneeled not quite in front of her but a little to the side, so as not to spoil her view.

"So, have you come to lecture me on my recklessness as well? Please yourself, but be warned—my brother has worried the topic to exhaustion."

"Your brother thinks only of you. Yet what's done cannot be undone."

"Life is uncertain in all regards," Teiko said very seriously, then she managed a smile and waved a hand at the vast stretch of water nearby. "An appropriate setting, don't you think? I must look like a fisherman's wife now. What shall I do at Suma, Lord Yamada? Go bare-breasted like the abalone maidens and dive for shells? Learn to gather seaweed to make salt, like those two lovers of the exiled poet? Can you imagine me, hair loose and legs bared, gleaning the shore?"

"I can easily so imagine," I said.

She sighed. "Then your imagination is better than mine. I am a worthless creature now."

"That is not possible."

She smiled at me. There were dimples in her cheeks. "You are kind, Goji-san. I'm glad the years have not changed this about you."

She offered me a cup of tea from the small pot nearby, but I declined. She poured herself another while I pondered yet again the best way to frame one of the questions that had been troubling me. I finally decided there simply was no good way, if I chose to ask.

"No lectures, Teiko-hime, but I must ask about the letter."

Her expression was unreadable. "Just 'Teiko,' please, especially now. So, you're curious about Kiyoshi's letter, of course. That poem was unexpected."

"You weren't Kiyoshi's lover," I said.

Teiko smiled a little wistfully. "You know I was not," she said. "But at the moment there is no explanation I can offer you."

"I'm not asking for one. What's done is done."

She sipped her tea. "Many things have been done, Goji-san. There is more to come, whatever our place in the order of events may be. Speaking of which, my brother in his own delicate way hints that there is another matter you wish to speak to me about."

"I am going to Suma," I said.

"That is noble, but pointless. Your life is in Kyoto."

"My life is as and where it is fated to be, but still I am going to Suma," I repeated. "Do you require me to say why?"

She actually blushed then, but it did not last. "You say what's done cannot be undone. Perhaps that is true, but you do not yet know all that *has* been done. As at our last meeting, I must ask you to listen to me, and then decide what you will or will not do. Please?"

"I am listening."

"You left Court because people were starting to talk about us."

"Yes. When the Emperor bestowed his favor on you, Lord Sentaro—"

"Did no more or less than what I asked him to do."

For a little while I forgot to breathe. I idly wondered, somewhere above the roar in my ears, whether I ever would again. "What? You . . . ?"

"It's unforgivable, I know, but I was not much more than a child, and both foolish and afraid. Once I had been chosen by the former Emperor there could be nothing between us nor even the rumor of such. I knew that you would do what you did, to protect my reputation."

"I would have done anything," I said, "if you had asked me."

"That is the true shame I have borne these past fifteen years," Teiko said softly. "I let this person you detest be the one to break your heart because I lacked the courage to do it myself. I heard later that he took undue pleasure in this. I must bear the blame for that also."

Fifteen years. I could feel the weight of every single one of them on my shoulders. "Why are you telling me this now?"

"Because I needed to tell you," she said. "More importantly, you needed to hear it and know just how unworthy I am of your regard before you choose to throw your life away after mine. Or do you still wish to speak to me of things that cannot be undone?"

Perhaps it was a test. Perhaps it was a challenge. Perhaps it was the simple truth. I only knew what remained true for me. "My decision is not altered," I said. "I would like to know yours."

There were tears in her dark eyes. "There are things we may not speak of, even now. If it is our fate to reach Suma together, speak to me then and I will answer you."

⛩

The demons were teasing me in my dreams; at least, so I believe. In a vision I saw Teiko and myself on the beach at Suma. The land was desolate, but the sea was beautiful and it met most of our needs. We walked on its shore. Teiko was laughing. It was the most exquisite of sounds, at least until she started laughing at me, and it wasn't Teiko at all but some ogress with Teiko's smile.

"What have you done with Teiko?" I demanded, but the demon just mocked me. I drew my sword, but the blade was rusted and useless; it would not cut. I looked frantically at the sea, but there was nothing but gigantic waves, one after another racing toward the beach. Sailing against them was one small boat. I could see Teiko there, her back turned to me, sailing away. I ignored the demon and chased after her, but the sea drove me back again and again until her boat was swallowed by the attacking sea.

"—amada!"

Someone was calling me. The ogress? I did not care. Teiko was gone.

"Lord Yamada!"

I was shaken violently awake. Kanemore kneeled beside my blankets, looking frantic.

"What . . . what's happened?" I said, trying to shake off the nightmare.

"My sister is missing! Help us search!"

I was awake now. "But . . . how? Her guards worked in paired shifts!"

Kanemore looked disgusted as I scrambled to my feet. "The fools swear they never took their eyes off of her, that Teiko and her maids were sleeping peacefully, and then suddenly Teiko wasn't there! Nonsense. They must have been playing *Go* or some such rot. I'll have their heads for this!"

"We'll need their heads to help us search. She could not have gotten far. Go ahead. I will catch up."

Kanemore ran through the camp with me not far behind, but when I came to the place where I knew Teiko and her ladies had been sleeping, I paused. The two maidservants were huddled together looking confused and frightened, but I ignored them. There was a small screen for some privacy but no way Teiko could have left the spot without one of the guards seeing her. I looked in and found her bedding empty and undisturbed. I pulled her coverlet aside and found a crumpled piece of paper.

"She's up there!"

I heard Kanemore call to me from the shore of the lake and I raced to join him. Just a little further down the shoreline was a place where the mountains dropped sheer to the water. On the very edge of that high promontory stood a small figure dressed in flowing white, as for a funeral.

"Teiko, no!"

I started to shout a warning to Kanemore, but he was already sprinting ahead, looking for the quickest route up the slope, and I followed hot on his heels, but it was far too late. In full sight of both of us, Teiko calmly stepped off the edge.

With her broad sleeves fluttering like the wings of a butterfly, one could almost imagine Teiko's fall would be softened, but the sound of her body striking the water carried across the lake like the crack of ice breaking on the rivers of Hokkaido in spring.

One could also imagine, first hope having failed, that there would be nothing in the water to find except, perhaps, a few scraps of paper. One tried very hard to hold on to this hope and only relented when the fishermen from a nearby village helped us locate and remove the cold, broken body of former Princess Teiko from the deep, dark waters of the sacred lake.

⛩

The moon was high again and cast its reflection on the river. The modest funeral rites for Teiko were well under way, and once more I stood on Shijo bridge, staring down at the moon and the dark water beneath it. I saw the *onibi* flare out on the water. I knew if I waited long enough, the ghost-lights would be followed by the graceful spirits of women who had drowned themselves for love in Kamo River.

I had seen them before; they would soon appear just above the water in solemn procession, drifting a bit as if with the currents below. The legend was that men unfortunate enough to stare at them too closely would drown themselves out of love as well. I wondered if I, before I drowned myself in turn, might see one small figure with the face of Princess Teiko.

I didn't know what Kanemore intended when he appeared beside me on the bridge. At that moment I did not care. I simply gazed at the moon's reflection and waited for whatever might come.

"I was told I could find you here," he said, then placed a small scroll on the railing in front of me. "This is for you, Lord Yamada," he said formally.

I frowned. "What is it?"

"A letter," he said, "from my late sister. I have already opened and read the one intended for me."

I didn't move or touch the letter. "Meticulous. She had this planned before we even left the city. She never intended to go to Suma."

"The shame of her disgrace was too much to bear," he said. He sounded as convinced as I was.

"I rather doubt," I said, "that there was anything your sister could not bear, at need."

"Then why did she do it?" he asked softly.

A simple question that covered so much, and yet at that moment I didn't have a clear answer. I think I understood more of what had happened than Kanemore did, but the "why" of it all was as big a mystery to me as it was to him. I shared the one thing I thought I knew for certain: "I've only been able to think of one clear reason. I have been drinking for the past day or so to see if I could perhaps forget that reason."

"Have you succeeded?"

"No."

He leaned against the rail with me. Out on the water, the mists were forming into the likenesses of young women. Kanemore glanced at them nervously. "Then share that reason with me. Preferably someplace else."

I smiled. "You must drink with me then."

"If needs must then let's get to it."

I picked up Teiko's letter, and we left the ghostly women behind. From there we went to the Widow Tamahara's establishment, since it was the closest. As usual, it was filled with drinking, boisterous *bushi* and other retainers currently not at service. We found a relatively quiet corner, and Kanemore ordered saké, which the smiling Widow Tamahara delivered personally. Kanemore poured out two generous measures, and we drank in companionable silence, as Prince Kanemore eyed the drinking *bushi* with distaste.

"A sorry lot, and yet they are the future."

I frowned. "These louts? What makes you think so?"

He sighed. "Think? Rather, I know. Every year more and more land and wealth is concentrated in the hands of the provincial nobility, and their private armies are filled with these *samurai*," Kanemore said, now using the more common, corrupted word, "whose loyalty is first to their lords and not the Emperor, as is right. It is for this reason only that upstarts like the Abe Clan can make so much trouble."

"Darker days are ahead if you are correct."

"Dark enough at present," Kanemore said, then he could stand the waiting no longer. "So, what is the answer you drink to forget?" he asked, as he topped off his cup and my own. "Why did Teiko kill herself?"

"The only obvious and immediate answer is, upon her death, you would be free to return to the capital and look after Takahito."

He frowned. "But you were going to be with her."

I sighed deeply. "Which did not alter her plans in the slightest, as apparently I was not an acceptable alternative."

"That is a very sad thing to bear," he said after a while, "and also very odd. I know my sister was fond of you."

"Maybe. And yet . . . "

"Yet what?"

I took a deep breath and then an even deeper drink. "And yet there is a voice deep in my brain that keeps shouting I am a complete and utter ass, that I do not understand anything, and the reason Teiko killed herself had nothing to do with me. Try as I might, *drink* as I might, that troublesome fellow only shouts louder."

"You have suffered greatly because of my family," Kanemore said. "And I know that I have no right to ask more of you. Yet it was my sister's wish that you read her letter. Will you grant her last request?"

I didn't answer right away. "I once asked what you were afraid of, Kanemore-san. I think it only fair to tell you what *I* am afraid of. I am very afraid of what Princess Teiko will say to me now."

Yet there was never really any question of refusing. I took out the letter. After hesitating as long as I dared, I broke the seal. In doing so I discovered that, when I feared the very worst, I had shown entirely too little imagination.

And, yes, I was in fact a complete and utter ass.

The letter was very short, and this is most of what it said:

The crane flies above
The lake's clear shining surface.
White feathers glisten,
Made pure by sacred water,
As the poet's book was cleansed.

At the end of the poem she had simply written: "*Forgive me—Teiko.*"

I thought, perhaps, if one day I was able to forgive myself, maybe then I would find the strength to forgive Teiko. Not this day, but that didn't matter. I had other business. I put the letter away.

"*Kampai*, Kanemore-san. Let us finish this jar of fine saké."

I knew Kanemore was deeply curious about the letter but too polite to ask, for which I was grateful. He hefted the container and frowned. "It is almost empty. I'll order another."

"No, my friend, for this is all we will drink tonight. From here we will visit the baths, and then go to sleep, for tomorrow our heads must be clear."

"Why? What happens tomorrow?"

"Tomorrow we restore your sister's honor."

The Imperial Court was composed more of tradition and ritual than people: everything in its time, everything done precisely so. Yet it was astonishing to me how quickly matters could unfold, given the right impetus.

Kanemore kneeled beside me in the hall where justice, or at least Fujiwara no Sentaro's version of it, was dispensed. The minister had not yet taken his place on the dais, but my attention was on a curtained alcove on the far side of the dais. I knew I had seen that curtain move. I leaned over and whispered to Kanemore.

"His Majesty Reizei is present, I hope?"

"I believe so, accompanied by Chancellor Yorimichi I expect. He will not show himself, of course."

Of course. The acknowledged presence of the Emperor in these proceedings was against form, but that didn't matter. He was here, and everyone knew it. I was almost certain he would be, once word reached him. Kanemore, through another relative in close attendance on His Majesty, made sure that word did so reach him. I think Lord Sentaro convened in such haste as a way to prevent that eventuality, but in this he was disappointed. He entered now, looking both grave and more than a little puzzled.

Kanemore leaned close. "I've sent a servant for a bucket of water, as you requested. I hope you know what you're doing."

Kanemore was obviously apprehensive. Under the circumstances I did not blame him. Yet I was perfectly calm. I claimed no measure of courage greater than Kanemore's; I simply had the distinct advantage that I no longer cared what happened to me.

"What is this matter you have brought before the Imperial Ministry?" Lord Sentaro demanded from the dais.

"I am here to remove the unjust stain on the honor of the late Princess Teiko, daughter of the Emperor Sanjo, Imperial Consort to the late Emperor Suzaku II," I said, clearly and with more than enough volume to carry my words throughout the room.

There was an immediate murmur of voices from the clerks, minor judges, members of the Court, and attendants present. Lord Sentaro glared for silence until the voices subsided.

"This unfortunate matter has already been settled. Lady Teiko was identified by my nephew, who died a hero's death in the north. Consider your words carefully, Lord Yamada."

"I choose my words with utmost care, Your Excellency. Your

nephew was indeed a hero and brought honor to the Fujiwara family. He did not, however, name Princess Teiko as his lover. This I will prove."

Lord Sentaro motioned me closer, and when he leaned down, his words were for me alone. "Shall I have cause to embarrass you a second time, Lord Yamada?"

Up until that point I almost felt sorry for the man, but no longer. Now my blade, so to speak, was drawn. "We shall soon see, Lord Minister of Justice. May I examine the letter?"

He indicated assent, and I returned to my place as Lord Sentaro's stentorian voice boomed across the room. "Produce my nephew's letter so that Lord Yamada may examine it and see what everyone knows is plainly written there."

A few snickers blossomed like weeds here and there in the courtroom despite the seriousness of the proceedings, but I ignored them. A waiting clerk hurried up, bowed low, and handed me the letter in question. I unrolled it and then signaled Kanemore, who signaled someone waiting at the back of the room. A young man in Taira livery came hurrying up with a bucket of clear water, placed it beside me, and then withdrew.

Lord Sentaro frowned. "Lord Yamada, did you neglect to wash your face this morning?"

More laughter. I was examining the poem closely and did not bother to look up. "The water is indeed to wash away a stain, Lord Sentaro. Not, however, one of mine."

The letter was not very long, and mostly spoke of the things Kiyoshi had seen and the hardships of the camp. There was one strange bit that caught my attention—there was a reference to Lord Sentaro and my father, and some "mistake" that Kiyoshi hoped to correct. Whatever the matter was, it had apparently been rendered irrelevant soon after, as my father had been executed on that very expedition.

Curious.

Still, my father was long dead and our family's honor and future had been burned to ashes with him. I forced my attention back to the matter at hand. The lover's poem actually came after Kiyoshi's personal seal. I unrolled the letter in its entirety, no more than the length of my forearm, and carefully dipped the paper into the water.

There was consternation in the court. Two guards rushed forward, but one glare from Prince Kanemore made them hesitate, looking to Lord Sentaro for instruction.

"Lady Teiko's sin dishonors us all," Lord Sentaro said, and his voice was pure sweet reason, "but the letter has been witnessed by hundreds. Destroying it will change nothing."

"I am not destroying the letter, Lord Sentaro. I am merely cleansing it. As the poet Ono no Komachi did in our great-grandsires' time."

Too late the fool understood. Once, long ago, a Lady of the Court had been accused by an enemy of copying a poem from an old book and presenting the piece as her own work. She faced her accuser and washed the book in question in clear water, just as I was doing now, and with the same result. I held the letter up high for all to see. Kiyoshi's letter was, of course, perfectly intact.

Except for the poem. That was gone.

More consternation. Lord Sentaro looked as if someone had struck him between the eyes with a very large hammer. I didn't wait for him to recover.

"It is a sad thing," I said, again making certain my voice carried to every corner—and alcove—of the court, "that a mere hundred or so years after the honored poet Ono no Komachi exposed this simple trick, we should fall for it again. The ink in Fujiwara no Kiyoshi's letter is of course untouched, for it has been wedded to this paper for the past fifteen years. Clearly, the poem slandering Princess Teiko was added within the month."

"Are you accusing me—" Lord Sentaro stopped, but it was too late. He himself had made the association; I needed to do little else.

"I accuse no one. I merely state two self-evident facts: that Teiko-hime was innocent, and that whoever wrote the poem accusing her had both access to the letter," and here I paused for emphasis, "and access to a Fujiwara seal. These conclusions are beyond dispute, Excellency. At the present time the identity of the person responsible is of lesser concern."

The man was practically sputtering. "But . . . but she was here! Why did Princess Teiko not speak up? She said nothing!"

I bowed low. "How should innocence answer a lie?"

The murmuring of the witnesses was nearly deafening for a time. It had only just begun to subside when a servant appeared from behind the alcove, hurried up to the dais, and whispered briefly in Lord Sentaro's ear. His face, having slowly turning a bright pink, now turned ashen gray. Kanemore and I bowed to the court as the official part of the proceedings were hastily declared closed. The proceedings that mattered most, I knew, had just begun.

That evening Kanemore found me once more on Shijo Bridge. The moon was beginning to wane, now past its full beauty, but I still watched its reflection in the water as I waited for the ghosts to appear. Kanemore approached and then leaned against the rail next to me.

"Well?" I asked.

"Teiko's honors and titles are to be posthumously restored," he said. "Lord Sentaro is, at his own expense and at Chancellor Yorimichi's insistence, arranging prayers for her soul at every temple in Kyoto."

"If you'll pardon my saying so, Kanemore-san, you don't sound happy about it."

"For the memory of my sister, I am," he said. "Yet one could also wish we had discovered this deception soon enough to save her. Still, I will have satisfaction against Lord Sentaro over this, Minister of Justice or no."

I laughed. "No need. Even assuming that the expense of the prayers doesn't ruin him, Lord Sentaro will be digging clams at the beach at Suma or Akashi within a month, or I will be astonished," I said. "It's enough."

"Enough? It was *his* slander that killed my sister! Though I must ask, while we're on the subject—how did you know?"

I had hoped to spare us both this additional pain, but clearly Kanemore wasn't going to be content with what he had. There was that much of his sister in him.

"Lord Sentaro did not kill your sister, Kanemore-san. We did."

One can never reliably predict a man's reaction to the truth. I thought it quite possible that Kanemore would take my head then and there. I'm not sure what was stopping him, but while he was still staring at me in shock I recited the poem from his sister's letter. "I trust you get the allusion," I said when I was done.

From the stunned look on the poor man's face, it was obvious he did. "Teiko *knew* the poem was a forgery? Why didn't she—?"

At that moment Kanemore's expression bore a striking resemblance to Lord Sentaro's earlier in the day.

"You understand now. Teiko knew the poem was forged for the obvious reason she did it herself. She used a carefully chosen ink that matched the original for color but was of poorer quality. I don't know how she acquired the proper seal, but I have no doubt she did so. It's likely she started the original rumors as well, probably through her maids. We can confirm this, but I see no need."

Kanemore grasped for something, anything. "If Lord Sentaro thought the letter was genuine, that does explain why he didn't destroy it, but it does *not* explain why he didn't use it himself! Why didn't he accuse Teiko openly?"

"I have no doubt he meant to confront her in private if he'd had the chance, but in court? Why should he? If Takahito was Kiyoshi's son then the Emperor's heir was a Fujiwara after all, and Teiko, the Dowager Empress, would be under Sentaro's thumb thanks to that letter. Until that day came, he could continue to champion Prince Norihira, but he would win no matter who took the throne, or so the fool thought. Teiko was not mistaken when she said Sentaro was searching for the letter—he wanted it back as much as she did."

Kanemore, warrior that he was, continued to fight a lost battle. "Rubbish! Why would Teiko go to such lengths to deliberately dishonor herself?"

I met his gaze. "To make her son emperor."

Despite my sympathy for Kanemore, I had come too far alone. Now he was going to share my burden whether he liked it or not. I gave him the rest.

"Consider this—so long as the Fujiwara preferred Prince Norihira, Takahito's position remained uncertain. Would the Teiko you knew resign herself to that if there were an alternative? *Any* alternative?"

Kanemore looked grim. "No. She would not."

"Just so. Your sister gave Sentaro possession of the letter solely to show that he *could* have altered it. Then she likewise arranged for the letter to disappear and for us to find it again. In hindsight I realize it had all been a little too easy, though not so easy as to arouse immediate suspicion. Those *shikigami* might very well have killed me if I'd been alone, but Teiko sent you to make certain that did not happen. Her attention to detail was really astounding."

Kanemore tried again. "But . . . if this was her plan, then it worked perfectly! Lord Sentaro was humiliated before the Emperor, the Chancellor, the entire Court! His power is diminished! She didn't have to kill herself."

I almost laughed again. "Humiliated? *Diminished*? Why should Teiko risk so much and settle for so little? With the responsibility for her death laid solely at his feet, Lord Sentaro's power at Court has been *broken*. The entire Fujiwara clan has taken a blow that will be a long time healing. No one will dare openly oppose Prince Takahito's claim to the throne now or speak ill of your sister in or out of the Imperial Presence. It was Teiko's game, Kanemore-san. She chose the stakes."

Kanemore finally accepted defeat. "Even the *shikigami* . . . Goji-san, I swear I did not know."

"I believe you. Teiko understood full well what would have happened if she'd confided in either of us. Yet we can both take comfort in this much—we did not fail your sister. We both performed exactly as she hoped."

Kanemore was silent for a time. When he spoke again he looked at me intently. "I thought my sister's payment was in gold. I was wrong. She paid in revenge."

I grunted. "Lord Sentaro? That was . . . satisfying, I admit, but I'd compose a poem praising the beauty of the man's hindquarters and recite it in front of the entire Court tomorrow if that would bring your sister back."

He managed a brief smile then, but his expression quickly turned serious again. "Not Sentaro. I mean you could have simply ignored Teiko's final poem, and her death would have been for nothing and my nephew's ruin complete and final. She offered this to you."

I smiled. "She knew . . . well, say in all fairness that she left the choice to me. Was that a choice at all, Kanemore-san?"

He didn't answer, but then I didn't think there was an answer. I stood gazing out at the moon's reflection. The charming ghosts were in their procession. I think my neck was extended at the proper angle. The rest, so far as I knew or cared, was up to Kanemore.

I felt his hand on my shoulder; I'm not sure if that was intended to reassure me or steady himself.

"You must drink with me, Goji-san," he said. It wasn't a suggestion.

"I must drink," I said. "With or without you."

PART TWO

A pyre, once it burns
On the barren Plain of Smoke
Can never be doused.
The mountain gives up no one.
Yet may a good name return?

It was four months, through the end of fall and all through that winter before I finally managed to crawl out of the saké haze I'd hidden myself in, mostly due to the fact that the last of Teiko's gold was exhausted.

On the evening of the third day of the fourth month, I received a letter containing a single poem, written in a delicate, flowing hand. I read the poem through for the third time, but even one so unused to the intricacies of courtly communication as I could not mistake its meaning. Mount Toribe and the plain at its eastern foot were the traditional burial grounds of the capital, the Plain of Smoke: the place where all funeral pyres were lit. Not my father's, however; he had been executed in Mutsu province and burned there. Still, his good name and my future had both gone up in smoke that day, almost literally, so the metaphor was apt.

"Tamahara-san, who brought this letter?"

The Widow Tamahara paused in her sweeping of the veranda outside my rooms, and poked through her iron-gray hair to scratch a spot that was apparently troubling her. "I'm not sure,

Lord Yamada. Some street child," she said. "No, wait, I think it was Nidai. Yes, I'm certain. He wears that tattered red sash."

"I think I've seen that one before. I gather he didn't wait for a reply?"

She grunted. "Not even so much as a '*Ohayo*, Tamahara-san' before he was away. No manners, but then what would one expect?"

What indeed?

"Thank you, Tamahara-san," I said.

The old woman hesitated. "Lord Yamada . . . "

"The rent, yes? I have not forgotten. Soon, I promise."

The Widow Tamahara just looked glum. "Very well."

I wasn't certain how much longer the Widow Tamahara's indulgence would last, even for one of my alleged station. She had a certain respect for even such minor and landless nobility as myself, but there were limits to all things, and the Widow Tamahara's patience was a leaky boat even on the calmest of seas.

So, someone had just dangled something they thought I wanted right under my nose. The only obvious reason was they, whoever "they" might be, wanted something from me in return. What that something might be rather depended on whether the hints I had just been offered were intended as inducement or bait, and as things stood, I had no way of knowing which.

I had enemies and more than a few, but only a few in a position to attempt anything and fewer still who would bother with subtlety if they meant to do harm. Furthermore, the text of the poem was written entirely in flowing *kana* script with no Chinese characters, suggesting the author was a woman. While it was true that more than one lady of my acquaintance might have had reason to be annoyed with me, I could think of none who had cause to want my head on a spear.

The messenger, such that he was, had not waited for a reply. Clearly, this meant the author of the poem intended to choose the time and place to contact me again. That only left the choice of whether I wanted to wait. I decided against it.

I returned to my rooms long enough to fetch a long dagger and tuck it into my sash. While I was perfectly within my rights to bear weapons on the streets of the capital, such things were considered a little ungentlemanly. The long *tachi* especially was really a weapon of war and tended to attract attention. I wore it only when the situation dictated it would be foolish not to do so.

The Widow Tamahara's establishment was in the area near the Gion Shrine, between Shijo-dori and Sanjo-dori; the foot traffic on these streets was good for business, she said. They were also good for losing one's self in the mass of people, if one wished it so or not. Even though the boy called Nidai tended to haunt the area, finding him might take considerable time. Still, without a current mission or patronage or the means for more saké, it wasn't as if I had anything better to do.

I was, I confess, curious.

Since I had no idea where to begin, I let myself wander where my feet took me, swept along on the current of people. I passed the magnificent shrine itself as I followed Shijo toward the river, while the crowds thinned but never quite abated. Just past the last of the shrine outbuildings, an *asobi* had set up to perform in the shade of a maple. A small crowd had gathered to watch the lady dance, and I, noting no one I recognized as Nidai in that crowd, started to move on.

I'm not certain what made me hesitate. *Asobi* were common enough in the capital, dancing and singing for their livelihoods and, more likely than not, providing more personal entertainments as well; because there were many unattached young men of means associated with the Imperial Court, the *asobi* were in great demand.

Yet there was something odd about this dancer. Nothing immediately obvious—she was charming and quite skilled. I judged her age at around thirty, perhaps a little less. Her gestures and movements were precise, flowing, and graceful; when the dance required that she spin her fans in the air, she did both at once in perfect precision as nimbly as a juggler, catching both as if there had never been any question of the matter. It occurred to me that I had never seen a better execution of this particular dance since my brief time at Court.

Not even at Court, I thought after some reflection.

In a moment or two, I realized what had caught my attention, aside from the woman's beauty and skill; it was the *asobi*'s hair. She wore it long, as nearly all women did when their circumstances permitted, and it reached just past her knees. There was nothing unusual about that, but the way she had dressed it was; she had confined her hair in a sort of loose ponytail tied at the middle of her back with a bright blue ribbon that matched her pink and blue *kimono*. What was unusual was the second blue ribbon, tied much closer to the nape of her neck. I don't think I had ever seen that done before. Perhaps it was a new style, but such things were no real concern of mine, and certainly no reason to delay my search.

In recognition of the *asobi*'s skill, I would have contributed if

I had any means to do so. I did not and had no reason to remain. I moved on past the shrine and down to the river, but there was no sign of the boy. When I returned to the Widow Tamahara's establishment, there was another message waiting for me, but this time the sender had not bothered to conceal his identity:

> *The stung badger retreats*
> *to his new burrow to heal.*
> *Struck once by the wasp,*
> *He will remember the nest.*
> *Even wasps must sleep sometime.*
> *—Kenji*

I sighed and lay the scroll aside. While I had to admire the attempt, I sincerely prayed that Kenji's efforts at refinement didn't take; the idea of getting poetry from him on a regular basis was too terrible to contemplate. Besides, I didn't have the faintest idea of what he was talking about. I idly wondered if Kenji himself did, but there was only one way to find out, and since the hunt for Nidai had proved fruitless, there was no reason not to change targets. Not that I believed that finding Kenji would be difficult; the man's habits were more fixed than a watchman's.

Sure enough, one more brisk walk brought me to the Demon Gate at the northeast corner of the city, and there was the priest Kenji in his mendicant aspect, sitting beside the gate with a broad straw *boshi* covering his head and face, his begging bowl resting in front of him. Around fifty, he had one of those young-old faces that seemed infinitely adaptable to a man's intentions. Kenji could look pious or lecherous as the mood took him, and one would think that either expression was perfectly normal for him.

"They say that evil spirits enter the city by this gate," I said. "Clearly this is true."

Kenji didn't look up. "And friendly greeting to you as well, Yamada-san. Now sit down and listen for a change."

Kenji had a tone of voice that he used rarely, but I'd learned to pay attention. It meant he was serious. I found a relatively clean spot beside the gate and in the near vicinity of Kenji. The people coming in and out of the northeast gate continued to do so, and no one paid us the least attention.

"Now," I said, "what's this about a badger avoiding wasps? Sounds like proper advice, but I'm not a badger."

"It's proper advice for anyone, but of course you're not the badger. The badger is Lord Sentaro," Kenji said, though his eyes were on the people passing through the gate.

"I think you're marking a trail, but I can't seem to find it. What has this to do with Lord Sentaro?"

Kenji sighed, and when he spoke again he sounded more as if he was talking to himself than to me. "It's possible? He hasn't heard? I didn't think he'd been drunk *that* long."

"As the mountain complains about the depth of the sea . . . I've had my fill of poetry for the moment. Speak plainly."

"The edict of banishment against Lord Sentaro has been lifted."

I just sat there for many long moments. Kenji seemed in no hurry to resume the conversation, and I was glad of that. It seemed that my capacity for surprise would never cease to be tested.

"Lord Sentaro is coming back to the Imperial Court? That's not possible." At least, I hoped it wasn't, nor did I understand how it could be so. Even a man like Lord Sentaro didn't suffer the suspicion of the death of a princess and resume his office as if nothing had happened. Such a blow could force even an Emperor to retire.

"I never said it was possible. I never said he was coming back to Court," Kenji pointed out. "I said the Edict of Exile had been *lifted*. There were, of course, conditions. A few days ago Lord Sentaro took the tonsure at Mount Hiea."

Which at least explained how Kenji had been privy to this information; doubtless he had several acquaintances within the monastic community, where such news would travel quickly.

"Lord Sentaro? A simple monk? This is priceless."

"Again you assume too much. Is your brain pickled?" Kenji sighed. "Lord Sentaro? A monk? Hardly. Yamada-san, he's been named Hojo of Enryaku-ji, as the former holder of that position felt the sudden need to retire to a more austere monastery somewhere in the vicinity of Edo. Need I spell out the implications?"

He did not, and I was feeling a chill to the depths of my being. The temple complex on Mount Hiei had first been established by order of the Emperor Kanmu, to protect the northeast entrance to his new capital from evil spirits. While the founding priest, Saicho of the Tendai Sect, had been a humble and devout man, Enryaku-ji had soon grown far beyond his original tenets. Not only was the temple deeply involved in Imperial affairs, these days it had its own private army of warrior monks, easily outnumbering the guards of the Imperial household. Lord Sentaro might not be returning to the Imperial Court directly, but as Chief Priest of the temple, he would have the power base he needed to work behind the scenes. If, in fact, that was his intention.

I had thought I was done with Lord Sentaro. Now I wondered if he was done with me. "This is very disturbing news." I went on to tell Kenji about the poem that had arrived that same day.

Kenji looked thoughtful. "Lord Sentaro?"

"It was written by a woman," I said.

He dismissed that. "It may well have been," he said, "but that doesn't mean that he didn't choose the words, and if you think being Hojo of Enryaku-ji will mean that he has no women about him, you're more simple than I think you. And that's not even speaking of the nuns housed there."

I smiled then. "If Lord Sentaro's renunciation of the world actually meant anything, he would not do so, but we both know that's probably not the case. Apparently his contrition must have appeared sincere, at least enough to satisfy His Majesty."

Kenji just sighed. "You know that, whatever Lord Sentaro really intends, taking the tonsure was an entirely appropriate action on his part, considering the cloud of suspicion hanging over him. I imagine the Emperor would have been in a very delicate position in regard to this, had he refused."

I considered this and realized Kenji was probably right. Go-Reizei would not be the first Emperor forced by the Fujiwara into an early retirement, should he make such a political missstep. The form of Lord Sentaro's contrition was correct, and in the Imperial Court, form was paramount.

"So Lord Sentaro gives up little and gains much," I said, "including release from exile and a base of power. I'll give the man his due: this was well played. Still . . . "

"Still what?"

"Assuming that the earlier poem did indeed come from the former Lord Sentaro, what are his intentions? He must know that there is no way my fortunes could be restored in this manner, and I'd hardly be fool enough to believe so. As for my father's good name, well, that moment has passed as well. As bait goes, that was rather weak."

"So you'd like to believe."

I shrugged. "All right then, I admit it—I'm interested, but it's impossible. Even if there were some way to prove the charges against my father were false, his lands have all been given away to Court favorites or awarded as prizes to provincial lords. Even the Emperor could not restore them now. Whoever sent the poem was hinting at what cannot be."

"Even so, what if his ultimate intention was not to entice you?"

"Then, pray, tell me what his intentions are?"

Kenji turned his eyes towards the heavens. "You know very well that Lord Sentaro's goals remain as they were before the death of Princess Teiko—to place a Fujiwara on the throne. While I don't know all the details of the events that led to Lord Sentaro's disgrace, I *do* know you were deeply involved and that Lord Sentaro does not regard you kindly. I'm guessing revenge would simply be pickles for his rice, not the main ingredient. Your earlier message might be some part of this or it may not. It might not even be from Lord Sentaro, but I think it's in your interest to find out. Whatever the result, you can rest assured that this matter is far greater than you."

"Most matters are," I said, then added, "thank you, Kenji-san."

He frowned. "Gratitude? I'm astonished."

" 'Even the devils take their fee.' You've told me something I needed to know and shown concern for my well-being, and gratitude is the only appropriate response. Especially since, at the moment, I have nothing else to give."

Kenji glanced wryly at his begging bowl. "Typical, and a common condition these days, alas . . . oh."

"What is it? By the way, have you seen Nidai?

"I see an opportunity. Pardon me while I redirect my business. As for Nidai, try the southeast gate. He often loiters there."

Kenji rose quickly and, at a near run, caught up with a bent old man who had just hobbled through the gate. "Grandfather, may I speak to you?" he asked in an overly loud voice.

Kenji's shout caused several pairs of eyes to turn toward him. The old man turned as well, frowning. "Yes, priest? What do you—"

Kenji didn't give him time to finish. In one swift motion he pulled a piece of paper from his sleeve and slapped it on the old man's head.

"How dareeeekkkkkk!"

The last bit came out as a shriek as the "old man" immediately shimmered and transformed into an even uglier creature of middling height with black wings and a large, beak-like nose.

A tengu . . . ?

The crowd around Kenji and the goblin gasped and drew back. Snarling, the *tengu* tried to rake Kenji with his claws but the monk had quickly stepped back out of reach. It glared at Kenji but took a look at the quickly forming crowd, including several *bushi* serving as escort to an oxcart carriage who were now drawing their swords, and the thing took to the air with one beat of its powerful wings and was soon out of sight over the mountains to the east.

"An evil spirit entered the city before our very noses," Kenji said to the people assembled. "You saw. No one is safe. Yet with my talismans . . . "

I didn't wait around to hear the rest. For a moment I wondered if Kenji had been in league with the *tengu* to drum up business, but that notion was a little farfetched, even for Kenji. I worked my way around the crowd as Kenji for his part worked the crowd itself. Once I was clear of the mob, I turned away from the northeast gate and headed south toward Rashamon. Karasuma-dorii was the most direct route and I took it, even though it passed uncomfortably close to the Imperial Compound. I kept to the far side of the street but wasn't otherwise overly concerned. If anyone in the Palace was looking for me, my exact position within the city would have been of little consequence.

The western gate to the Compound was shut, and the way was physically blocked by several *bushi* in Minamoto colors. While of course the entrances to the Imperial Compound were guarded, it was unusual to see them closed off in that manner. I wondered idly if there was some festival or ceremonial observance involved, but I couldn't recall any specifically that fell on this date. I shrugged. Whatever the reason, it was—I hoped—no concern of mine. I kept moving.

I was already tired of walking; my four months inside a saké cup had taken their toll; in more ways than one, I realized. It was, now that I thought to look, a fine spring day. The *sakura* were in bloom all through the city. I took it as confirmation of my wretchedly demeaned state that it wasn't until this, my second trip of the day out into the city, that I finally noticed. At least I wasn't *beyond* noticing. I didn't know if this was a good sign or not, but I appreciated the fact for what little it might be worth. I ignored the ache in my legs and kept moving until the Rasha Gate came into view.

Kenji hadn't steered me wrong; I found Nidai playing at tops with a group of children not thirty paces from the southeast gate. He was, as the Widow Tamahara had said, immediately recognizable by his tattered red sash. No telling where the boy had acquired it, but he wore it among the other city children like a badge of honor. The other children immediately scattered as I approached. Nidai didn't budge.

"Lord Yamada," he said, ignoring his red spinning top as he gave me a formal bow. "She said you'd come."

I stopped. "She?"

"The one who hired me to deliver your message earlier today," he said. "That is who you're really looking for, isn't it?"

I smiled. "You seem to know a great deal of these matters."

He sighed. "Very little, really, my lord. Not even the lady's name, as she refused to tell me. She covered her face, too."

I'd suspected no less. So, a woman had not only written the poem but had arranged for its delivery. It was nice to have this much confirmation. "Well, then," I said, "it seems I've walked a long way for nothing."

Nidai pulled a piece of paper from his sash that had been folded into a long strip and tied into a lover's knot. "The second task of my hire," he said. "When you meet the lady, tell her that I did everything just as she said. I am a good messenger."

"I will be sure to tell her," I said, noting that Nidai had said "when" and not "if."

I took the paper, and Nidai immediately scooped up his faltering top and ran off to join the other children disappearing into the streets around the gate. I found a comfortable stone and sat down to read the message. I untied the knot in the paper and unfolded it, anxious despite myself. Kenji's news today was disturbing and more than a little; I wasn't entirely certain that the earlier poem didn't have something to do with it, not that this new message gave much in the way of enlightenment. There was no poem, and very little else. Just a date, two days from now, directions to a particular place in the city, and an approximate hour which, this time of year, would be just after sunset. The message was written in the same delicate precise calligraphy of the earlier letter.

The message itself was obviously an appointment. All that remained was to decide if I wished to keep that appointment. It occurred to me I'd be a fool to accept not knowing what awaited me, but I'd perhaps be a bigger fool not to do so. I thought of visiting Seita for information; the ghost's bridge was a fairly short walk from the Rasha Gate, but I didn't have the fee; it seemed I was adrift and left to my own devices.

I smiled, remembering the old proverb: "The man who dances is a fool. The man who does not is also a fool. If both are fools, one may as well dance."

One may, indeed.

When I returned to my rooms that evening, the Widow Tamahara greeted me with a bowl of rice and a bit of fish and a question. That question was not, as I dreaded, the usual one about the rent.

"Wasn't that the most awful thing?"

"Ummm . . . "

"Honestly, Lord Yamada, your obvliviousness is really quite astonishing," the Widow Tamahara said, correctly interpreting my blank stare as total incomprehension. "You have not heard? The news is all over the city!"

I wasn't so certain of that. Counting my travels to the northeast and southeast gates, *I* had been "all over the city" and had heard no great news. Then again, I had spoke to no one save Kenji and Nidai. "What is it?"

"One of Princess Ai's attendants has been murdered! Within the Palace Compound itself! Can you imagine?"

I could imagine, and from what I knew of life at Court, I was just surprised that it happened so seldom. Princess Ai I also knew, or at least remembered. She was a principal wife of the current Emperor and known as much for her bad temper as her beauty. If one of her attendants had been murdered, I'd have placed odds that Ai herself was responsible, acting on some fit of pique or another. Perhaps this explained why the western gate of the Imperial Compound had been sealed off; priests would have been summoned and purification rites begun as soon as the body was removed. Even so, the Princess and all her attendants would be ritually impure for the next month and probably "exiled" from the Compound proper to one of the various outlying mansions within the city until said impurity was removed. I could also imagine what a good humor that would place Her Highness in.

"A tragedy," I said. Considering that the Widow Tamahara had just brought me my evening meal despite my being late with the rent, I had no wish to antagonize her by revealing my disinterest. "I'm afraid I spoke to no one today who had heard the news. If

69

it's not indelicate to ask, how was this done? Do they know who is responsible?"

Tamahara-san rubbed her scrawny neck. "That's the strangest part of all. What I have heard suggests that there were no marks on the poor girl, no wounds. Even most poisons leave some sign, but there was nothing. Perhaps she was smothered in her sleep."

I frowned. "Most poisons" perhaps, but not all by any means. Still . . . "This happened during the night? Among the other attendants?"

"Yes, as I understand it."

Now that was indeed a bit strange. If the girl in question had slipped from Ai's chambers to, say, keep an assignation with a lover then her separation from the others made the possibility of an attack much more likely. Yet if the girl had been sleeping in a group with the other close attendants, as was usual, then for someone to slip inside and do violence to one without alerting the rest the culprit would either have to be very stealthy or everyone else present had to be complicit.

"If there were no wounds, why is it presumed the poor girl was murdered?"

"That's a good question, Lord Yamada. I do not know. Yet my sources were quite emphatic on that point."

The incident was more than a little curious, assuming that the Widow Tamahara's information was good, but I knew better than to put too much faith in the old woman's sources; in general they were no better than the typical street gossips. No doubt the unfortunate girl had died of some unknown but virulent ailment; the gods and demons of disease were a busy lot and sometimes not detected and exorcised quickly enough, even among the upper classes.

"Doubtless the one responsible will be found out," I said. "The Palace has great means at its disposal."

"I suppose," Tamahara-san said, chewing a fingernail thoughtfully. "Is there a possibility you will be engaged in this matter?"

Again, the rent; I knew we'd get back to the subject sooner or later. "It's possible. I guess we'll have to wait and see."

The Widow Tamahara looked almost hopeful as she left me to my rice. For my own part, I put what remained of my faith in the Widow Tamahara's rice and fish. It was all I could really count on, though probably not for very much longer. Given that reality, I took time to savor my simple meal, hungry as I was.

I had barely finished that meal when I received yet another message. The author of this one, however, was not in the least bit mysterious, nor was the messenger. The young man kneeling on my veranda under the watchful eye of the Widow Tamahara was dressed in the familiar red and black colors and bore the butterfly *mon* of the Taira.

He held out a small scroll with both hands and announced, "From Prince Kanemore."

The scroll itself would have told me that much once I broke the seal—I recognized Prince Kanemore's hand immediately. There was no poem, and frankly, I would have been surprised if there had been. The message had all the signs of Kanemore's blunt style:

Lord Yamada, please do me the honor of accompanying the bearer wherever he directs, and do not worry. I will explain upon your arrival. Kanemore

That was the extent of the message. I looked at the young man. "Where are we going?"

"My apologies, my lord, but I am not allowed to say."

I sighed, and directed the young man to wait while I changed my clothing to something at least somewhat cleaner. For all I knew, Kanemore planned to bring me to the Imperial Compound itself, and my clothing was in even sorrier condition than it had been during my last visit. I really just wanted to find a clear spot on my floor and go to sleep, but refusing the summons was out of the question. This time, however, I did put on my *tachi*. While I was more than willing to trust Prince Kanemore with my life, the part of his message that said "don't worry" was having the opposite effect. The young Taira *bushi* glanced at the sword when I returned to the veranda but made no objection.

"Lead on," I said.

When we first headed north I was afraid my worries were accurate, but instead of turning west toward the Imperial Compound we turned east. The light was failing rapidly, but the young man had not brought a lantern and showed no inclination to find one. He moved quickly and surely along those narrow streets, and it was all I could do to keep up. It wasn't until we had reached the gate that I realized our destination was Zenrin-ji, a temple on the eastern edge of the city not too far from the cremation grounds near Mount Toribe. We passed two other Taira *bushi* outside the gate, and though they were clearly in a high state of watchfulness, they did not challenge us. We proceeded directly to the Lotus Hall, greeted by the steady drone of monks chanting a *sutra*. At the far end of the hall I could see a statue of Kwannon, Goddess of Mercy. On a raised wooden bier before the statue there lay the body of a young woman in funeral white. I was taking all this in and barely noticed when the *bushi* escorting me suddenly kneeled and bowed low, then discreetly withdrew.

"Yamada-san, thank you for coming."

"I am at your service," I said.

I had recognized the voice. Prince Kanemore stood at the rear of the hall with a scowling older monk who, by his demeanor, I took to be the man in charge of the temple. Kanemore confirmed this at once.

"Lord Yamada, I do not believe you have met this gentleman. He is Master Kintei, Chief Priest of Zenrin-ji."

"I am honored." I bowed to them both, and the priest's bow of acknowledgment was little more than a nod of his head. He quickly turned his attention back to Kanemore. I didn't bother asking any questions; I knew the time for that was coming soon. As for the two of them, they immediately resumed a discussion that had clearly been interrupted by my arrival.

"And I must say again, Highness, that this matter is highly irregular. If the Ministry of Justice has no issues, why do you? Yes, highly irregular." The chief priest's voice was rough and whispery.

"I know that, yet I must respectfully ask for your indulgence in this . . . situation. I must also ask that you accept my assurance that the gravity of the matter leaves me no choice. You have my word that there will be no insult to the unfortunate young woman. I . . . I know her family well."

"I will hold you to that promise, Highness. I would be negligent in my duties otherwise."

Kanemore bowed slightly to the old man who merely nodded curtly in my direction and reluctantly withdrew. The chanting never stopped, but after a moment I realized it was coming from outside the building and that Kanemore and I were alone in the Lotus Hall. He smiled at me a little wistfully, and it was only then I saw the weariness in his eyes. I realized to my shock that he looked as bad as I felt.

"It's good to see you again, despite the circumstances," Kanemore said, then hesitated. "Are you well?"

I almost laughed. "If by 'well' you mean 'sober,' then yes, I am quite well. Disgustingly, annoyingly well."

He smiled faintly then. "Yet I must, under the circumstances, be grateful for this unfortunate condition."

"The 'circumstances,' I confess, I don't quite understand."

"Lord Yamada, the young woman on the bier is—or was— Taira no Kei, an attendant to Princess Ai. She died, apparently, in her sleep sometime last night. I know there have been rumors."

"The rumor is that she was murdered."

Prince Kanemore let out a breath. "I should have realized the story would spread. But yes, I believe she was."

I frowned. I had assumed that Tamahara-san's talk on the matter had just been gossipy chatter, and what I had said in return merely idle speculation, and yet here was the matter again, real and immediate in the dead body of this young woman.

"How? It was my understanding the unfortunate girl died in the foyer adjacent to Princess Ai's chambers, surrounded by a throng of attendants. From what I know of such arrangements, chances are that no one could possibly have reached the girl without stepping on at least three others. Or am I mistaken?"

Kanemore looked grim. "No, that's exactly where she was when she died, and before you ask, no, there was no sign of any of the more common poisons. For that matter, I do not believe she *was* poisoned. The new Minister of Justice instructed me to make certain the body was examined for wounds, even the smallest, while it was being prepared for the funeral rites. My people were meticulous; there was not so much as a bug bite found. There was a bluish cast to her face as if she'd been strangled, but it was faint, and there were no marks on her neck, other than her own."

"Her own?"

"When she was found, she had both her hands at her throat as if she had been choking, but the other girls insist she had eaten nothing since the evening meal. The size of the marks on her neck suggest those marks came from her own fingers."

"Then how, if she was murdered, was it done?"

"That is what I had hoped you might be able to answer. I apologize for the ritual impurity this will entail. You won't be able to participate in a temple ceremony or enter the Imperial Compound for a month."

"Prince Kanemore, you know very well I give less than a pail of slops for either ceremonies or, no offence intended, being inside the compound."

He smiled a rueful smile. "As do I in principle, but in practice I cannot afford to be away from the Palace now. Besides, I likely would be forced to quarter with Princess Ai in the Sanjo mansion, so I believe I must decline."

I almost laughed, but then I thought of the grim duty before me, and the impulse faded. "Very well. I would ask that you guard the doors, but I see you've already arranged for it."

Kanemore grunted. "I don't expect Kei's nearest family to

arrive before tomorrow, but it's best to be cautious. We shall have ample warning of any early arrivals."

Quite sensibly so. The last thing either Kanemore or I needed was for the girl's father or uncles to arrive and find a stranger taking such liberties with the remains of their child.

It was clear why Prince Kanemore had interrupted the funeral rites so that he and I were alone in the hall with the body of the dead girl. What was less clear was what he expected me to find that the priests and the current Imperial Minister of Justice, Lord Sentaro's replacement, had apparently missed. Still, there was no point in delaying the matter, and plenty of reason not to do so. I reluctantly approached the bier.

One wished to keep one's detachment at such times, but it was difficult. With her face painted white and her eyebrows drawn black, Taira no Kei looked like a little girl napping after a long day of playing grown-up. While it was true that life was uncertain and transient, there was something about looking at the dead body of a girl who could not have been older than twelve that tipped my balance of right and wrong. Whether a *kami* of disease was responsible or something more sinister, Taira no Kei's death was simply *wrong*, and nothing Kanemore or I could do would set it right again. One was left only with questions such as "how?" and, perhaps more to the point, "why"? Answering the first might lead one well along the path to the second. I leaned close.

Fortunately there was no need to disturb the girl's clothing. When Kanemore said the body had been thoroughly examined, I had no good reason to doubt his judgment in that regard. That fact spared me some awkwardness but did not leave me much to go on. The bluish pallor was easy enough to spot, once I rubbed off a bit of the white makeup near her jaw line. The marks on her neck were very clear to see, even through the makeup. I examined them closely, then carefully ran my fingers over the girl's throat.

Curious . . .

I then combed my fingers through the dead girl's hair as close to the scalp as I could manage, and then down to the nape of her neck. There was some slight swelling at the back of her head, but nothing to indicate a fatal blow.

No matter how lifelike the body appeared, there was no way to mistake the lack of warmth and the stiffness of the corpse for other than what it was—a shell whose spirit had fled. There was nothing left now, save the mortal flesh soon to be burnt on the slopes of Mount Toribe.

Prince Kanemore had thoughtfully supplied a basin of water and I washed my hands. It wouldn't remove the ritual impurity, but it made me feel better. I dried myself on the cloth also provided and left the bier.

"I know you have already made your own inquiries, so let me ask you: given Kei's age, may I assume there were yet no spurned lovers? What about personal rivalries or jealousy among the attendants themselves?"

"Kei was a beautiful young girl, so neither is impossible," Kanemore admitted, "but extremely unlikely; she was too young for such things, even by the standards of the Court. I uncovered one or two flirtations, but nothing more serious. Also, she seems to have been well regarded, even by Princess Ai . . . though with Her Highness that is a relative term. Why do you ask?"

"Before I say anything else, Prince Kanemore, there is

something else I need to ask: what made you believe the girl was murdered?"

He sighed. "Only my eyes and my instincts, Lord Yamada. I have seen too many deaths by violence to mistake them for anything else. Whatever killed Taira no Kei, I believe she fought it, and lost."

"There are many disease *kami* that will choke off a person's wind and make them turn blue as they die."

Kanemore looked grim. "You do not see her now as I saw her then, Lord Yamada. I know I am right."

I did not argue, as I shared his opinion completely. "Yes, Prince Kanemore. I believe you are."

"Then how was it done?"

"She strangled herself."

Kanemore scowled at me. "But that's impossible. And even if she did manage it, that would be . . . "

"Suicide? No, and for the reason you just pointed out: strangling yourself with your own two hands simply cannot be done. You can hang yourself, certainly, or twist a cord around your own neck and secure the ends if you're very determined, but anyone who simply tried to strangle themselves would lose consciousness and relax their grip well before death claimed them, no matter how sincere the attempt. They would wake up with a headache, but little the worse otherwise. No, the only way this could work was if the girl was compelled by a will other than her own. Again, as you pointed out, the marks on her neck were made with her own two hands. Now, certainly the instinct may be to put one's hands to one's throat if one were choking, but would you then attempt to crush your own windpipe? I think not."

"But . . . then how was this done? Sorcery?"

That was a very good question, which, at the moment, I could not answer. "I do not know, and I readily acknowledge the entire notion is rather far-fetched. Yet, like you, I am certain I am right."

I couldn't tell if Prince Kanemore felt either relief or justification, because his face showed neither. Rather, he was clearly worried, and that made me worry too.

"Prince Kanemore, if it's not impolite to ask, what is your interest in this girl?"

"As I told Master Kintei, I know her family and the Emperor has requested that I be acting Captain of the Palace Guard while I am in the capital. Since I must remain at Court for the time being, I have chosen to make myself useful."

"That is a reason," I said, "and certainly understandable, but it's not your real concern, is it? Nor is that the reason you remain at Court despite your avowed intent to renounce your title and start a new family clan."

He met my gaze squarely. "Whatever killed Taira no Kei could easily kill others. The reason I choose to remain where I am is due to unfinished business, Lord Yamada. I think you know of what I speak."

I did: Takahito. For his sister's sake, Kanemore would not allow himself to be separated from his nephew until the young man was crowned emperor just as Princess Teiko had wished. Despite his sympathy for the unfortunate girl's family, Kanemore's real concern was for Teiko's son. That was my concern as well.

"Then I must remember that you remain Prince Kanemore, and not simply my friend, Kanemore-sama."

"For the moment," Kanemore sounded reluctant but then

continued, "then there is the matter of Lord Sentaro, now the chief priest at Enryaku-ji on Mount Hiei."

"Yes, I assumed you had already heard about that. Something I fear even Princess Teiko did not foresee."

"Perhaps, but she certainly knew the matter did not end with her," Kanemore said dryly. "You never asked the contents of my sister's letter to *me*."

I frowned. "That is so. I will ask now, if you will share the information."

He smiled. "It only said, in essence, to be wary of the Fujiwara, that the danger was not past. I did not understand what she meant at the time, but now I think I do. I wonder if the danger will *ever* be past. I should have killed Lord Sentaro when I had the chance."

I sighed. "You never had the chance, Highness. We both know the Emperor would not sanction such a duel. You'd have been treated worse than a common murderer; the Fujiwara would have seen to that."

He scowled. "At least Takahito would be safe."

"Oh? And is Lord Sentaro the only Fujiwara who does not wish to see Takahito on the throne? Are you so certain that Lord Sentaro—or whatever priest name he's conveniently adopted—is behind this?"

I saw a little of the fire go out of Kanemore's eyes. "No, I am not. I only know that there is now apparently an assassin who can evade guards and strike within a crowd of people without being detected. This," he said with characteristic understatement, "is a problem. Yet if Takahito were the real target, why is he alive and this poor girl now lying here in his place? I have justly suspected

Lord Sentaro of many things, but incompetence is not among them. That Princess Teiko fooled him does not change that; she fooled us as well. The matter of this unfortunate girl makes no sense to me."

"Nor to me. And, frankly, I find this situation as disturbing as you do."

Kanemore looked at me. "Lord Yamada, I need to understand what happened here and who is behind it, before the assassin moves again and against a target even less to either of our liking."

"You have my aid, for whatever I can do, Highness. You know this."

After Teiko's death I, no less than Kanemore, was honor-bound to see this matter through. Even so, I reluctantly accepted payment from Prince Kanemore for three reasons. The first was that I certainly could not explain why I should not. The second was that I could now placate the Widow Tamahara and thus not have to worry about being cast out into the streets of the capital before I unraveled the knot of Taira no Kei's death—assuming that there was an answer within my poor reach, and I was determined to find out. The third reason was that now I would have the means to buy a little information.

Even so, it was too late in the evening and I was far too weary to attempt a visit to Seita's bridge now. I asked Kanemore to gather some information for me from the Imperial Compound and specifically Princess Ai's quarters. We arranged to meet the following afternoon, and I then allowed the young Taira *bushi* to escort me back to my rooms. I must have pulled my bedding out at some point, but in truth I have no memory of doing so before I fell asleep.

That night I dreamed of Taira no Kei. Her ghost kept trying to serve me tea. She was gentle but very persistent. I tried to explain to her that she was dead, and that whatever she meant to bring to me no longer belonged in this world. I remember being very insistent on this point. She looked unhappy but did not relent. I must have tea, if not now, then later. It was very important. Since I had been of no help to the girl while she lived, I did not want to refuse her, even though I knew I should.

"If I take tea later, will that be all right?"

She looked at me very seriously then, and the image burned itself into my memory: her painted white face, white funeral robes, and glittering black eyes. "You must take tea with *oneesama*. Please be kind."

"Your older sister? Why? Who is she?"

"She is in pain. Please be kind," the ghost repeated, and then Taira no Kei faded with the rest of the dream, leaving one more question of the day unanswered.

The next morning dawned bright and much too early. While I recognized the possibility that I had been visited by Taira no Kei's ghost in the night, I knew it was equally likely that the girl's appearance was no more than the jumble of the day's events working their way through my exhausted brain. There was no way to tell which, so I did not bother putting either possibility to the scale.

That was the problem with dreams—when it came to seeking a basis for future plans, or the keys to a mystery, dreams were simply not dependable. It was possible I had learned something very important during the night, even if I didn't understand what it might be. Yet knowing this, what could I do? Other than, perhaps, finding out if Taira no Kei did indeed have an older sister and attempt to have tea with this person. None of it made any sense.

Rather than dwelling on the dream, I made myself busy, first by settling accounts with the Widow Tamahara, then by locating the house where my unknown correspondent had asked for a meeting.

There was a once-fine house near the northern edge of the city. It was where my directions indicated, but the house was not in use and had not been so in a long time; that much was evident at first glance. The gate to the compound wall was askew, there were bushes and wild grass throughout the garden, the screens were in disrepair, the pond was choked with weeds. I stood some distance away, satisfying myself of these facts, when a very odd thing happened: a large group of workmen arrived and began repairs on the gate while I watched. In almost no time at all they had the gate set to rights and had begun work inside. I accosted the man who appeared to be in charge as he came outside to direct the delivery of wood and supplies, and give several just-arrived carpenters their instructions.

"Can you tell me who lives here?" I asked.

The man gave me a small bow, clearly distracted. "Sir, no one lives here at the moment," he said. "We were engaged to make repairs with a bonus for working quickly, and that is all I know."

"Who hired you?"

"A lady. She did not give her name, but her gold was good."

The man was busy and I did not keep him. I had already learned more than I expected. While I had seen it myself a few times, the exchange of gold was not a common thing, even among the nobility, where normal payment for goods or services was in rice or, at most, the old bronze Chinese coins that some used as trading tokens. Such rare payment as gold easily explained why the workmen were being so quick and diligent. I well remembered similar reactions before the last of Teiko's gold had been squandered on drink. I idly wondered just how much these men would manage to do before the appointed hour, and was this for my benefit or no?

Curious.

Still, I had no time to loiter. I made my way back south to the Gion district and the Widow Tamahara's establishment, where Prince Kanemore and I had agreed to meet. I sometimes wondered how the prince felt coming to such a place, but surely in his travels as a soldier of the Emperor he had known far worse. In truth, when I arrived to find Kanemore already established at a corner table, the man looked perfectly at ease, both with his less than refined surroundings and the *matsu* cup he was using to drink one of the Widow Tamahara's finer grades of saké. I knew any concerns he might have were for far greater matters.

He nodded in my direction. "Lord Yamada."

I bowed as I kneeled at the table. "I'm sorry to have kept you waiting."

"I used the time. Would you care for a drink?"

"I would care a great deal. Which is why, perhaps, I must decline."

He sighed. "Thoughtless of me, I know. Still, it was an . . .

interesting morning." He drained his cup and set it aside. "I suppose we should eat something. Surely you will join me there?"

I smiled. "With enthusiasm."

The Widow Tamahara personally brought out rice and tea, and grilled eel with *miso* and pickles. I don't think I realized just how hungry my morning walk to the north of the city had made me. As for Kanemore, this was much simpler fare than he was accustomed to in the Imperial Compound but not beyond his experience during campaign. He attacked his portion as heartily as I did my own, and for a while neither Prince Kanemore nor I said anything; it was only when our bowls and cups were empty that we got to the matter at hand.

"I checked the ceiling, Lord Yamada. Nothing had been disturbed until I myself moved one of the boards. Frankly, if anyone had done so and attempted to lower himself from there, the dust would have had everyone awake and sneezing in unison long beforehand. What about some sort of winged creature?"

"Who would have needed to negotiate tight quarters and then hover like a hawk over the girl all the while." I told Kanemore about the *tengu* that had tried to enter the city two days before, and the power of the downbeat of its wings. "Even assuming that such a creature had reached the girl and physically forced her to place her own hands about her neck, there is simply no way it could have done so without either it or the girl awakening anyone who was not themselves already dead."

Kanemore looked morose. "I knew it was unlikely, but now we're back where we started. What you and I both believe happened still appears to be impossible."

"It *did* happen," I said with emphasis, "and so cannot be impossible. The question of 'how' does remain, I'm afraid."

Kanemore sighed. "I must return to the Imperial Compound. I don't dare remain away for long, especially now."

"I assume Prince Takahito has taken over his mother's quarters? He's guarded, of course?"

"Of course. I have trusted men at every door and around the grounds. If I do any more, he'll have more guards than the Emperor himself. Still, at least no conventional threat will get by them."

"I have no answers for you as of yet. But rest assured that this is my purpose. What was the girl's family told?"

"The current Minister of Justice, Lord Noruboshi, personally assured the girl's father that she died in her sleep of some unknown ailment."

"Did you tell the minister of your suspicions?"

"I told him at the very beginning of his alleged 'investigation', but he pronounced my suspicions impossible, and how could I argue otherwise? I'm actually rather fond of Lord Noruboshi. He has a good heart, for a Fujiwara, but at best he's a genial idiot. He will not be of any help, I'm afraid."

"I wasn't counting on it. We'll need to find our own sources of aid."

"What about your ghost?"

I smiled. "Seita? He's not 'my' ghost, Prince Kanemore, but you've seen how accurate his information can be. Yet I must emphasize that he is neither infallible nor omniscient, nor, let it be said, always reliable. But, yes, I was thinking along just those lines. I will send word when I learn anything, assuming I do."

"I pray that it be so."

There wasn't anything else to be said. Kanemore departed for the Palace grounds, and I returned to my rooms to rest since I had no idea how long or how late the coming evening, for me, was to be. I tried to nap but sleep would not come, so I wound up lying on my back on a rather tatty cushion pondering over and again what had happened, judging the various elements, considering all aspects of the matter that my tired mind could hold. It was more frustrating than restful because all of my mental journeys, like a circular road, brought me back to the same understanding that had left Prince Kanemore and myself stranded earlier in the day: what had happened to Taira no Kei was simply not possible.

I smiled ruefully. *So then the girl is not dead. The smoke of her burning did not rise up the slopes of Mount Toribe, and her family did not mourn, and her ashes were not buried or scattered. None of that happened. None of it could have happened. Like Kei's visit to me, it was merely a dream.*

I sincerely hoped that Seita's understanding was greater than mine, but I was hard-pressed to understand how it could be less. As things were, I had to confess myself totally baffled. I finally managed a bit of fitful sleep as evening approached, but there were no dreams that I could recall.

When I awoke from a shallow sleep the sun had not yet set, but was not long for the sky. I informed the Widow Tamahara that I would not be taking supper in my rooms that evening. I then left her and followed Shijo-dori until it crossed Karasuma, then turned south toward Rashamon.

My rather vivid memories of my last trip through the Rasha Gate had me a bit on edge as I exited the city proper, but there were no incidents, no sound of rustling paper, nothing. The Rasha Gate's reputation as an entranceway for evil spirits was matched only by that of the northeast, or "Demon," gate through which the *tengu* had entered the city the day before, though the demands and direction of travel required that the northeast gate be well-used despite this reputation. There was less traffic and travel to the south, and only fools or those with compelling reason would find themselves as I now found myself—alone on the southern road within sight of Rashamon. I imagined there could be no one else to which this would apply *and* be in search of a ghost as well, but that was why I was there.

The moon was high when I reached the ruined wall of Seita's home, if such it had been, and approached the bridge that crossed the now overgrown stream, its banks covered in wild vines and briars. I could smell the *sakura* in the former garden, now grown wild.

"Seita-san? I need a word with you."

Seita did not appear. There was a flash of red to one side of the bridge on the opposite shore, then another close to the water. It winked out like a firefly, then reappeared on the other side of the bridge.

"Seita, is that you?"

It was several long moments before I received a reply, almost too faint to hear.

"Lord Yamada?"

I frowned. "I don't have a great deal of time, Seita-san. Why so elusive?"

"Being elusive is not always a fault. Sometimes it is a necessity. How do I know that you are really Lord Yamada, and not something with Lord Yamada's face *pretending* to be Lord Yamada?"

I think the voice now came from beneath the bridge, but I wasn't even certain of that. "You mean the way the *shikigami* impersonated you? And who knows this aside from you, myself, and Prince Kanemore? All the creatures were destroyed."

Now Seita did appear on the highest point of the half-moon shaped bridge. "A good point, Lord Yamada," the lantern said. "But one cannot be too cautious these days."

I sighed. "Seita-san, not to be indelicate, but you are already dead and have been so for a considerable time. What have you to fear?"

"Spoken with the true arrogance of the living," Seita said dryly. "So, what do you wish of me?"

"I have come about a girl who was murdered in the city yesterday."

The lantern dimmed, then brightened again. "One? There were at least three that I am aware of. Could you be more specific?"

"The circumstances of the one I speak were very specific," I said. "A girl surrounded by her friends, and all saw nothing. No wounds, nothing except marks around her throat she apparently made as she strangled herself."

"Cannot be done," Seita said.

"It *was* done," I said, feeling just a bit annoyed. "What I need to know is *how* and *why*."

"You're referring to Taira no Kei?" he asked.

"The same. I imagine the rumors would have reached you quickly."

"Yes, but I asked because she wasn't the only one. Four people

89

have died in the city under similar circumstances within the last month . . . except they didn't strangle themselves. At least, there was no mention of it."

"How did they die, then? Have any become ghosts who would, perhaps, speak to us?"

"We're well past idle conversation now, my lord," Seita said. "And I am hungry. One bowl to start, or my memory might fade."

I had expected no less. I produced a measured bag of uncooked rice from Prince Kanemore's stipend and placed a pair of *hashi* upright through the mouth of the bag.

"For the good of my friend, Seita-san," I said, bowing formally.

I didn't look as the bag floated off of my outstretched palms, though I knew what was about to happen. When I looked again, the rotted remains of the cloth bag were drifting away on the breeze like falling leaves. Seita let out a sigh of deep contentment.

"Much better. Now, to answer your first question: I don't know. I only remarked on the matter because their manner of death was unusual and much remarked upon among those left behind after the departed's passing. Thus, those rumors reached me. If your information concerning Princess Ai's attendant is correct, that merely reinforces what I have already heard, save for the nonsense about self-strangulation. In answer to your second question: at the moment I don't know but consider it unlikely. Most people pass immediately from this world at death."

"You did not," I pointed out.

Seita looked thoughtful. "Lord Yamada, when you look at me, what do you see?"

The question rather took me by surprise. "What do I . . . ? I see a red lantern, about half my height, with a rather large eye and a smaller mouth. Is this not the manifestation you have chosen?"

"I chose nothing. In my mind I am as I was. My family compound, which you have assured me on many occasions is a ruin, I see as I remember it, a happy place. Sometimes I think I can hear the voices of my mother and father, my wife, just in the next room. I know this is not as things are, but while I linger they remain true for me. Why should I leave? What do you think is waiting for me beyond this realm?"

It seems that even a ghost may be haunted. "I don't know," I said. The lantern sighed, and I felt a chill on the evening breeze. "I do. It's what awaits anyone who is not an 'Enlightened Being,' as the priests say. There are many hells, all waiting to burn away the impurities and delusions of this life for however many ages that shall take. For our own good, of course, and yet you wonder what the dead should fear? Death is easy, Lord Yamada. What comes after is the difficult part."

"No doubt I'll find out soon enough. For now I have other problems."

"Which only my memory of hunger, which will not leave me alone, forces me to see as my own."

I didn't argue the point. "That there were other deaths of a similar nature should not surprise me, as my understanding of the matter is so limited I don't know what is to be expected and what is not. Which is why I have come to you, Seita-san. Can you help me or not?"

The ghost hesitated. Before this I was merely annoyed. Now I was worried. Seita had been acting strangely before and now it was even more apparent. Normally by now he would have named his price and been halfway to collecting it from me. Yet at the moment he just hovered, silent, at the highest part of the bridge.

"You don't see it, do you?"

I sighed. "Seita-san, if you keep asking me questions, before long I'll be demanding rice of *you*. What are you talking about?"

"A darkness has come over the city, like a great cloud. Can't you sense it? Even in the daytime? It's there, though much more powerful at night."

"I have not your . . . sensitivity, to such matters. What is it? Some sort of magic? A demon?"

"I do not know," Seita said. "Nor do I wish to know. This darkness has eyes, Lord Yamada. It has intentions. What it chooses to notice, it sees. I do not want it to see me."

"Is this 'darkness' you refer to what killed Taira no Kei and the others?"

"I am not sure . . . " Seita looked about as agitated as I had ever seen him. He finally sighed again, looking resigned. "Damn my hunger. Damn you and your rice, for that matter. Give me some time, Lord Yamada. Perhaps someone within my circle knows more than I do. See me in the evening after two days' time. Four bowls, if I have your answer. One if you want me to keep trying."

"Done, if you'll tell me who and where in the city those similar deaths occurred. There may be no common thread, but I must look anyway."

Seita obeyed, and somewhat hastily. "Now please leave me. No offense, Lord Yamada, but the darkness sometimes seems deeper when you are around."

I didn't argue that point, either. "I will look for you two days from now."

"Yes," Seita said, "and please, not before."

He floated back across the bridge and disappeared. It occurred to me that it was little wonder I was usually alone, if even ghosts did not wish my company.

As I walked back into the city through Rashamon I considered the new information that Seita had given me, trying to see what possible link to Taira no Kei there might be. I had not yet even gotten as far as Karasuma-dori when I came to the inescapable conclusion that there simply was no connection.

The other four mysterious deaths consisted of a retired prostitute near the Gion Shrine, a nine-year-old orphan girl in service to a fishmonger, a young monk at Kiyomizu-dera, and the wife of a provincial lord from Hokkaido. I went through a quick mental map of the city to locate where each death had occurred, and the pattern, if one could call it that, seemed completely random within the range of the city where such incidents had been identified. While it was always possible there was a connection I was too dull to see, I certainly was not seeing it. If any of the victims, other than possibly the former prostitute and the fish-seller's servant, had even met each other before I would have been greatly surprised. A prior meeting was definitely not the case with the governor's wife; she was from the province originally and had never even set foot in the city before, if Seita's information could be trusted.

New disease spirits sometimes arose, ones for which the priests had yet to locate the proper prayers. Sometimes the death tolls rose quite high, and the malady turned into an actual plague before it could be brought under control and the correct deities assuaged. Perhaps Taira no Kei and the others were merely victims of one such, and as the threat progressed and was thus recognized, spiritual counter-measures would be discovered. My reasonable side said this was so; every instinct within me—and in Kanemore as well, it seemed—denied this.

The darkness has eyes. It has intentions.

Seita's words came back to me, unbidden. It occurred to me that there was another in my circle who might understand at least a little of what Seita was talking about. I judged the lateness of the hour by the height of the moon and thought, perhaps, there was still enough time. Instead of taking Shijo-dori back to the Widow Tamahara's establishment when it crossed Karasuma, I continued north toward the Demon Gate.

Kenji wasn't hard to find. There were only seven wine shops in the immediate vicinity of the Demon Gate, and the reprobate monk had his favorites; I found him slouched by a low corner table in the third establishment I tried, drinking quietly. This was not a good sign. Clearly Kenji had progressed from the "loud and boisterous" portion of his evening and was well on the way to the "stagger off somewhere and pass out" portion. If I wanted to get any sense into or out of the man, I knew I must proceed quickly.

"Lord Yamada, you great sullen fool," he said by way of greeting. "Have a drink."

Now this was odd. Kenji never willingly offered his wine to me or to anyone who wasn't young and female. More to the point, his speech was not slurred, nor was he otherwise incoherent. Clearly, I had been wrong about the man's state. Yes, he was drinking, but he was nowhere near drunk. If the eyes through which he regarded me were a little reddened, they were still clear and focused.

"Not that I mind, since I do need to speak to a man rather than the sad remains of too much bad saké, but why are you sober?"

"That is a good question," Kenji said. "Frankly, I would like to know the answer myself. No women about. No gamblers willing to lose to a monk. I even have the means to drink as much as I might want this evening. And yet . . . well, I am puzzled."

At first I thought the man was mocking me, but on closer inspection I realized he was, indeed, puzzled. There was fear, too.

"You're starting to sound like Seita."

"You're comparing me to the dead? That's bad luck, and I don't need yours on top of my own."

"I meant only that Seita seems worried. So do you. Would you mind telling me why?"

Kenji took another drink, and then made a face. "I don't know that. I don't even know," he said, taking one more drink and then scowling, "why this fine saké tastes like ditchwater on my tongue. I had thought my spotting that *tengu* was an opportunity, but ever since I helped drive it out I've been jumping at shadows. Perhaps the wretched creature cursed me."

I took the opportunity to ask a question that had occurred to me long since. "Why would a *tengu* try to enter the city in the first place?"

Kenji shrugged. "They are tricksters not unlike foxes, but their special delight is misleading the righteous."

"Then you certainly had nothing to fear from it, and I can understand the attraction since the capital has so many temples and monasteries. So why, then, are we not overrun with the creatures?"

Even the deliberate insult did nothing to either provoke a

response or lighten Kenji's mood. "Simply because we *are* thick with temples and monasteries, and powerful ancient shrines, Lord Yamada. The spiritual forces arrayed against any such intrusion are great, especially in the direction of the Demon Gate. That's why Enryaku Temple was founded to the northeast of the city in the first place."

"And yet it felt it could saunter in through that very gate, albeit in disguise, in broad daylight. Perhaps our defenses have been weakened." I then told Kenji what Seita had told me, 'dark cloud' references and all.

"From which direction does this dark spirit come?" he asked.

I frowned. "I don't know. Sullen fool that I am, I didn't think to ask."

"Well, you *should* have asked. Directions and paths of advancement or retreat are crucial in these matters, so it could be important. Perhaps this dark spiritual energy is what I have been sensing. It would explain why the barriers were low enough to let a *tengu* inside the city in the first place, and why everything seems so wrong."

So Kenji did indeed sense what Seita had referred to, and perhaps the same thing that, in my own dull way, had been troubling me as well. "That's the way I feel about that girl's death," I said, because it was true.

"I think perhaps this extends beyond even that," Kenji said. "But I do not know how or what this thing might be."

I had an idea. "Meet me at Rasha gate, at sunset two days from now. I have an appointment with Seita, but these matters are closer to your understanding than mine. Perhaps you can think of some questions that would not occur to me."

"Doubtless true," Kenji said, rubbing his chin. He looked thoughtful, or at least as thoughtful as Kenji ever did.

"You're going to meet the person who sent the message about your father tomorrow, yes?"

While I had thought of myself as ambivalent on the matter, when Kenji asked the question straight out my answer came of the same spirit. "Yes, I am."

"Do you think that is wise?"

"I most certainly do not. I have no idea what I'm getting into."

"Then perhaps you could persuade Prince Kanemore to accompany you. Just a thought."

I sighed deeply. "First of all, I can take care of myself. As for Prince Kanemore, he is a friend but he has his own concerns, and this is my family business, not his."

"Even so."

"Let us get back to the matter at hand. There is no need to stall, Kenji-san. I know it is a long walk to the southeast gate, and this really isn't your affair. I have patronage at the moment, so I can make it worth your while."

"No need," Kenji said, sounding reluctant. "It occurs to me that perhaps this *is* my affair, though I wish it were not so. If this 'darkness' does indeed have eyes, then perhaps it has already seen me through that *tengu*."

As with Seita, I did not argue. Kenji might very well be right, and as I had said, such matters were closer to his realm than mine. In two days, perhaps we would know. As for myself, tomorrow I was to meet the author of that poetic message concerning my father. With the events surrounding Taira no Kei's death, the matter had been given rather short shrift in my concerns, but now as the time grew nearer—and despite the fact that Teiko's brother and son required my foremost attention—I found my curiosity growing. Who even remembered my father or cared about the loss of my family's lands and future? My hopes were not terribly high, but I thought that perhaps tomorrow there would be at least one question answered.

⛩

The following day I spent most of my hours in matters of little consequence, and that evening as the waning moon rose I presented myself at the newly repaired gate of the once-ruined mansion. After a short delay it was opened by Nidai. He still wore his tattered red sash, but his clothing otherwise had been much improved and his hair freshly cut.

"Lord Yamada," he said, bowing low. "Welcome."

I suppressed a smile. "So you have progressed beyond simple messenger, Nidai-kun. What is your involvement in this affair?"

"Thanks to my proper conscientiousness as a messenger I am now a lady's servant, Lord Yamada. Certainly better employment than fighting my comrades for fish-heads stolen from the market. Mistress is expecting you, so if you will follow me . . . "

"Lead on, then."

I had to say that the workmen had been more than diligent. While the water in the small garden pond was now a muddy brown, at least the worst of the water weeds and scum had been cleared away. As for the rest of the garden, the brush had been cleared and the path relined, and the trees properly pruned. On the house itself, two of the sliding screens facing the gate had been replaced completely and the rest expertly patched. Another day or two and the place would be better than presentable.

Nidai kneeled again by the main screen serving as the doorway and slid it aside, bowed me through, and then closed it again. I entered warily enough, but the half-expected ambush did not materialize. Instead, I was in a large central room; the floor had been freshly scrubbed and cushions spread near a small dais. The setup reminded me of Princess Teiko's audience chamber, though on a smaller scale and with only Nidai and myself in attendance. The lady, if any, was nowhere to be seen.

"So, do I now await the pleasure of your mysterious employer? If I am to do so, I will at least be comfortable." But before I could sit, Nidai quickly steered me away from the floor cushions and up onto a low stool on the dais itself.

"Your seat is up here, my lord. It is my mistress who craves audience."

"Well," I said, for want of something more clever or to the point.

Curious.

Nidai bowed low. "Will you see my mistress now?"

"That is why I am here," I said.

Wearing a three-layered *kimono* with formal overcoat, the woman entered through the left-hand door and more floated than walked to a cushion in front of the dais. She then kneeled in one smooth motion and bowed low to me. I followed all this with an interest that was slowly overshadowed by a growing certainty. I knew her. The lovely face, the long black hair tied back with two separate ribbons, the grace and beauty of her movements, all as I remembered.

"You are the *asobi* at Yasada Shrine in Gion. I saw you dancing near there."

She did not look up. "I am honored that you noticed this worthless person. I am called Hikaru-no-Yuki."

Shining Snow.

It wasn't an actual name; rather a professional or use-name of the sort *asobi* often adopted. A girl of a poor family was often apprenticed—sold, really—to an older *asobi* with no daughters of her own, thus to be raised by the older woman and trained to become an *asobi* in her turn and support her mentor when the older woman could no longer make her living as a dancer, singer, and courtesan. Yet there was training, and then there was being born to, raised with, and living a higher esthetic for the entirety of one's existence. If the exquisite creature kneeling before me now had ever been a peasant, then I was the Goddess of the Sun.

"I would like to know your true name," I said. "And please look at me as we speak."

She raised her head. "This is my true name, Lord Yamada, so far as such things matter to either of us. You must realize that I once bore another, and I do not deny it. Please also realize that I am trying my best to forget that name. It no longer belongs to me."

I could have insisted, but even if I had done so there would have been no way to tell if she spoke the truth or not; she had as much as said that she had no intention of doing so, at least so far as her name was concerned. I wondered if I would hear any truth at all this evening. I had been pondering that very question long before keeping the appointment, and was no closer to knowing the answer now.

"Why am I here?" I asked.

"Because I can help you," she said.

"Then perhaps a better question might be 'why are *you* here?' "

She smiled a grim smile. Even so, her dimples reminded me very painfully of Princess Teiko's.

"Quite properly asked, Lord Yamada. As a woman forced to make her own way in this world, I full well understand the necessity of fair exchange. I am here because I believe you can help *me*."

Now, perhaps, we were getting to the core of the matter. "What do you want of me, Lady Snow?"

She sighed. "I am no lady, as surely you know. But I thank you for the courtesy."

"And I am barely a lord, as surely *you* know. Courtesy for the same, or call it a whim of mine. Now please answer my question . . . oh, but before you do—surely you know that Nidai is listening at the door?"

She smiled again and raised her voice just slightly. "Nidai-kun, if you are not well away from that door before I finish speaking, you will consider yourself dismissed. Are you still there?"

The frantic scramble out on the veranda did, in fact, begin well before Lady Snow had finished speaking, and the sound of Nidai running across bare wood had already ceased by the time she had gotten to her final word.

"He's a good boy," she said, "in his way."

I grunted. "He'll be a bandit or worse before he's fifteen."

"More than likely. Unless an alternative presents itself."

"Which you seem to have done. Lady Snow, I gladly concede your perhaps misplaced benevolence toward that little scoundrel, but you have made implications in my regard which I know full well are beyond your power or anyone else's to implement."

"Mine? Of course. I have no power. Yet do not be so certain of the latter, Lord Yamada. Will you at least listen?" I indicated assent and she went on. "Now then, your father was executed during one of the northern campaigns, some seventeen years ago, yes? Upon his death it was revealed that he had, in fact, been an agent of one of the northern clans in league with the barbarians, yes?"

"Whether this is true or not, the 'facts' of the matter are common knowledge . . . among those who need to be aware of such things," I said.

"You'd be surprised how many things become 'common knowledge' far from their original spheres, Lord Yamada. You're of course right to wonder why one such as myself should have any interest or knowledge of this, but I trust it soon will become clear to you. Now then, if you'll pardon my bluntness, I must ask—was your father guilty of what he was accused of?"

I shrugged. There was no point in evading the issue so far as I could see. "I believe he was, which is one reason I have my doubts anything can be changed now."

"That seems a rather harsh view of your father's honor."

I almost laughed. "My father was never more than a very minor provincial lord completely under the domination of the northern branch of the Fujiwara. Like many others, he had a little and wanted more. It does my father no discredit to admit he was ambitious. It is simply the truth. If he saw treachery as the best means to an end, he very well might have seized it."

"So certain of that, are you? Suppose I tell you he was not a

YAMADA MONOGATARI: TO BREAK THE DEMON GATE

traitor, and that the persons deliberately responsible for his ruin and disgrace are still alive?"

I didn't answer for a moment. I wondered if this small emotion I was feeling was hope or resignation. "I would need proof, and very definitive and substantial proof at that."

"Which is the one thing I do not have, unfortunately. Yet. That little omission also brings me back to your question. In this matter, at least, our desires can be said to be in harmony."

I frowned. "I don't understand. What concern is this matter of yours? Did you know my father?"

"Yamada no Seburo? No. But I knew an acquaintance of his. His name was Fujiwara no Kiyoshi."

Again, that name. For a man dead fifteen years who *didn't* happen to be a ghost, Kiyoshi certainly managed to insert himself repeatedly into my life. Judging from what happened the last time his name resurfaced, I wasn't sure I liked the turn this conversation was taking. I chose my words very carefully.

"Again, what is he to me?"

"He was your friend," she said softly. "And he was my lover. I was barely sixteen when he was murdered."

I frowned. "Murdered? He died in battle."

She looked at the floor. "I know the official account of the battle as well as you do, Lord Yamada, and I repeat: murdered. As was your father."

My mind was spinning like a boulder falling down a mountain. I thought I saw something to grasp, and I did. "You are Taira no Hoshiko?"

Her expression was unreadable, but the ice in her voice seemed to lower the temperature of the room. "Lady Hoshiko . . . that creature with no mind or will of her own, that brittle, simpering little doll? Do not insult me so, Lord Yamada. Please understand—I have no doubt Kiyoshi would have made the little fool his official wife, or at least attempted to do so. Her family connections were second only to his own, and he did have some fondness for her, whereas I . . . well, we know my circumstances. But he belonged to *me* nonetheless, and he was stolen. You asked what I wanted from you, Lord Yamada, and I will tell you: I want you to help me win justice. If we achieve it for Yamada no Seburo, I achieve it for Fujiwara no Kiyoshi as well. The two were slain by the scheming of the same man."

"Who?"

"Fujiwara no Sentaro. Formerly the Emperor's Minister of Justice and now known as Dai-wa, Chief Priest of Enryaku Temple."

PART THREE

The spring sakura
Hides not from the bitter wind,
or the frost of night.
These things blight or not at whim.
Does the flower heed its fate?

Lady Snow had, after dropping her metaphorical rock upon my head, paused to prepare tea. I continued my stunned and silent brooding while she poured for us. I took my cup and sipped. I already knew that the woman was not who she appeared to be and I should have been concerned about poison, but I really wasn't; if she'd intended that and nothing more, there would have been far easier ways to go about it.

"You don't believe me," she said finally.

"No," I said. "I'm sorry, but I do not."

She didn't look insulted. She looked, rather, as if she had expected no less. "Why not, may I ask? I assure you that Kiyoshi and I *were* lovers. I had barely begun at my trade when we met. He was my first. He was kind. I only later learned how rare a trait that was."

"You do realize, do you not, that your relationship with Kiyoshi is *not* the portion of your story with the least credibility?"

She smiled faintly. "Lord Sentaro."

I sighed. "Exactly. While I willingly concede the man is both ambitious and lacking in scruple, perhaps even to an excessive degree, you're telling me he arranged the murder of his own nephew!"

She sipped her tea. "Yes. That is exactly what I am telling you, because it is a fact."

"Kiyoshi kept out of political matters and, as I personally knew, had no ambition in that regard. He was neither a rival nor a threat to his uncle's position. What possible reason could Lord Sentaro have to wish him harm?"

"Kiyoshi learned of his uncle's plot against your father and meant to expose it. That is why he was killed. Perhaps Lord Sentaro did so reluctantly; I do not know. I only know what happened."

"And how could you possibly know this?"

She set her cup aside, and instead of answering, asked a question of me instead. "Do you know a man named Murakami no Fusao?"

I frowned; another name associated with Kiyoshi. "Yes, I remember him. An old retainer of the Fujiwara and Kiyoshi's chief attendant."

She smiled then. "More like Kiyoshi's shadow. His proximity was not always . . . convenient, for us."

That much I could believe. He was an old man even when I knew him, but he had been Kiyoshi's personal attendant and servant almost from birth, and his devotion to his young charge was beyond question. You seldom saw one without the other.

"What of him?"

"Soon after Kiyoshi's death, he left the Fujiwara's service forever and took up trade as a painter in Otsu. Did you not think anything odd in that?"

"I had other matters on my mind at the time," I said.

She bowed in apology. "Of course. You wouldn't have known that the choice was his; he was not dismissed. He left because of what he knew and dared not say."

"What did he know, then?"

"Your father, as I said before, was innocent. He was accused of acting as a spy for the Abe Clan, which had allied itself with the northerners even then. He was executed at Lord Sentaro's order."

"And as *I* said before, everyone knows this. Lady Snow, your company is charming and your tea delightful, but I'm beginning to think you're wasting my time."

"Here's something you do not know: Lord Sentaro himself ordered your father to meet with the barbarian prince. That was the meeting that Sentaro in turn claimed proved your father's guilt. I learned this from Fusao himself. He learned it, in turn, from Kiyoshi. That is why Kiyoshi was killed, and almost certainly on Lord Sentaro's orders. Fusao says the arrow that killed his Master was fired from his own ranks."

I was intrigued despite my better judgment. As I recalled, one of my father's frequent letters had mentioned instructions from Lord Sentaro. Yet what did that prove? It could have been a reference to almost anything, taken by itself. As for Kiyoshi . . .

"Targets can be uncertain in wartime. Accidents happen."

"This was no accident. You forget that Fusao was present during the battle, and he says he saw the man aiming quite deliberately at Kiyoshi but too late to sound a warning. Afterwards the archer could not be found."

I considered. "Interesting. Can Fusao attest to this? Would he be willing?"

Lady Snow looked unhappy. "Unfortunately, no. He has since died. We met through an intermediary last year. It seemed the old man knew his time was short and wished for a bit of . . . comfort, toward the end. It was not until I actually arrived that we recognized one another. He told me everything he knew."

"An interesting story but a bit of a coincidence, don't you think?"

She looked resigned. "If one accepts that one's destiny is fixed, then there is very little that is really 'coincidence'. Yet I do acknowledge that what I say strains credibility. You do not know me, Lord Yamada. I suppose I cannot blame you for doubting what I tell you, though I did hope for better."

I grunted. "There's a part of the story you're leaving out and, frankly, the part that strains my belief even more than your chance meeting with Fusao: why would Lord Sentaro bother to betray my father? I know the man, and a minor noble of my father's stature would be beneath his notice, save as a useful tool. What did he possibly have to gain?"

Lady Snow met my gaze squarely. "I do not know."

Now that answer did surprise me. Assuming that everything Lady Snow had told me from start to finish was a fabrication for reasons I could not yet fathom, she would certainly have no difficulty coming up with a suitable lie for such an easily anticipated and basic question.

"You really do not know?"

"How could I? Fusao did not know. Perhaps only Kiyoshi himself knew the whole story. I certainly would think there had to be more to it, for my lord to be willing to expose the machinations of his own uncle."

I rubbed my chin. "Lady Snow, thank you for the tea and the very interesting tale. I am quite entertained, but I feel I must be going."

She looked disappointed but far from defeated. "What reason have I to lie to you about this matter or any other? What would it take to convince you?"

I sighed and got to my feet. "Lady Snow, as to the first I do not know but gladly concede that it's an interesting question which I must ponder at some later point. As to the second, proof would go a long way toward easing my doubts. Yet, by your own admission, you have none. If your story does not sway me, a man with a personal stake in the matter, consider how much less weight it would have at the Imperial Ministry."

She looked thoughtful. "I'm afraid I must defer to your judgment there. Perhaps I let my eagerness get the better of me."

I hesitated. "Lady, I do not, as I said, know what possible reason you might have for lying to me. Yet whether what you say is true or not, there are those who would not like to hear such tales spread around. I urge discretion, for your own sake."

She smiled at me then, not bothering to cover her face. "I will certainly take your warning to heart. Yet I will not promise that this is the end of the matter, Lord Yamada. Suppose I find something that would satisfy even you? I have some avenues that I wish to explore yet, but travel may be required. Compensation can be arranged, if perhaps you were willing . . . ?"

I sighed. "Lady Snow, even if I believed all you have said, I have other pressing matters within the capital just now and simply cannot leave. If you learn more and still wish to persuade me, send word. You are very agreeable company and I am still prepared to listen. I can promise no more than that."

She blushed just slightly and bowed low. "Short of your good opinion, which I must warn you I still seek, your promise will have to do. Good day to you, Lord Yamada."

"And good fortune to you, Lady Snow."

I found Nidai nervously pacing near the gate. He bowed to me. "Was I in time?" he asked.

I suppressed a smile and did my best to look severe. "Just barely. You are still in Lady Snow's employ for now, but I would mind my step from here on if I were you. I would certainly wash my face."

Nidai ignored my comment on his personal cleanliness. "Lady Snow? That is a nice name. May I call her that? She has only permitted 'mistress' before now."

"I think you had better ask her," I said. "But, just between the two of us, I do not think she will mind."

The moon was starting to set as Nidai closed the gate behind me. While I didn't mind walking the dark streets as much as some, caution was never a poor option. Already I could see *onibi* flaring here and there, the ghost-flames an unmistakable sign of unquiet spirits. As I walked I saw more and more.

While ghost-lights were common in the city at night, it *was* a bit unusual to see so many. At first I put the matter down to the location; for some reason the ghosts around Lady Snow's home were particularly active. But after I had walked some distance from the repaired home, the *rei* activity did not abate; if anything it intensified. Besides the *onibi*, other manifestations began to appear: a paper umbrella with one eye hopped quickly past me and disappeared into a narrow gap between two storehouses. A dark, shadowy *neko-rei* howled from a rooftop and, once it had my attention, gave me a startled look as if I had surprised it and not the other way around. It disappeared, leaving a scent like cat-urine.

"Phew. I hope I do not meet many more like that."

My wish was not granted. In an alleyway an entire family of ghost cats hissed and spat at each other. Again, as I passed they scattered, but when I was past I could hear them again, snarling. A bent old monk in a straw hat and tattered *kesa* hobbled past me. He had no face. I might have dared question him, except that no face meant no eyes to see or mouth to speak, as well; plus he seemed in a great hurry, tottering along as quickly as his memory of arthritic old legs would carry him. I paused and watched him totter away.

When I turned around, the road was blocked by ghosts. They flowed toward me like a spring torrent. I had never seen such a massing of spirits in my life, and in so many different manifestations. They rolled toward me like a vast spiritual tide, and to my horror I realized I was about to be swept away.

"Yamada-san, put this on!"

I recognized Kenji's voice from behind before I spotted him, running to catch up with me. He dangled a talisman of some sort on a dirty silken string. I hurriedly placed it around my neck just as the wave of ghosts crested over us. For a moment I could see nothing but black shadows with glowing red eyes that somehow never quite touched me. I was well aware that ghosts, while not normally substantial, could easily cause physical harm if angered or determined to do so.

"I would say we should get off the street," Kenji said, "but I doubt if anyplace else would be much better."

"What has set them off, do you know? And for that matter, what are you doing here?"

"I followed you," Kenji admitted. "Since you wouldn't heed my advice about bringing a friend."

"I suppose a reprobate mendicant is better than nothing, especially considering what is happening now. I don't think Kanemore would have been much help." I examined the talisman on the end of the cord but, like most of Kenji's concoctions, it was little more than a piece of paper tied into a knot. I had no idea what was written on it and doubtless wouldn't have understood the spiritual resonances if I did. "What is this, anyway?"

"A simple ward," Kenji said. "Of the sort I always wear. It makes contact unpleasant for the spirits, so they're avoiding us, but it wouldn't stop a determined attack."

I frowned. "You mean this isn't one?"

Kenji sighed. "Take a good look around you, Lord Yamada. Do you really think so?"

Actually I did not, but couldn't immediately fathom what this "stampede" was all about otherwise. Seita notwithstanding, most ghosts tended to be elusive creatures and only manifested now and then, and for reasons or compulsions of their own. Besides there being so many, I had never seen them behave in this manner before. Behind the relative security of Kenji's ward, I took a closer look at the horde of ghosts moving through the streets of Kyoto as they flowed around Kenji and me as if we were two rocks in a river. Now I was amazed I hadn't noticed the common thread before now.

"You're right, Kenji-san. They're not attacking, they're running! From what?"

Kenji scowled. "I wish I could answer that. There's a pall over the city that makes *me* want to run, too, if only I knew what direction was 'away.' Ah!"

"What is it?"

He grinned. "Isn't it obvious? If you want to find the source of a river, you row against the current. Follow me!"

Now Kenji led the way into the very crest of the wave with me close behind. I understood his reasoning and could find no flaw in it as we worked our way back through the tidal wave of ghosts toward the origin of their panic. That did not mean I was very keen on the idea. I was far from certain I wanted to meet anything that could put such a blind terror into all the ghosts of Kyoto.

I wasn't sure how far we had come. It was dark, and landmarks were hard to spot. I did know we were heading in a northeastern direction.

"The Demon Gate?" I gasped out, sparing no more breath than I had to. I needed the rest for running.

"Hard to say," Kenji replied. "Possible, or a coincidence."

Definitely possible and hardly a coincidence, if so; Kenji knew that as well as I did. The northeastern gate of the city was the preferred method for evil spirits and their ilk to enter ever since the founding of the city. That was the reason the Ryakaku-ji complex had been built in the first place, to defend that entrance. But it didn't seem to be having much deterrent effect at the moment.

Kenji stopped so suddenly I had gone three paces beyond him before I even noticed, and as many again before I could stop. Ahead of me, the ghosts were disappearing.

"What in all the hells . . . ?" I heard him mutter.

Kenji didn't come forward. I didn't give him time. I quickly backed away to where he stood staring, and once there I pretty much did the same. The ghosts ahead of us were disappearing, being swallowed by, so far as we could see, nothing. Or rather, darkness. This darkness was not nothing, or perhaps it was exactly that; nothing in its purest form. Not the spiritual non-attachment, the bliss that the temple priests were always on about, but rather a nothing that could not tolerate anything of a real or separate nature within its sphere. A devouring sort of nothing. An extremely hungry sort of nothing.

I tried to shake off the feeling of dread that had crept over me. Perhaps I was seeing more than was actually in front of me, but I could not help the way the thing made me feel.

"It's there," Kenji said. "Whatever it is, that's it, and it's coming this way."

I already knew that. What I didn't know was if there was a chance in the world that we, now that we had been so foolish as to find the thing, could outrun it.

"It's alive, isn't it? Your senses are better than mine in this realm; do you not sense a presence within that darkness?"

"Yes," Kenji said. "Perhaps we should go."

I thought the same, but then I noticed the spirits on the edge of the *nothing* were now moving away from it, or rather escaping. The darkness was not moving, and I would have sworn by any god or scripture you'd care to name that just moments before it had been moving, and swiftly.

"It has stopped," I said. "See for yourself."

"Fortunately for us," Kenji said. "I've seen enough."

"I haven't."

I didn't blame Kenji in the least, but now I had been foolish enough to find the source of the ghosts' terror, I wasn't going to be so foolish as to abandon my position without learning as much as I could. I only hoped the price would not be so high as my life.

"Don't be a fool, Lord Yamada. While I'm rather proud of the quality of my wards and talismans, I tell you bluntly: the best I could make probably would not even slow that thing down."

"How do you know," I asked, "if you don't know what it is?"

"I know what it isn't," he said. "It is not a man or a woman. For all I know, it is a ghost that devours other ghosts. Perhaps the spirit of an ogre or worse."

"Worse," I said. "You and I have already known an ogre's ghost, and it was nowhere near as malevolent as this. I'm going closer."

Despite my brave words, it took several long moments and as many deep calming breaths before I could force myself to do as much as take a step. I doubt the shadow of a post moved any slower than I did as I slipped closer and closer to the mass of darkness.

Now that I *was* closer, I noticed some things that had been invisible from my former position. While there was still no discernible shape to the blackness, I did realize it wasn't totally black. There were graduations of nothingness, like the transforming aspects of a cloud as it flies across the face of the sun. Here and there a flash of light, very faint, almost like a firefly in a fog. The one thing that did not change was the feeling of total malevolence that came over me whenever I looked at the thing.

There came a point, when I was perhaps no more than fifteen paces from the wall of darkness in front of me, I realized nothing on heaven or earth or beyond could compel me to take one more step in the thing's direction.

When Kenji's hand touched my shoulder I had my *tachi* a good hand's breadth out of its scabbard before I realized he was there. I let out a breath and sheathed the weapon again.

"Surprising a frightened man is a good way to lose your head. I thought you stayed behind."

"And let you be a fool by yourself? Where's the humor in that?" he said, but he wasn't looking at me. His eyes were trained on the darkness. "Incredible."

I looked around, but my immediate surroundings were unfamiliar. "Where are we? I know we were traveling eastward and crossed the river at some point, but this place is not familiar."

"A bit south of the Demon Gate," Kenji said. "A loose organization of mendicant priests operates a hostel just across the street."

I could see it now. I could see a great deal more. "The darkness is withdrawing to the east."

"Yes," Kenji said a bit distractedly. He was chewing his lower lip and his mind was plainly elsewhere.

I think I knew the reason. My own feelings at that point were difficult to describe. I knew the darkness was present; I was well aware of this after we had caught up to it, saw the ghosts devoured, felt the hatred and malevolence it—barely—contained. But despite my fear and wonder at the scale and nature of the thing, I don't think I fully appreciated just what a blight the thing had been on my surroundings until it was gone. I felt I could see and breathe and think again, whereas before all three traits had seemed arguable.

A man staggered out through the gate of a small family compound and into the street, his eyes wild. Most decent folk kept off the streets after dark when demons and ghosts were felt to be at their most powerful and present, which is why I had not been surprised that Kenji and I had been just about the only non-spirits about during the incident. What could have possessed this man to leave his home now?

For a moment I don't think he really saw either Kenji or myself, but then his eyes came back into focus.

"H-help, sirs, please," he finally said. "My poor wife . . . "

I hurried to his side with Kenji close behind. "Is the lady ill? My friend is a priest," I said. I didn't bother to mention he wasn't exactly a pious priest or a very good one, outside of his specialty. This did not seem like the time. "Perhaps we can be of assistance?"

The increasingly frantic man led us into his home. There was just the one room, and still lying twisted in their bedding was the body of an older woman. That she was dead was obvious from the beginning. The man put his hands together and wailed while Kenji slowly kneeled and began chanting a sutra. Kenji's droning voice finally calmed the man down enough for me to try and get a coherent sentence out of him.

"I am sorry for your wife. What happened?"

"I don't know," he said. She was struggling, as if something gripped her. I saw nothing, I asked her how I could help, what I could do . . . "

I'm not sure why it took me so long to understand what had just happened. Perhaps I was getting old, or, at least, older than my years.

"You saw nothing?"

"Nothing," he said. "Is she . . . ?"

"I'm sorry."

Five other men arrived as we spoke and hesitated at the doorway, but Kenji, who obviously knew them, waved them inside. Mendicants from their garb, from the hostel Kenji had mentioned, no doubt called by the commotion. Two of them joined in with Kenji and chanted the sutra while another, obviously unconcerned with ritual purity, gently straightened the old woman's limbs and composed the body. The others took the old man from me, wrapped him in a cloak, and made him drink a cup of saké. I considered this probably the best course, at least as far as the bereaved man was concerned. I did not think I would learn any more than I already had from him that night.

Kenji left the chanting priests and joined me by the door. "My brothers and I will do what is needed tonight," he said. "Munikata-san can contact the priests at Senrin-ji tomorrow for the formal arrangements."

"You know this man?" I asked.

"He's a weaver. I know most of the folk near here," Kenji said simply. "My second home, aside from the Demon Gate. I've spent many of the colder nights in the hostel across the street."

"You may be a scoundrel, but you're also a fully ordained priest," I pointed out. "Should you be associating with these men?"

"As opposed to, say, the Chief Priest at Senrin-ji? Or perhaps His Immanence, Dai-wu of Enryaku-ji?"

I remembered the old man at Taira no Kei's funeral rites. "I see your point."

Kenji sighed. "Go home, Lord Yamada. The danger, whatever it was, has passed for the moment. This is priest's work now. I will join you as planned tomorrow."

I took my leave then, but not before I took a closer look at the body as I paid my respects. The faint bluish pallor and the contortion of the limbs before the mendicant had straightened them, all told me plainly that whatever had killed Taira no Kei had killed this woman as well, and in the same manner. The only difference was that, this time, someone saw it happen.

And saw absolutely nothing.

⛩

The following morning just after sunrise, I left a message for Prince Kanemore with one of the guards at the Imperial Compound's eastern gate.

The sun was only a little more on its way toward its zenith when Prince Kanemore joined me on the grounds of the Gion Shrine. I had rather hoped that Lady Snow would be entertaining at the same spot where she had been a couple of days ago. Not only could I have used the entertainment, but I would also have been grateful for the distraction. Yet that was not to be. Fortunately, the crowds were not heavy, and it was possible to find a quiet place to sit and talk, out of earshot of passersby. I quickly related the events of the previous day, save only my conversation with Lady Snow; I was not yet certain how much of that I either needed or wanted to share.

"A ghost and yet not a ghost," Kanemore said thoughtfully. "This does not put my mind at ease."

I grunted. "Nor should it. A spirit with the power to kill, apparently at whim, is not something to be treated lightly. Did you notice anything like this the night of the attack on Kei?"

"I'm afraid not. I was asleep at the time, as was nearly everyone except, one hopes, the guards. I will find out who was on duty that night and talk to them. So, do you attach any significance to the fact that the creature absorbs other spirits it encounters?" Kanemore asked.

"I've never seen that before," I said. "Whether it draws its strength from those spirits or can overwhelm them *because* it's already so much stronger, I do not know. There is still too much I do not know."

"Surely, if Takahito was the target, he would have been attacked before now. Yet if the attacks *are* random, it cannot be said that he—or indeed, anyone—is safe."

"True, and come to that I'm not convinced the attacks *are* random. I remember what Seita told me. The darkness has eyes. It has intent, perhaps unfathomable as yet, but present. Do me one favor, if you will. Question the guards of each gate as a separate group from those of the other gates."

"Certainly, but why?"

"For my own curiosity, if nothing else. Their differing perspectives might give us some understanding that we do not as yet have."

"I'll be certain to do so," Kanemore said. "Is there anything else you require?"

I hesitated. "Prince Kanemore, there are a few more things I want to ask you, but they have little to do with our current business."

He frowned. "Oh? Such as?"

"How much do you remember from your first campaigns in the north?"

Prince Kanemore smiled a little wistfully. "I remember it mostly as a grand adventure. After all, I was only fourteen or so at the time. While those early conflicts were little more than scouting expeditions compared to today, I think my mother thought they would cure my martial interests."

"We can see how well that worked," I said dryly.

He smiled again. "Just so. But I don't think my boyhood outings are what you're really interested in."

"I was wondering about my father."

"I'm rather surprised you hadn't asked about this before now," Kanemore said.

"I didn't think there was much point before now," I said, "and I'm not sure that this isn't still the case. Yet I must ask."

Kanemore sighed. "There isn't much I can tell you. I was certainly not privy to the councils of Lord Sentaro and my uncle, Prince Yoritomi. My duties at the time consisted mainly of not getting myself killed and staying out from under foot. There were documents, I was told, but I never saw them."

I frowned. "Lord Sentaro was there?"

"As a representative of the Court; he was certainly no field commander, but yes, he was there. The actual incident of your father's arrest and execution happened when I was away from the camp; I had been part of the honor guard for a barbarian king Lord Sentaro was negotiating with. Naturally, those negotiations ceased in acrimony after your father's death."

"What about Fujiwara no Kiyoshi? Were you present when he fell?"

121

Kanemore sighed. "No, it also happened while I was away. His detachment surprised a barbarian raiding party crossing the border. The enemy was routed, but Kiyoshi was killed."

I looked up. "He was the only one?"

Kanemore frowned. "Yes, I believe so."

I thought about this. "As a strategist with the hindsight of the last seventeen years, what do you make of that early campaign?"

"I think we had a real chance to prevent at least some of the trouble that's come on us now. Without the support or at least active indifference of the barbarians, the Abe Clan would never have dared show such defiance. We've been seeing increased skirmishes, ignoring of Imperial edicts . . . I do not think this rebellion will end soon. I think it is going to get much worse. I mean no disrespect to my late Uncle to say this much. I think he would agree."

"So the discovery my father was a spy for the barbarians broke the fragile trust that Lord Sentaro was trying to build with the barbarian king?"

"I think it fair to say so. Still . . . "

I frowned. "Yes?"

"The timing could not have been worse. An agreement had already been reached in principle. After this incident, that agreement was never formalized."

I shrugged. "Things often happen at the worst possible times. I must bear some of my father's guilt in this."

"You cannot blame yourself for your father," Kanemore said, though his mind was apparently elsewhere.

"Is there something you're not telling me?" I asked.

"Not deliberately so," Kanemore said. "Yet, thinking as

a strategist, I know the worst possible time from your own perspective may well be the best of all possible times for someone else."

"Meaning anyone who wanted to prevent any such accord could not have chosen a better implement than the incident with my father?"

"I can't think of one. The *gaijin* prince's raiding, apparently at your father's request, did not help but it was not unusual. It was almost expected. Yet the spying business . . . " Kanemore sighed. "Forgive my idle musing. No one stood to gain by such a thing. Not the *gaijin* prince and certainly not my uncle, or even Lord Sentaro though I freely confess I have always disliked the man. It would have been quite a boost to his standing if the negotiations had succeeded."

"No doubt," I said. "Thank you."

"For what little I have done, you are welcome. But I've been away from Takahito for too long. He will begin to think he has lost his shadow and try to slip off and flirt with Lady Hayako again. Not that I can blame him; she is quite the little charmer."

"Do what you must. Perhaps one day Takahito will even appreciate it."

Kanemore smiled. "I do not ask for miracles, Lord Yamada. Just as much as men can do. I can only hope that what we do in the days to come is sufficient to the need."

"As do I. Until we meet again."

When Kanemore left, I remained on the shrine grounds for a while and pondered. Kanemore hadn't told me much I didn't already know, but perhaps more than I had expected. I hadn't realized Kiyoshi had been the only one to fall that day. That was odd but not suspicious; it was a relatively minor skirmish, and such things happened. Even assuming Lady Snow was correct and my father had been betrayed, I did not see what Lord Sentaro or anyone in the Emperor's camp stood to gain from the breakdown of negotiations. For that matter, I did not see what anyone on the opposite side had to gain. Unless, perhaps, the chief of the Abe Clan and the barbarians had been in agreement even then. Yet why wait seventeen years to start a war they supposedly wanted from the start? Was anyone capable of containing such determined aggression, with both the subtlety and the patience to wait so long to see their labors come to fruit? While I was willing to grant that such was possible, I would not have cast a wager against the odds. The premise simply did not make sense to me.

I turned my attention back to the matter of the ghost cloud, or whatever it was. This manifestation didn't make a lot of sense either. That a vengeful spirit would attempt to hound, harass, and otherwise drive to destruction someone they felt had wronged that spirit in life was not a strange thing. Frankly, I was surprised such vendettas didn't happen more often. Yet there was apparently no connection among any of the victims so far, except that they happened to be in the capital at the time they were attacked. Women had died, and men. Young and old. High and low. By all appearances, whatever killed them had struck at random.

I knew that, understood that, even willingly conceded that all the facts as we presently knew and understood them pointed to the random nature of the attacks. I simply did not believe the attacks did not have a purpose. As one lived a life, one came to the inescapable conclusion that either everything was random, or nothing was, and there came a time to choose. I had long since done so, and my choice told me there was meaning here. I could almost smell it. I could almost, yet not quite, touch it.

Unfortunately, all I could do for the moment was wait and hope that, by this evening, Seita had an answer for me. Any answer would do.

The *sakura* were still in bloom, and I took advantage of my idleness to appreciate a fine spring day on the grounds of Gion Shrine. My idleness did not last nearly as long as I had expected, but I couldn't say the interruption was unwelcome.

Nidai appeared on the path, carrying a cushion and looking extremely solemn. He bore a large fan thrust through his sash with the handle protruding like a sword. Lady Snow was close behind in a two-layered *kimono* of blue and red, following demurely as Nidai-kun led the way.

"I must say I'm curious as to how you found me," I said, "since I told very few people where I would be." That was a bit of an understatement, as I had told no one save Kanemore.

Lady Snow bowed, and after favoring me with a frown, Nidai did the same. "I have no explanation save for that of a happy coincidence, Lord Yamada," Lady Snow said. "In truth, I was not looking for you."

I raised an eyebrow. "Oh?"

"No, after my morning performance I merely came to appreciate the *sakura*, as indeed you seem to be doing. May I join you?"

"Certainly," I said.

Immediately Nidai hurried up with a small brush and proceeded to sweep the leaves and debris from the cobbles nearby. Then he placed the cushion on the cleared space for Lady Snow to kneel.

"That will do for now, Nidai-kun," she said. "Please make my request to the fish-monger. You have the instructions written down; show that to him if there is any confusion."

He bowed low. "I will not be long, My Lady."

She smiled then. "Oh, I think I am safe enough in Lord Yamada's care. He does not wish me any harm, I think. At least, not yet."

After Nidai had disappeared down the path I looked at Lady Snow. "Yet?"

"I told you I had not given up," she said. "So you may expect more attempts to persuade you to my cause."

"Please understand—I do not take you lightly, Lady Snow. If what you say can be proven, it is my cause as well. I just do not think you have done so as of now, nor is it likely you will be able to."

She smiled then, covering her face with her fan. "I may yet surprise you."

"I don't discount the possibility," I said. "At present, that is all I can do for you. I am sorry I missed your performance this morning."

"As am I, since I do not think I will be performing in the city for a while. I will have other matters to attend."

I frowned. "If you'll pardon my saying, that house you have taken must be a severe expense. How will you manage, if you spend your time on this quest?"

"I have a patron, Lord Yamada. He prefers that my performances be more . . . private."

"Yes," I said. "I would assume so."

She sighed then. "You think ill of me, I suppose."

While it was true the news saddened me for reasons I couldn't quite name, I thought no less of Lady Snow. What I knew of *asobi* and their lives was no more than what most men of my alleged class knew; they were skilled dancers, singers, and sometimes—more likely, often—courtesans. Rare indeed was the noble outing or moon-viewing party that was not graced with one or two of these entertainers, and quite often several. "Slipping your boat into the reeds" with an *asobi* was practically a proverb for the culmination of a successful party. She was as life and her opportunities had made her. I had no pretense to greater virtue in my own.

"Why would you think so? I make no claim to know the fit of sandals I've never worn. While I do not think my duties the same as yours, I consider patronage a fortunate state on the whole. Are you of a different opinion?"

"With the right patron," she said, "matters may be better than unpleasant. My master does not ask too much of me. Even so, for his business and my own I must be away from the capital for a few days. I will want to speak to you when I return."

I bowed. "Gods willing, I will be here."

The hour was growing late by the time Nidai returned, and I hastily took my leave of Lady Snow. It occurred to me I had tarried perhaps longer than I should have, but I found myself in no hurry to leave, even though we said very little else to each other for the rest of the time it took Nidai to complete his errand. Yet it was nearly dark when I finally reached Rashamon.

Kenji sat with his back against the gate. "You are late, Lord Yamada."

"Forgive me, Kenji-san. I was distracted."

He gave me a sharp look. "By whom, if I may ask?"

"Lady Snow."

"Ah," Kenji said. I was rather surprised this was *all* he said. He used his staff to help lift himself off the ground. "Let's be off, then."

Kenji led the way, and I fell into step beside him. "I am surprised," I said finally.

"At what?"

"At you. No questions? Hectoring?"

"I'm certainly in no position to do so," Kenji said. "You have been alone for a long time, and that was even before Teiko's death."

I scowled. "It's not like that with Lady Snow. As for Princess Teiko, that matter is closed."

Kenji just shrugged. "As you say. You were late for our appointment, so I merely asked for the courtesy of an explanation, which you have given. You need not justify your actions to me."

He was right of course, and I had no one to blame but myself since I had volunteered more than Kenji had asked. I'm not sure why I would not let the matter go. Maybe I wanted him to understand. Maybe I wanted to be sure I did.

"She's a very talented and beautiful lady. Any man would be glad of her company. In some ways she does remind me of Teiko."

Kenji grunted. "If you'll pardon my saying so, Lord Yamada, that's more than enough reason for caution right there."

I couldn't suppress a grin. "I would not argue that point."

"Are you ready to tell me what you discussed with Lady Snow?"

"Today was little more than polite chat. As for yesterday . . . " I related the salient bits of my conversation with Lady Snow from the previous day. Kenji looked thoughtful and did not interrupt until it was plain I had no more to say on the matter.

"Interesting. Do you believe her?"

"I know it's foolish, yet part of me wants to believe that my family fortunes can be resurrected. It's impossible, but I want to believe it anyway."

"Because you wish it were so, or because it is Lady Snow telling you these things?"

I thought about that. "I do not know," I said finally.

Kenji grunted. "That's honest, at least, not to mention troubling. But until we know her true intentions, it doesn't hurt to know what she wishes you to believe."

"She may be telling the truth, at least as she understands it."

"I concede the possibility," Kenji said cheerfully, "but no more than that. Now, what about yesterday evening? We have not had the chance to discuss that as yet."

"You know as much about that as I do," I said. "You were there."

"Do you think it a coincidence Munikata's poor wife died at the border of that cloud-thing's travel?"

"I concede the possibility," I said, using Kenji's own words.

Kenji grunted again. "I'll take that as a 'no.' Neither do I, and I have no more idea of what that creature may be or why it attacked that woman than I had yesterday. It has some of the characteristics of a ghost, in the same sense that a tiger shares some common traits with a house cat. Still, it would be dangerous to confuse the two."

"I've asked Kanemore to question the guards about the night

that Taira no Kei was found dead. Perhaps I can confirm that something similar happened then."

Kenji frowned. "That was a moonless night, if I recall correctly. They might not be able to distinguish one patch of darkness from another. Nor are other folk as sensitive to the presence of spirits as you and I. Still, it is worth trying," Kenji said. "Yet suppose they saw the cloud or darkness or *something* as well. What then?"

"Then we can associate this thing with two deaths. Even if we still do not know for certain that the creature, whatever it is, was responsible. Still, it would be the prudent wager and I think we'd be wise to proceed with that in mind."

"I agree," Kenji said. "Though I'll admit I'm very curious to hear what Master Seita has to say on the matter."

"As am I." Indeed, I realized that, as the conversation progressed, the more anxious I was becoming. Everything Kenji or I said just emphasized to me how very little we did know, and how much we needed the sort of information Seita had proved himself capable of providing time and time again.

We reached Seita's ruined compound shortly thereafter and proceeded through the broken wall, then into the overgrown garden to Seita's bridge.

"Seita-san!"

We waited, but the red lantern did not appear. I called again, with the same result. I pulled out one of the bags of uncooked rice to give him the scent, but even that made no difference. The moments dragged by, and still Seita did not appear.

"Is he in hiding?" Kenji asked.

"Possibly. He was uncharacteristically nervous the last time I saw him. Can you do a conjuration?"

Kenji grunted. "My talents are mostly in the realm of protection against spirits, moving undetected among spirits, and banishing spirits. I'm not so well-versed in the art of summoning them. It's a foolish conceit, as most respectable people know. Indeed, you'll find very little call for that, even among the bereaved."

I should have realized this was so. Seita's long presence at his family's former estates notwithstanding, the proper goal of any bereaved family was to make as certain as possible the departed's spirit had been properly sent out of this world and on to the next, to be judged as their *karma* demanded. To do otherwise was a failure of obligation.

Calling a spirit to one was a different matter altogether, and such summonings were more into the realm of Chinese and Daoist magic than Buddhist. I did know one or two practitioners of the Chinese arts whom I dealt with when need dictated, but it never occurred to me that I might require their services to track down Seita. He was more wont to appear when he wasn't needed than to disappear when he was.

I was contemplating crossing the bridge and looking for Seita, both beneath it and on the other side, when Kenji frowned and kneeled down at the foot of the bridge, sniffing like a hound.

"What are you doing?"

I'm not even sure Kenji heard me at first. He was sniffing about and muttering to himself almost as one deranged. He finally gave out what I could only interpret as a shout of triumph and picked up a small scrap of paper. He sniffed this too.

"Kenji-san, would you mind telling me what you're on about?"

"Camphorwood. Cinnamon. Both were burned as incense here. The first is easy enough to obtain, but the second is dear, indeed. Obviously I've never used it myself, but I've been told of its efficacy more than once."

"Efficacy in what?"

"Exorcism," Kenji said, as he finally stood back up and brushed off the dirt. "A rite of exorcism has been performed here."

"Seita?" It was a foolish question, but I had to ask it, and Kenji confirmed my fears.

"Almost certainly, Lord Yamada. Seita has been banished from this world."

I felt cold. "But why? He wasn't harming anyone."

Kenji shrugged. "I don't know. I do know that, whoever it was, must have wanted it done a great deal. The supplies used were precious and whoever performed the rite was a master. Neither would have come cheaply."

"Which could also mean whoever was involved had no need to worry about the expense," I said. "Yet I've seen you do exorcisms before, Kenji-san. You used only the proper sutras and prayer. There was no burning of incense."

Kenji sighed and rubbed the stubble on his head. "Because both the correct prayer and the correct sutra are easily obtained at the cost of a little time for study, which is usually all I have to spend. My methods are not the only ones."

"It would seem so."

So much for my hopes for some sign of a coming dawn; with Seita gone, I was pretty much back where I began.

"You don't suppose Seita's exorcism is simply a coincidence?"

"I concede the possibility," I said grudgingly. "But only just. Who knew about Seita? I mean, specifically my connection to him?"

"If you're looking for culprits, you'd best start with me," Kenji said. "I knew. And more, I have the skills required to do the deed."

I almost laughed. "And if you'd been paid to do so with the wasteful methods indicated, you'd have used your own methods and kept the difference."

"My clients are fools sometimes," Kenji said. "I try not to be." It was as close to an admission as he was going to make, but I didn't need confirmation.

"So that leaves Kanemore," I said, though it did cause me some discomfort to put the thought into words. "At least, of the ones I know for certain. It's possible there are others, if someone really wanted to find out."

"Kanemore certainly has the means, if not the skills," Kenji said thoughtfully. "You don't seriously suspect the prince had the rite performed? Would he do such a thing?"

That was the question I knew I needed to ask, but unlike so many others lately it was one I could answer. "Prince Kanemore serves a purpose higher than his own interests," I said, "and if banishing Seita or killing you, or me, or a hundred better served that purpose, he'd do it with perhaps regret but absolutely no hesitation. Yet I can't imagine what reason he might have. Especially now, if it's true that Seita had information that might protect Takahito. I simply do not see cause."

Kenji shrugged. "Nor I. There must be some other explanation."

I hoped Kenji was right and there was, indeed, some other explanation. There had to be.

Our walk back into the city was far more sober than the trip down through Rashamon. As usual the streets were deserted, or nearly so. All decent people were at home. Which left me, Kenji, and whatever other lowly reprobates, thieves, demons, and ghosts might be about. Yet, not quite completely buried in the gloom and uncertainty, a thought occurred to me.

"Kenji, where are you going now?"

He shrugged. "To the hostel. There are signs of rain, and I'd rather not get caught out in a storm later tonight."

True enough. There was an ominous cast to the northern sky, but I read nothing supernatural in that. It just looked like rain. As the breeze freshened, it even felt a bit like rain.

"Let me go with you, at least so far as the streets near where we walked last night."

"Glad of the company," Kenji said, "or do you have another reason in mind?"

"Say rather I'm curious about something. Another trip to the area south of the Demon Gate might satisfy that curiosity."

"You're being mysterious," Kenji said. "I hate that."

"The object of my curiosity isn't clear enough in my own mind to be much more than that. Not a suspicion, or anything easily explained. Likely not even relevant. When I know more, I'll be glad to share that poor knowledge with you."

"As you will."

As we walked, we saw nothing more or less than we expected to see. It had been something of an exaggeration to say that *no* decent folk were about. Say rather there were many, none of whom wanted their faces to be seen. Lovers walked by, their faces veiled but their intentions clear, hurrying off to their chosen trysting places; now and then a servant nervously made his or her way through the darkened streets with only a small lantern for light, sent on business that could not wait until morning; and, here and there, were ghost-lights and moving shadows with eyes. As we drew closer to the scene of the previous night's events, I waited for something, anything, to change.

Nothing did.

We reached the hostel. Kenji acknowledged the monk on duty but did not enter. "Well?"

"Walk a little further with me, and perhaps the matter will be clearer to both of us."

We kept heading north, closer and closer to the demon gate. We were nearly there before Kenji finally let out a gasp. "The ghosts! They're still here!"

We stopped. "Yes."

Kenji frowned. "But we saw then absorbed into the darkness! Did it miss these?"

We both paused to watch a ghost in the form of a walking stick hop by, and I was somewhat startled to see a pair of lanterns just beyond the city gate, but neither was Seita.

"We both saw the nature of that cloud. How could it have missed anything? How could these have escaped? I'm guessing they didn't escape at all. They were absorbed, but not permanently."

I called after the walking-stick ghost, but of course it ignored me, as did the second and third spirit I tried to contact. It was the reason sources of information like Seita were so highly prized in the profession of nobleman's proxy: ghosts made the best spies and informants of all. No human could match them for either stealth or access. Yet most ghosts were so involved in their own interests and concerns they simply ignored humans, unless that human happened to be one they bore some grudge against.

It was nearly impossible to get a ghost to speak to you that did not wish to do so. Just as it was also nearly impossible to shut one up if it did. I had been very fortunate to find Seita, who had retained most of his worldly desires and simply wanted a bit of rice now and then, otherwise to be left alone with the memory of his former life. Now it seemed our luck in this regard was at its end, for both of us.

"The ghosts know what happened," Kenji said. "They may even know what that thing is."

"Possible," I conceded. "But getting any of them to answer our questions will be very difficult. Since by your own admission this is out of your realm, it may require a specialist."

"You know my opinion of that," Kenji said.

I did. While Kenji might be one of the worst excuses for a priest who ever lived, he was still primarily a *Buddhist* worst excuse for a priest who ever lived. The idea of Yin-Yang or Daoist magic made him very uncomfortable. Even those dedicated to the ancient Way of the Gods did not always get full respect from Kenji.

"Do you have an alternative?" I asked.

"No," he said. "I do not. But I'll have no part in it. Do as you think you must, Lord Yamada. You can be certain that at least I will not interfere. But if you find yourself changed into something grotesque or worse, do not look to me to set matters right."

I smiled faintly. "I wouldn't think of it. Goodnight, Kenji-san."

Kenji went to the hostelry, and I turned south toward Gion; while the ghosts were most active now, there was nothing more I could do that evening, nor much chance I could do more in the morning if I did not get some sleep. Despite my weariness I took the long way home, past the compound of Lady Snow. There were no lights within, and the gate sealed from the outside.

"Lady Snow has, indeed, taken her leave of the city. At least she told the truth about that."

It wasn't much to be cheered by, and yet I was a little. So much had gone wrong that day I was grateful for even the slightest bit that bothered to go exactly as I expected.

The next morning there were warrior-monks from Enryaku-ji on the streets of the capital. Armed, but in no large numbers; no real force. They appeared in groups of two, three at most. I saw them walking on Shijo-dori and Sanjo-dori, and then again on Karasuma-dori. They did not accost or otherwise pay any heed to the throngs of people moving about the street and so passed through the crowds leaving no disturbance or, indeed, little to remark on in their wake. Yet they did leave small eddies of people who whispered to each other in very low tones and shot many furtive glances in the monks' direction.

The monks did not belong there. We knew it, and they knew it; and yet here they were, walking with the unhurried pace of people with no particular destination in mind and all the time in eternity. Still, I had no doubt they could move quickly enough if the need arose. Yet who would determine that need?

Curious.

I found Master Chang Yu seated at his worktable in his small shop off Karasuma. Unlike some Daoist practitioners he really was, as his name implied, Chinese. He was a short and round little old fellow with a drooping gray mustache and a none-too-clean yellow robe. The image he displayed was no more or less than the truth, but one did not have to scratch his genial surface too hard to find dross.

He was, in most regards, a charming charlatan.

The way of things dictated he would always remain a foreigner in his adopted country, but he had built that very strangeness, that "otherness" into a fairly lucrative concern. I had to admire his ability to turn a disadvantage to his favor; it was no surprise his reputation was greater than his reality, nor when it came to the true measure of his abilities that there was a great deal of chaff mixed with the rice. Still, what he could do, he could do, and for the proper consideration he would attempt nearly anything. Profit made him reckless. Frankly, I was surprised he'd lived as long as he had.

"Lord Yamada. How can this humble one serve you this morning? I have a wonderful cure for the excesses of rice wine."

"The only cure for rice wine is more of the same. That's not why I am here, Chang-san. I need to conjure a ghost."

"You always have such strange requirements, when the right herb cures most ills. I think you should try some."

"I think I must find someone else." I said and made as if to leave.

He scowled. "I should let you go, you know," he said. "I think it would be wisest."

"Since when have you done what is wise?"

"True, and this hardly seems the time to start." The old man sighed. "Can you pay? Forgive my asking but, well, just forgive me."

"Yes. But no more than four bags of uncooked rice."

He shrugged. "So long as it is a small ghost."

"What about if the ghost has been exorcised?"

Chang Yu laughed. "There isn't that much rice in China. Besides, summoning a ghost from hell upsets balance and order. In order to remain true to the Way, I must avoid such things."

I sighed. "I'll settle for a small ghost then. But it has to be one that normally haunts the area just south of the Demon Gate."

He frowned. "Any one?"

"Anyone who can speak."

He tugged at his scraggly beard. "Most spirits can converse with the living, after a fashion, if properly motivated. For an extra bag of rice, I'll undertake that as well."

I wasn't in a mood to argue. Kanemore's means were vast but not inexhaustible, and I had already spent more than I wished. Still, I needed this answer very badly, and unless I had been mistaken in Kanemore all this time, so did he.

"Agreed."

"Two bags now, but I'll need time to prepare. Return as evening falls with the balance, and we'll see what can be done."

I gave Chang Yu the payment and went looking for Kenji. While he of course would have nothing to do with Chang Yu and his Chinese magic, now there were other matters to discuss. I found him near the Demon Gate as usual, but he was neither hawking talismans nor begging alms. Instead he merely sat in a shady spot with his back to the wall near the gate, looking. He nodded to me as I approached.

"Sit, Lord Yamada. I think I know why you have come."

"The monks of Enryaku-ji," I said. "I assume you have seen them?"

"Oh, yes. I have indeed," he said, but that was all.

"And?"

He took a long breath and let it out slowly. "The city is not their rightful place. They should not be here."

"You'll find no argument from me on that score," I said dryly. "What do you think it means?"

"I don't know. But it echoes a very troubling precedent."

"You mean this has happened before?"

"Not exactly. Yet I believe there are parallels . . . do you remember the Emperor, Kammu Tennou?"

"Since he died over two hundred years before I was born, no," I said, and Kenji sighed gustily.

"Even you spent some little time in the Great School, so you know very well what I mean. Do you remember the stories of his reign?"

"A very active Emperor, if I remember my lessons. He made war against the Ezo—the barbarians—in the north and expanded the Imperial domains," I said, considering. "And he moved the capital, which was then in Nara, to its present location."

"Very good," Kenji said. "Now, do you recall *why* he moved the capital?"

"Oh." Now I thought I could see where Kenji's rather meandering path was leading. "To escape the power of the temples. Now, if only the Fujiwara were as easy to elude."

"Be that as it may," Kenji said, "the point remains that, like Emperors before and after, Kammu sought means of consolidating his power without undue interference. The temples at Nara had grown wealthy and influential under Kammu's reign, so much so he realized his only method to escape them was simply to move and leave them behind, cutting them off from their base of power which was, ironically enough, the proximity of the Emperor Kammu himself."

"So why was one of his earliest official acts to endow Enryaku Temple?"

Kenji smiled. "Did he have a choice? The northeast is an unfortunate direction, regardless of your location. How better to defend the city from evil influences than to locate a temple in that very direction, acting as a buffer between the northeast and your shining new city? Besides, it was not the Eightfold Way he sought to escape, merely the power of the chief priests at Nara. From that standpoint, his action was a complete success. The temple complexes at Nara faded. Yet now . . . "

"Yet now, two hundred years or more after his death, you see the same dynamic at work?"

He looked at me. "Don't you? Enryaku-ji had its own private army for some time before Lord Sentaro became *hojo*. Do you consider it mere happenstance that now we find armed monks wandering the streets of the capital?"

"Not in the least. Yet all we've done so far is discuss history with, perhaps, some idle speculation. What have you heard?"

"Not much," Kenji admitted. "I sent a letter to Master Saigyo at Mount Oe just this morning, so I do not expect a reply for some weeks. Even so, I consider it very unlikely he's heard anything— Enryaku-ji is a world unto itself. Even the temples within the city do not have extensive commerce with it, but I intend to find out what I can."

"The Emperor is in residence," I said. "Not on pilgrimage or under any ceremonial spiritual obligations that would require his absence?"

"There is nothing on the calendar that I am aware of," Kenji said, frowning. "Why do you ask?"

"I find it very hard to believe the monks of Enryaku-ji have been allowed into the city without the Emperor's permission, or at least his forbearance. If that's the case, it's possible Kanemore might have some knowledge of the matter."

"I'll leave that to you," Kenji said, rising. In a moment I followed his example, and we stood facing each other beside the Demon Gate. "The mendicants will be gathering in their usual places. I will seek their watchfulness in this as well."

That was sound thinking. The mendicants covered most of the city in their daily search for alms and, in some cases, mischief. They could prove useful, but if so it would be Kenji's field to harvest. I had, I hoped, my own; again I went to the easternmost gate of the Imperial Compound, but the guard there said Prince Kanemore was away, and no message could reach him for at least a day. Instead, Kanemore had left a letter for me.

I thanked the guard and took Kanemore's sealed scroll back to my rooms at the Widow Tamahara's establishment to read:

> *When treeless mountains*
> *Uproot and walk as pilgrims,*
> *Then might another*
> *Seek an opposite true path*
> *and in their footsteps wander.*

At the end of the poem, Kanemore had simply written: "I would welcome your thoughts on my pilgrimage, for I know such things are of interest. Until my return—Kanemore."

While it was required of all men of Kanemore's rank to be

accomplished poets, Kanemore was not the subtlest I knew. That was a good thing; despite Kenji's confidence in my education, my ability to follow the classical allusions was somewhat less than my alleged station in life should require. It had been a long time since my days at the Imperial University, and I was quite out of practice.

Still, "treeless mountains" was a pretty obvious reference to the monks of Enryaku-ji, with their bald heads and their current habit of walking within the city proper. Unless I badly misread the piece, Kanemore had gone to Enryaku-ji himself. Now, it was quite possible that a stranger who intercepted Kanemore's message could decipher it as I had. Even so, I understood the context where another might not, and so Kanemore's poem acted as a workable cypher despite its limitations as art.

This fact left many questions, one of which was why he bothered. Kanemore's communications tended to be fairly straightforward as a rule: "Meet me at Gion Shrine tomorrow afternoon," or "I am going to Mutsu Province for two months"—that sort of thing. It rather fit his temperament and helped explain why he had chosen the *bushi* path, when most men of his station considered a poetry contest a better judge of a man's worth than whether he could ride or shoot. Kanemore's martial interests were looked at rather askance at Court, but that had never stopped the Emperor or his ministers from making use of those skills when it suited them.

Of course, Kanemore could write poetry at need, but as a general rule he didn't bother writing poems to *me*, and why was he going into the viper's den that was now Enryaku-ji? Had he gone on the Emperor's behalf or his own? It was one tangle I was not going to unknot without Kanemore's help, and there was nothing for it but to wait and speak with him upon his return. Until then I was on my own pilgrim's path and very uncertain where it would take me.

My meal had arrived in my absence and I ate it cold, more concerned with its benefit than the proper savour of the food. After that I rested for the coming evening, as there was little else I could do, but I did not feel inclined to enclose myself in my shabby rooms while the day passed. I took the last of the tea out onto the veranda so I could enjoy the garden in the Widow Tamahara's courtyard. Granted, it was not much of a garden to one who had been privileged to walk the gardens on the grounds of the Imperial Palace. Yet it was what it was, and the sight was pleasant enough as I sipped my tea.

I was, however, somewhat surprised when the Widow Tamahara joined me. With Kanemore's patronage I had stopped dreading the old woman's presence as much since I wasn't tied to thinking up excuses for my tardy obligations. Even so, there was a hesitation in her manner I found a little disconcerting. It was simply not in the Widow Tamahara's nature to be either shy or tentative, and yet she was positively demure as she kneeled some distance from me and waited until I had acknowledged her presence.

"Yes, Tamahara-san? Is there something you wish of me?"

"I was wondering, Lord Yamada, if you had heard anything. I mean, about the priests of Enryaku-ji taking over the city. Do you know what that is about?"

I sighed. "I do not know what you have heard, Tamahara-san, but I am quite certain they have done no such thing. The guards at the gates and the Imperial Compound are not changed."

"I suppose, but it is very strange. Rumors have been flying like a flock of crows, and nothing but ill comes on their wings. Evil spirits have entered the city, and people are dying. You've not heard these things?"

"I've seen the priests wandering the streets," I admitted, "and it is certainly unusual. Yet what reason would the good monks of Enryaku-ji have to rebel against their Emperor?"

"I am sure I do not know why they should bother," the old woman admitted. "The city is nearly run by priests and monks as it is; this temple or that, this shrine or that. The Gods I do not mind so much, Lord Yamada. They accept their offerings and advance as is their right and retreat as is their wont. One knows one's obligations in their regard. But the saints? Feh. Useless."

I frowned. "Indeed? Then why did the emperors install the temples to protect the city?"

"Protect who? People are dying, Lord Yamada, dying in strange ways. The monks are charged with keeping evil from the city, and yet instead of remaining in their temples praying, they are swaggering about the streets. Let them have their way, and they'll turn all the poor merchant women out into the streets and close the wine shops and brothels. Before long we'll all be shaving our heads and denying our natures, and the evil spirits will be the least of our worries."

"If I hear of any such edicts," I said, "I will do my best to give you ample warning."

"You're smiling at me, I know it," she said. "But you mark me, Lord Yamada—those monks are up to something."

I couldn't very well argue with the woman on that score, since

I was rapidly coming to the same conclusion. Or rather, that Lord Sentaro was up to something and his current base of operations meant the monks of Enryaku-ji were part of it as well. Indeed, it would be foolish to assume otherwise. Even if Lord Sentaro's renunciation of the affairs of the world was as sincere as a crow on a corpse, for the man to forego all politics and scheming was simply beyond his nature. Whatever was afoot, I was fairly certain it would not require the Widow Tamahara to take the tonsure herself and I told her so. She just shrugged and took her leave of me, but I know she was not convinced.

When the sun touched the mountains to the west, I made my way back to Karasuma-dori. The warrior monks were no longer in evidence, but whether this was because they had withdrawn from the city as evening approached or merely dispersed themselves within it, I did not know. It did occur to me that, if they were quartering at one or more of the temples throughout the city, this fact should not be difficult to uncover. I put the matter aside for a later time and concentrated on the matter at hand.

Chang Yu was waiting at the doorway of his shop, apparently unconcerned, but I could tell he was scanning the dwindling crowds along the Karasuma-dori as evening approached.

"Are you ready to get started, Chang-san?"

He grinned. "Started, Lord Yamada? My part is all but done. Come see."

Since Chang and I understood each other, perhaps to a greater degree than his normal run of clients, I was spared most of the, shall we say, more ceremonial accouterments of his craft. At the rear exit of his shop he contented himself with one brief droning utterance that could have been an invocation, or could have been a comment on my parentage. While I had certainly given him cause to do so now and again, he did understand that such would be lost on me. I thought it more likely the chant actually *was* an invocation, since Chang understood my interests in his methods were far less than my interest in the results. Which, I had to admit, the old man had delivered as promised.

"Honestly, Lord Yamada, it was almost too easy."

The alley behind his shop was part of the maze that led to residence compounds, gambling establishments, and even more obscure little shops. In the alley there hovered what in all appearance was a walking stick with two great bulging eyes and the tiniest slit of a mouth. Those huge eyes were currently staring down the alleyway, and the creature's agitation was plain.

"His name's Gintaro," Chang Yu said. "If you want anything else from him you'll have to ask it yourself; I'm weary of talking to the silly thing."

I looked at the creature in the alley, then at Chang Yu. "I have to ask this: how are you holding him?"

Normally the fine details of the conjuration were of little interest to me, but in this case my curiosity was aroused, simply because there didn't seem to be any means employed. The ghost was plainly trapped and not liking that fact in the least, but I couldn't see what was holding it. I expected a barrier of some sort, perhaps a rope hung with talismans and anchored with images of the Buddha, or *something*, but the ghost merely hopped up and down in place and did not move right, left, forward or backward. I did see it levitate once, to a height of about ten feet, but it soon came down again.

The old man grinned. "He's under a spiritual obligation

147

to the god of the earth, who is currently residing to the west. Therefore he can only advance west to east until the god relocates. Normally, when he reaches the western gate he simply vanishes and reappears at the Demon Gate to begin his journey again. You've seen the same thing among the living . . . except for the vanishing and reappearing part."

I had, though I heard it more often used as an excuse; something along the lines of "I would go home now as you wish, my sweet lady, but I am under spiritual obligation to avoid advancing to the north, where my home is. Surely you would not turn me out into the cold streets?" Still, many people took such things seriously. As apparently did this ghost.

"Well then, why does it not advance to the west?"

"Because I can't, of course," said the walking stick. "That fat tick of a charm merchant has blocked my way. And it's very rude to talk about someone when they're within hearing, you know."

"You call me a fat tick and you speak of discourtesy?" Chang Yu asked. "Feh. I'll set your wood on fire if you take that tone with me again."

The walking stick glared but did not continue its invective. I leaned close to Chang Yu and whispered, "If I needed to release him, how would I do it?"

I was adept at neither conjuring nor banishing spirits, but the one thing I did have experience in was the extraction of useful information from them. Now, Seita had been an easy case. He was, at his core, a Hungry Ghost. Feeding him always assured his co-operation. This thing, on the other hand, seemed to operate on a more religious level. I would have to use that if I wanted to find out what I needed to know.

"Just dig down two inches into the dirt of the alley where that white pebble sits. When you find the barrier you'll know what to do," Chang said.

I acknowledged Master Chang's instructions and then turned to the ghost. "Gintaro-san, were you near the Demon Gate two nights previous?"

The walking stick looked sullen. "Aren't you in league with this corpulent sorcerer? Why should I tell you anything?"

"Because if you do, I'll set you free. If you don't, I'll let you sit in Master Chang's back alley for weeks or months before the god relocates. I think he will be very cross with you for not fulfilling your obligations."

"It's not my fault! The god will know it is not my fault!"

"Will he care? Gods understand obligations very well. One thing they are less clear about is excuses. Do you want to take such a chance? I would not."

The thing scowled. "What do you want?"

I shrugged. "A few trifling questions you can easily answer, and then be on your way. Is that so much to ask?"

"Get me into trouble, they will. I know it," the thing said, though each word seemed to cost it in pain and aggravation. "Ask."

"Were you within a bowshot of the Demon Gate two nights ago?"

"Yes."

"Was there a dark cloud of spiritual energy present that night?"

"Yes." The answer came slower this time but not because the thing was confused. I think it understood very well what I was asking about.

"I may require an answer that goes beyond a simple yes or no," I said.

"That has not happened as of yet," the walking stick pointed out.

"Do you know what the cloud was?"

"Yes. Considering the rather basic nature of the questions so far, I assume you eventually ask what you really want to know?"

I started to rebuke the ghost harshly, but it occurred to me that the thing had said nothing more or less than the truth. "What was that thing?"

"Everything," the walking stick said. "Everyone."

"What do you mean 'everything, everyone'?"

"Just that. We were joined with it. It was ... Satori. Transcendence. I lost it. I lost it."

"You're telling me you were one of the ghosts consumed by that thing?"

"Consumed? No. We were all still there, ourselves and yet not. Knowing each other. Understanding each other, for the first time. Can you imagine what that was like, to know that and to lose it? We all did. It will be back. We will be waiting. This time we will not run, those of us who shared that night. We will embrace the darkness."

"Waiting? Embrace it? Why?"

"To become one with God."

PART FOUR

Your sleeves remain dry,
nor even the dew applied
to feign your heart's ache.
How can I believe your love
on such threadbare evidence?

"The assumption has always been that evil enters the city through the northeast gate," Prince Kanemore said. "We must face the possibility that the evil, whatever it may be, is already here."

Kanemore had not returned to the city for three days, and when he finally did come back it was another day before we could arrange a meeting. The insight I had hoped to gain from his visit to Enryaku Temple was even slower in coming.

We sat together at an isolated table at the Widow Tamahara's establishment. He sipped rice wine and I sipped tea. I rather wished we could trade cups, but at that moment I was afraid should I once more crawl into a saké cup, I might never have the strength to crawl out again.

"The pattern of attacks seems to argue otherwise," I said. "The one thing those attacks have in common is that none, so far as I can determine, happened more than two miles from the Demon Gate."

He sighed. "I don't argue that point. Just that this may simply mean the focus of the creature, whatever it is, requires that it originate there. We have no real evidence it's using the gate as a portal."

I wanted to argue because I firmly believed otherwise but, strictly speaking, Kanemore was right. We did not know and could not prove the entity was entering through the gate, yet that had been my base assumption from the time I finally spotted some pattern to the attacks, and that was their proximity to the northeast gate. There was no other common thread and this was, so far as I was concerned, the only trail worth following. I didn't like being reminded of just how tenuous a path it was, but Kanemore had said no more than the truth. As he sipped his wine, it was soon clear he had more to say.

"There has been an unspoken assumption all along in this matter," Kanemore said. "We felt that Enryaku-ji was somehow involved."

"Culpable, if not actively engaged," I said. "How could anything like what I've seen enter the city without Enryaku-ji knowing?

"Master Dai-wu thinks that what we're dealing with is a culmination of decadent and impious influences within the city. That in some regard the attacks are the work of the spirit of the city, attempting to cleanse itself."

" 'Master Dai-wu'? Do you mean Lord Sentaro?"

"I mean Master Dai-wu," Kanemore said softly. "Goji-san, I know what you are thinking, and believe me, I thought the same. But I've met the man. He has changed."

I sipped my tea. The fact that Kanemore had used the more familiar "Goji-san" rather than "Lord Yamada" was not lost on me. He was telling me that he was a friend, in case I had forgotten, and he spoke as one.

"Prince Kanemore, you and I both know Lord Sentaro is incapable of being anything other than what he is. This is the same man about whom you once said: 'to call him a pig is an insult to pigs.' Did I remember that right?"

Kanemore reddened slightly. "I've met the man since, Lord Yamada. You have not."

Again, I could not argue. As the willow bent to elude the wind, so I considered what Kanemore had told me. "What sort of 'impious influences'?"

"The un-ordained priests, for one. Always going about alms-begging and drinking and whoring. Their numbers are huge within the city."

"So why does the cloud not attack them, if it is angry with the mendicants?"

"I do not know. Perhaps the city is merely angry. Like a wounded thing, it strikes blindly."

"Do you really believe that?"

Kanemore sighed. "Not really. Yet I stand by my opinion that the man once known as Lord Sentaro has undergone a transformation. I'm as astonished as you are."

That part, at least, was the Kanemore I knew. I had known him to be fierce and headstrong but never quick to anger, and certainly not indecisive. His uncertainty now in this matter was troubling, more for the fact that some of it actually made sense. Not the part about Lord Sentaro, of course; I don't know what false geniality Lord Sentaro had used to seduce Prince Kanemore, but I knew it could not be genuine. Still, the ghost had said something about being one with all. It was rather vague, but if the spirit of the city itself was on a rampage, how then would any single spirit or ghost subsumed into that maelstrom feel, think, or see? Perhaps they would have reacted the same as the little walking stick ghost that Chang-san had trapped in his alleyway.

"I gather the Enryaku-ji monks within the city were sent as observers with the Emperor's permission?"

Kanemore indicated this was so. "I did not know the context at first and saw nothing of them from within the Palace Compound, so I thought little of the matter. Yet when I heard the Emperor was sending a delegation to Enryaku Temple for counsel, I volunteered. I wanted to see for myself what was going on there. I confess I rather thought to singe the dragon in its own den, but Master Dai-wu surprised me. He was quiet, calm, thoughtful, composed, and serene. None of which are attributes I've ever associated with Lord Sentaro."

"Nor I," I said, rubbing my chin. Was what Kanemore telling me actually possible? Had the man changed; was his devotion to his new station in life sincere? I could hardly believe it, and yet this new theory on the nature of the entity made as much sense as anything that had occurred to me so far.

"The monks will be back," Kanemore said. "Armed, this time. There has been agreement between the Emperor and the Master of Enryaku-ji to attempt to weed out any evil influences within the city. It is thus believed that the *kami* of the city may be appeased. You might . . . well, you might want to mention this to that somewhat disreputable monk you've been known to associate with."

"I might indeed. Prince, tell me if you know: how many monks are slated to enter the city itself?"

"No more than two hundred."

"How many guards are stationed at and around the Imperial Compound?"

"That is something I don't think I should reveal," Prince Kanemore said, taking a long drink. "Even to you. Forgive me."

I bowed. "No reason to apologize, and I did not mean to pry into matters that are not, strictly speaking, my concern. Yet are you going to tell me that such a large force within the city, a force whose loyalty is not primarily to our Emperor, does not concern you? Even from a tactical standpoint?"

"Of course it does, but the matter is out of my hands. Yet I will do what I think needs doing, Lord Yamada. Count upon it."

I bowed. "I expected no less. Can you tell me when the monks are returning?"

"Tomorrow."

"Well, then," I said, "I guess we shall see."

After Kanemore left, I went to the veranda outside my rooms and rested for a bit. I considered seeking out Kenji, but as it turned out the scruffy priest saved me the trouble. He appeared in the Widow Tamahara's garden.

"I heard Prince Kanemore returned today."

"You heard correctly. I've met with him."

"And?"

I told him about the ghost I had spoken to, and what Kanemore had said about the monks and "Master Dai-wu." Kenji looked thoughtful.

"If that is Enryaku-ji's opinion . . . well, it almost makes sense," he said grudgingly. "I think such a thing is at least possible."

"I think the same, which is the frightening part. In either case the monks will do as they have been charged to do. There's no help for that."

"I will spread the word among the mendicants. Those who have sense to listen may avoid the net. Those who do not, well, they at least cannot say they were not warned."

"And what of you, Kenji-san? You said the theory made sense. You did not say you believed it."

"Neither did you, Lord Yamada," Kenji said. "As for me, I'll try to make myself less conspicuous. I may be fully ordained, but this net may not make such fine distinctions. You know where to look for me at need."

"As do you."

The fourth month surrendered to the fifth as the last *sakura* fell from the trees to be replaced with the green of late spring.

Over the next few weeks and despite Kenji's efforts, several dozen itinerant priests were taken off the streets of the capital by the monks of Enryaku-ji, and placed in seclusion within the temple grounds outside the city. They were forced to bathe and meditate regularly, but were not otherwise mistreated.

The warrior-monks were now a common sight on the streets of the city. Many people had even come to welcome their presence, as they were polite and respectful and kept good order on the streets, even better than the Emperor's ministers charged with that duty. They had even persuaded visiting officials and provincial lords to keep the number of their *bushi* retinues in check, and those present under stricter control. This had reduced the Widow Tamahara's normal clientele somewhat, and she was not happy about it, but even she was of the opinion that things had not turned out as badly as she feared.

As for me, I was still worried; though I was, it seemed, just about the only one concerned. Even Kanemore viewed their presence with some detachment now, and told me as much when we met at our appointed time near the beginning of the fifth month on a warm afternoon.

"I have to admit," he said, "that our fears do not seem justified."

"Prince, it is far too early to close that particular scroll. I simply do not trust Enryaku-ji while Lord Sentaro is its master."

He sighed. "You well know I bow to no man in my hatred of Lord Sentaro. The Priest Dai-wu is another matter. I do not know how it happened. I only know when I look into the man's eyes I do not see Lord Sentaro. Not even a trace."

"That only means he's showing a blank face. He's a skilled enough manipulator for that."

"Not blank, my friend. Open and friendly and guileless."

I frowned. "Are you certain it is the same man?"

"His head is shaved, of course, but it is Lord Sentaro, or at least the man who once was Lord Sentaro. There's no doubt in my mind. Astonishment? I freely confess it. But no doubt."

I scratched my head. "I must yield to you on this, since I have no argument to make save my own past experience, which to a great degree you have shared."

"Just so. Then there is the matter of the attacks, which have apparently ceased. Nothing has happened since that poor man's wife you told me about . . . or at least nothing we can attribute to this 'dark cloud.' So perhaps Dai-wu was correct about the source."

I smiled. "I concede the possibility."

Kanemore sighed. "Lord Yamada, I honestly don't see what course we can take now. To all appearances, Dai-wu has been vindicated."

I bowed. "While naturally it is in my interest to continue pursuing the matter, at the moment I confess myself at a loss myself as to how to proceed. I serve at your pleasure, Prince Kanemore. What will you have me do?"

"You must consider yourself at leisure, at least for now. I think we have done all we can do, unless you know something I do not."

I thought, perhaps, I did. But it was nothing I could either point to or explain to anyone's satisfaction, including my own. "No, Prince Kanemore. I do have one favor to ask, if I may."

He smiled. "What is it?"

"If you are part of any more delegations to Enryaku-ji, I would like to be included, if possible."

"Since I would feel better if your sharp eyes could confirm what I think I saw, that can be arranged. Is there anything else?"

"Just be on your guard, prince. For all our sakes."

He grunted. "Always."

There was nothing more to be said, and we parted. I still did not believe the danger was past, but had to concede that Kanemore was right about the attacks. There had been none, and my observations of the spiritual activity radiating outwards from the Demon Gate likewise showed nothing unusual, not since the day of the last attack and not for the last several nights.

Could the presence of the mendicants actually have been the key?

Some were pious men who chose not to associate themselves with any specific temple for sincere and personal beliefs. Others did not do so because no self-respecting temple would have them. Kenji was something of a special case; he had taken his training, albeit reluctantly, at the temple on Mount Oe to the northwest and remained on good terms with its chief priest. He had a place to go, if it came to that. I just happened to know he had not left the city, nor did I expect him to do so.

Still, as Kenji more or less predicted, it was the most unsavory, least disciplined mendicants who had been most likely to be snared by the monks of Enryaku-ji and removed from the city. Had the spirits of the city been enraged, and had this been enough to soothe their outrage? How I could I be sure?

And then, not for the first time and I was certain not for the last, I realized I was being an ass. I slapped my forehead with the palm of my hand.

Baka!

If the mendicants and other lowlifes had indeed raised the ire of the resident spirit of the city, then why under the Heavens was the matter being addressed in the Temples of the Buddha? The proper avenue of inquiry was the Way of the Gods and their shrines. This went back to the spirit of the city, the spirits that resided in all things and was an older matter, a context if not in the ascendant, still well-entrenched and unlikely to fade from our world anytime soon. It went without saying such a thing would not occur to Kenji. He was Buddhist to the core of his reprobate soul. But this fact should very well have occurred to me.

I considered. Gion Festival was not due to begin for another month, so the shrine would not yet be caught up in preparation;

it might be possible to gain an audience with the priest of the shrine for a suitable offering . . . which now became a separate problem. For the moment, Prince Kanemore's patronage had ended. Even as a friend he would not risk insulting me by extending patronage when there was no work for me to do. While for my pride's sake I was grateful, the lack of means nevertheless posed a dilemma. I had seen the last of my rice safely turned over to the Widow Tamahara and thus secured room and board through the seventh month. At the time it seemed prudent. Yet now I was without a suitable offering, and I did not think the gods would look favorably upon my questions if I appeared in their sanctuary empty-handed. I was certain the priests would not.

What did I possess? My sword? It was truly a fine blade, a gift from a grateful father for extricating his wayward oldest son from a mess of the boy's own making. It would make a very suitable offering to the shrine, but under the circumstances I could not seriously consider parting with it. What did that leave? Clothes? Even my best were a little threadbare. There had to be something else and, after a while, the answer came to me, reluctantly but inevitably.

I stood on a storage chest and lifted a board in the ceiling, taking down the cask, its cord ties and seals still in place. My last extravagance from Princess Teiko's gold; a cask of exquisite *bejean* saké. I don't know why I hadn't drunk it already. For some time the anticipation itself was enough. After that I was usually already too drunk to get the sodding thing out of the ceiling. Now . . . well, even the best saké would not keep forever, and by the time I was ready for it the saké might be too far past ready for me. Better the gods had it than to let it go to waste. I took the cask under my arm and set out for the Gion Shrine.

Some hours later as I walked home on Shijo-dori it occurred to me that my saké was gone and I had nothing tangible to show for it; not even a decent bout of intoxication. Oh, the priests had been entertaining enough, waving their staffs with the white *shide* zigzags, purifying and invoking on my behalf and all that, but so far as I could see, nothing had actually happened. The priest had simply told me to ask my question in my dreams and the *kami* would answer, but he also said it was very important that I phrase the question correctly. This would be something of a challenge, since I wasn't completely sure what I should ask, and assuming I did, one rarely had control of one's own dreams long enough for anything as lucid as a question and an answer.

Still, I couldn't drink the saké myself anyway and couldn't bear to sell it, so I was really no worse off. As for the gods, well, we would see. If the dream failed me, it wouldn't be the first time I'd played all I had on a toss that did not win. Besides, my relationship with the gods of this world had not always been properly observed. While I firmly believed that the gods were content to be most concerned with those most concerned about *them*, a little show of respect now and then would do no harm.

It was late afternoon when I returned to the Widow Tamahara's compound from the shrine. Nidai-kun was waiting for me on the veranda outside my rooms. He had undergone even more of a transformation since our last meeting nearly a month before. For one, his clothes, face, and hands were clean. For another he was clearly better fed and turning into quite a handsome youth. His eyes had lost none of their mischief, but now you could begin to see less of the child and more of the man he might one day become.

"Being in service agrees with you, Nidai-kun," I said.

He bowed formally. "Thank you, Lord Yamada. If it pleases you, Lady Snow requests you join her for dinner tomorrow night."

So she has returned. I wonder what she has to say now?

"When did your mistress return to the city?"

"Only yesterday. As she wishes to renew your acquaintance, she said it would be her pleasure to cook for you. Will you come?"

"I suppose you've been instructed to tell me nothing of your journey or its purpose?"

He bowed again, but I caught the grin before his face was hidden. "Lady Snow sends her apologies but is of the opinion that, should you learn too much from this humble servant, there would be precious little incentive to visit her in her loneliness."

While I had little doubt Lady Snow was only lonely when she chose to be, I didn't see any point in involving myself with her further.

"It is a kind offer, but what if I am not inclined to accept?"

Nidai reached within the sash of his robe and produced a scroll. "In that case, Lady Snow instructed me to give you this."

I unrolled the small scroll and read what was written there; a poem, of course.

As mulberry bark
produces paper stark white,

so might a person
of dark and unworthy nature
uncover understanding.

So she anticipated me, as Teiko often did. Sometimes I think Teiko had done that just to vex me. Or perhaps I was simply a much more transparent person than I liked to believe. That aside, the poem, unless I badly misread it, said that this time Lady Snow had documentation; an interesting claim which, despite my skepticism, I knew I would have to check for myself. I had no doubt Lady Snow knew that as well.

Besides, it wasn't as if I was going to get a better offer that day or, indeed, anytime at all.

"Tell your mistress that Lord Yamada is pleased to accept her kind invitation, and will call upon her tomorrow evening."

Nidai bowed again, then hurried away to either deliver my reply or deal with whatever other errands Lady Snow had assigned to him that afternoon. I studied the poem Lady Snow had written a little more closely but could find nothing in it I had not already seen.

In the years since I had been at court, I'd come to appreciate the concept of just saying what you meant, or as close as understanding and literate expression allowed. Yet I knew that, in the Imperial Court especially and among the nobility in particular, saying exactly what you meant could earn you a quick pilgrimage to Suma. Worse still to say exactly what you meant in a communication that fell into the wrong hands. A person who wished to survive, never mind prosper, had to learn quickly clarity was not usually an ally. Classical allusion and obscurity became both tool and weapon, and had been so for many generations.

Without context even the most lyric poem could at once be a thing of the most incredible artistry, and still be impenetrable to anyone but the intended recipient. I could appreciate the subtlety of the art and yet still wish the world was not quite as it was. As things were, the incident did remind me of something I already knew and had yet not fully considered.

Lady Snow writes poetry. That would be part of her training as an asobi.

True enough. The nature of their profession required they blend in with the aristocracy at need. Indeed, for the higher-ranking courtesans such skills were indispensable. A gentleman of high station courted the favor of someone like Lady Snow with the same feel for love as both game and contest as that same gentleman would a Lady of The Court, though in the case of high-born women the stakes in terms of marriages or alliances could be much higher. However seriously it was or was not played, it was still the same game.

That did not explain why Lady Snow felt the need to send poems to me unless, like Kanemore, she felt that using a poem was safer and there was risk involved in letting it be known what she wanted to say or show to me—another sign of the lady's seriousness about this matter. Whether she actually believed what she was going to say to me, she acted as if she did and as if it was important to convince me as well.

So, tomorrow night and despite my better judgment, once again I would give her that chance. I thought, perhaps, I should just call myself a fool right then, and get the matter settled and out of the way.

The shadows had lengthened and were now starting to fade as

the sun disappeared below the mountains. The moon was rising. I thought of how lovely it would look from the Shijo-dori bridge and thought to bestir myself, but it was difficult. My period of rest on the veranda just emphasized to me how weary I was. I thought perhaps I could forsake moon-viewing for a good night's sleep, but compromised by watching the moon rise from right where I sat.

I must have dozed, because when I awoke I felt refreshed. The moon was high still and so near to full that the Widow Tamahara's garden was illuminated clearly. It was a lovely sight, and again I could only think how much more lovely it would appear from the vantage of Shijo Bridge.

Now I felt up to the walk. The path was simple enough; the Widow Tamahara's establishment flanked the street along the compound's northern wall. I merely slipped through the gate and joined the people walking east on Shijo-dori.

Apparently I was not the only one with this idea.

The street was nearly filled with people. There were many couples and families in their best clothes, lovers masked, noble parties with escorts, courtesans and shopkeepers, all heading in the general direction of Shijo Bridge. It was a little unusual to see so many people moving freely along the streets of the city after dark; normally this was the time for demons and ghosts. Still, there was safety in numbers, and the moon cast its reflection into the Kamo River for some time during its nightly excursion across the heavens. While moon-viewing on the Shijo Bridge could never compare to a moon-viewing party at the Imperial Court, it would do well enough for those of us now outside the confines of the Imperial Compound.

Lady Snow was there. I recognized her from the twin ribbons

tying back her long black hair. She was walking in the throng ahead, with the devoted Nidai officiously clearing a path for her. Then it wasn't Lady Snow at all but Princess Teiko I saw moving through the crowd. I couldn't see her face, but there was no doubt in my mind. I did not think it so very strange to see her there. I wanted to catch up to her, perhaps speak with her, and the impossibility of that did not occur to me at all. Just as I stepped forward, the pair of them slipped into a gap in the crowd ahead and were lost from view. It was only then I noticed something else peculiar about the crowd around me—they made no noise.

Not one sound. No voices, not even the click-clack that Lady Snow's wooden *geta* should have made on the cobbled street. Had I stumbled into a throng of ghosts unawares? I didn't think so, despite the presence of Teiko. Anyone who really believed ghosts were silent had not spent much time among ghosts. Still, the silence was strange. I meant to loosen my sword in its scabbard but discovered I was not wearing it. This was also strange. I sometimes wore the blade less often than was really prudent, but even I wouldn't venture out on the streets of the city at night without it. Yet here I was, and here it was not.

Oh . . .

No sooner had the thought occurred to me that everyone on the road stopped instantly and their heads swiveled in unison to look at me.

"Thinks he's figured it out," said Nidai, suddenly appearing beside me. He looked back the way I had come. "You've let the pretty star elude you completely. I have to go catch her, since you can't," he said.

"You mean Lady Snow?"

"Snow is not a star. Try to get to the bridge, Lord Yamada. Otherwise it's a waste of good saké." With that he ran off back down the way we had come and left me quite alone. Literally so. The throng of people had vanished utterly. Considering the circumstances, I thought it very odd that I had not disappeared myself. I no doubt would do so and soon. There was not much time, but I did not dare run, for the delicacy of the dream-world was legend. It would not take much to shatter it and leave me short of my goal. I walked as fast as I thought I could get away with.

"What is your hurry?"

Kanemore walked beside me, matching stride for stride.

"The dream will end soon," I said and kept walking.

"Plenty of time," Kanemore said, and in that instant we were both standing on Shijo Bridge as if we had been there all along, looking up at a beautiful full moon. I knew the moon wasn't supposed to be quite full yet, but I ignored that fact because it wasn't important. Too many facts tended to interfere with a dream.

I looked at Kanemore, who seemed content to gaze at the moon. His eyes were glowing faintly red, like two dying embers. "Lovely thing," he said.

"You're the *kami*, aren't you?"

"Is that what you wanted to know?"

"No." *Careful, Yamada . . .* "*Kami-sama*, what is the spirit that is attacking the people of Kyoto?"

"I do not know," said the image of Kanemore. "It's nothing of mine. It comes from outside."

I wasn't surprised. I had never really believed the gods of Kyoto were behind the attacks. Yet I had hoped they knew what was. "Do you know how to stop it? Will you tell me?"

The *kami* shrugged. "When the time is right, force it to leave."

"How?"

"The usual way," said the *kami*.

Before I could ask another question, any question, I ran out of time. The *kami* and Shijo Bridge were both gone. No matter how many times I opened my eyes and looked again, all I saw was the view to the Widow Tamahara's garden, faint and ghostly in the waning moonlight, from the veranda where I had slept. I rubbed my aching neck and considered what I had learned. Which, so far as I could see, was nothing I didn't already know except for the part about forcing it to leave, and that made no sense at all. Force it to leave? The usual way? What was the usual way, if I didn't even know what the thing was?

I had been warned to consider my questions carefully and I thought, perhaps, I had not done so as well as I might have. Even so, I couldn't think of any question, no matter how straightforward in human terms, that something so very far beyond my understanding as a god might give an answer equally beyond understanding. I gave up on getting any more answers that particular evening and dragged my weary carcass off to my rooms to gather what might remain of my sleep for the evening.

There was simply no help for it. Tomorrow I would need to find Kenji.

The next morning I was again reminded of why Kenji might be difficult to locate; the warrior monks were out in force. While the bulk of the citizens had come to treat them as just part of the city background, I could not afford to do so. I turned south toward the southeast gate. I found Kenji just beyond that gate on the side of the eastern road. He looked a little the worse for wear, but that was to be expected. Both customers and alms had to be a little skimpy at the southeast gate. He looked up and smiled at me.

"Lord Yamada. You're looking well."

"Coming from you, that sounds almost like an accusation." I found a shaded spot beside the scruffy priest and sat down without invitation. "I see your strategy is to leave the city without really leaving the city."

He shrugged. "It's a very good strategy in most respects. The monks of Enryaku-ji seldom venture south of Shichijo-dori for some reason. Too far for their delicate feet, I wager."

I hadn't noticed that specifically, but now Kenji had mentioned it, I realized it was so. I had seen none of them once I'd passed Gojo-dori. I held out a small bundle tied with a cloth.

"One way in which I suspect it is not such a good strategy is that customers are much thinner on the ground along this road. The Widow Tamahara was in a generous mood this morning but I wasn't hungry. Please take it."

Kenji didn't have to be persuaded. It was only after he'd eaten the rice, fish, and pickles to the last crumb and grain that he sighed and spoke again. "All right, what do you want?"

I told Kenji about the oracular dream I'd had the night before. He kept silent until I was finished. Then he scowled. "While I have no problem accepting the existence of gods—they are, after all, no more than beings of a spiritually purer state than humanity—they are not necessarily reliable."

"Even a 'purer state' than humanity is not good enough?"

Kenji sighed. "Yamada-san, you must understand that, from my perspective, even a being of higher spiritual state isn't very much better than a normal person. They both remain Unenlightened."

"Kenji-san, you are perfectly free to preach to the gods later if you can spare the saké to gain their attention, but I need your help right now."

Kenji patted his belly. "Lord Yamada, it's a good thing for you I am so easily bought. Now then, you want to know what you've really learned from this oracular dream? I'll tell you—nothing."

"If so, it was an expensive 'nothing,' Kenji-san," I said. "Though I do find it interesting there was so much of it I already knew."

"Rather, it told you what you were prepared to hear from what you already knew: the attacks were not the result of the gods of the city being angered; you didn't believe this to begin with. That the gods of the city do not know who caused them: neither do you. Shall I go on?"

"You're saying I simply dreamed, and the image of Kanemore was just an image of Kanemore?"

Kenji smiled. "No. I'm saying if this indeed *were* the case, you would have no way of knowing the difference. You were told to banish the entity in 'the usual way.' Now, if we knew what the creature was, that actually might be good advice. I can prepare wards against almost anything, but first I have to know what the 'thing' is."

"Is it a ghost, you think?"

"What sort of ghost can consume other ghosts and still leave them untouched at the end of the night? That kills with no regard of vengeance or righteous justice?"

"I don't know."

"And so, here we are again. Shall we enjoy the view?"

I couldn't argue with anything Kenji had said. Probably I had been wasting my time. One trouble with dreams is that they made very poor documentation. Perhaps what I had seen and heard in my dream was real. Perhaps not. I simply had no way to know except instinct, and that didn't always serve me well. Still, in the end it was usually all I had.

I got to my feet. "While I treasure our conversations, I have an appointment this evening and errands to run before then."

"Lady Snow?"

I hesitated. "How do you know?"

He smiled wistfully. "There's a look that comes over you when you mention her, Lord Yamada. I won't call it gentle. Say rather just a bit less brooding. You didn't mention her name, I admit, but I saw and recognized that look. I'd be careful if I were you."

I shrugged. "Lady Snow wants something from me, and I believe I know what that something is. She serves her own purposes, no more or less than anyone else. She's otherwise harmless."

Kenji looked serious, or at least as serious as Kenji ever did. "No one is harmless, Lord Yamada. And anyone who can soften your habitual scowl? Doubly so."

"I'll take that into account."

"Good day, Lord Yamada."

I left Kenji on the far side of Rashamon and returned to the city. To my own surprise, as I walked up toward the Gion district, I found myself considering what Kenji had said. Was I in danger of becoming enamored of Lady Snow? Certainly she was beautiful and talented, so much so that she did remind me of Teiko. She was not Teiko, however, and no one else could be. I considered this state of affairs quite fortunate.

Men often talked of love and wrote poetry to express their feelings. Sometimes it was done in earnest, at others simply because it more easily parted the curtains to a lady's chamber. Teiko and I had never mentioned the word. Spoken or no, I knew my heart as I thought I knew hers. I was still dealing with the consequences of what I thought I understood all these years later, and would be doing so for the rest of my life.

Perhaps Kenji had been right to be concerned. While I had never adopted the vows or the habits of monks, I did know pleasure was fleeting and of little consequence aside from itself. Love, however, was dangerous for all concerned. I resolved to remember that the next time Lady Snow smiled at me from behind her fan.

I did not meet any of the monks from Enryaku-ji until I was well up Karasuma-dori, almost to Shijo-dori. Remembering what Kenji had said about the monks' patrolling habits, I resolved to test the premise further.

Since I was, as Kanemore had put it, currently at leisure, I turned west when I reached Shijo-dori and headed away from Gion. When the road I walked spoke more of trees and gardens than city, I turned south again. I went nearly to the southwestern corner of Kyoto without seeing a single monk of any kind, except for the occasional furtive mendicant who, like Kenji, had apparently learned where in the city it was safe to beg for alms or otherwise make themselves known. Still, with their former hostel almost within sight of the Demon Gate, it could not be easy for them to manage now, even assuming the sympathy and piety of the citizens could be counted upon; which, in my opinion, could hardly have been a sure wager if Kenji's current state was any indication. No doubt many more of the itinerant monks had found their own way out of the city since the original edicts.

I turned north from there and made my way up the westernmost avenue of the city proper. After a bit I realized the presence of the Enryaku-ji monks had not reasserted itself.

"They've spread out from the Demon Gate to the Imperial Compound and Gion, but no farther," I said aloud to no one in particular. "Curious."

This put all of them within easy striking distance of the Imperial Palace, and the more important of the various mansions located outside the compound proper. If I meant to stage an attack, that is exactly what I would do.

Perhaps I was merely being overly suspicious, and I had no doubt that Kanemore was well aware of the warrior monks' disposition within the city. Still, with the bulk of the Taira and Minamoto *bushi* currently in the north, the situation did give one pause for thought even though on the face of it an attack from Enryaku-ji made no sense. Since the northern branch of the Fujiwara already controlled most of His Majesty's government, what could Lord Sentaro—whom I still could not think of as the apparently serene and pious Dai-wu—possibly have to gain by such an act?

I wanted to speak to Kanemore again though I had no new arguments to offer, but could not justify sending him a message. So I was somewhat surprised upon my return to the Widow Tamahara's late that afternoon, to find a young man in Taira colors waiting on the veranda with a message from Prince Kanemore. He waited politely while I read:

His Majesty is sending an offering of silk to Enryaku-ji as a token of esteem. We leave tomorrow morning after sunrise from the Demon Gate, and you are welcome to come if you wish to accompany us. Please leave your sword behind; I will guarantee your safety. Kanemore.

No poem this time as, in Kanemore's apparent opinion, there was no need for secrecy. Not that I was concerned—Kanemore's word was better than gold. Yet even without such a promise I would not have hesitated. Now perhaps I would get the chance to meet Master Dai-wu and see what Kanemore had seen.

"You may tell His Highness I will be glad to join him tomorrow morning," I said, and the young messenger bowed low and hurried away.

It was the second invitation in as many days. One could almost feel social.

As evening approached, I went first to the baths. I told myself it was simply to avoid offending Lady Snow's nostrils after all my exertions of the day, but in truth I planned to look as much the part of Lord Yamada as a humble nobleman's proxy could achieve. To do otherwise seemed rude and disrespectful, and I did not wish to give unnecessary offense since, as I was fairly certain, later this evening I would once more be forced to disappoint the lovely Lady Snow.

The breeze was pleasantly cool as, dressed in as close as I could manage to finery, I made my way to Lady Snow's home later that evening. I paused a moment to enjoy it south of the

Palace Compound, knowing full well that late spring would soon give way to days like furnace blasts and nights of smothering heat. Just a few more weeks and high summer would reign above even the Emperor's will.

Nidai, looking plump and prosperous, was waiting at the gate. He bowed and ushered me inside into Lady Snow's courtyard.

Clearly the workmen had been back since my last visit. The garden, once a completely overgrown wreck and only partly put to rights by my first visit, was now a thing of beauty, and for its size comparable to anything in the city not excluding the gardens of the Imperial Palace. I was impressed and said as much.

"Lady Snow directed the workmen personally," Nidai said with more than a touch of pride, "and in every detail."

"Your employer's taste is quite extraordinary." As was, apparently, the wealth of her unnamed patron. Taste was one thing—and in tradition-bound Kyoto, close to paramount—yet this marvel had to have cost a great deal. Still, with a concubine of Lady Snow's quality, clearly her master had felt the inclination—perhaps even the necessity—of indulging her to a considerable degree.

Nidai ushered me into the main room and saw me comfortably seated before running off to confer with his mistress. He returned before long.

"Lady Snow bids me welcome you and apologizes for the delay. Dinner will be ready shortly. In the meantime, I am instructed to keep you entertained. Unfortunately, I do not know how to do this."

I smiled. "Well, we could talk. You could tell me where you and your employer have been for the past month."

He sighed. "Lady Snow warned me about this subject very

specifically. I am free to discuss the weather and local gossip only. I've actually been gone too long from my old haunts to know much gossip."

"Speaking of that . . . do you miss your friends?"

"Some of them," he admitted. "Though most were friends of necessity rather than true affection."

"Strength in numbers?"

He shrugged. "Of course. I'm an orphan. I say this not as an excuse but as explanation. My life has been based on necessity, Lord Yamada. What I could do, what I had to do. I am not proud of much of it but not ashamed either."

At first I hadn't understood what Lady Snow had seen in this once-grubby urchin. Now I thought, perhaps, I was seeing some of it as well.

"We all do what we believe we must, Nidai-kun, for good or ill. In that we are no different."

He looked as if he wanted to say something else, but then we both heard the whisper of a *shoji* screen being slid aside, and Lady Snow entered the room bearing a steaming tray. While I had to admit I was famished, and the smells wafting across the room from the tray were intriguing, at first I could do little but stare at Lady Snow.

While Lady Snow's attire was not of the more formal *junihitoe* style suitable for Court, she had managed to capture echoes of Court dress with a multi-layered *kimono* and a Chinese-style over-jacket. The alternating green and blue motifs were impeccably correct for the season, and the ocean wave pattern on the green over-jacket had clearly been accomplished by a master weaver. I had known royal princesses who did not suit their clothing so well nor bore it as gracefully as did the *asobi,* Lady Snow.

Nidai discreetly withdrew as Lady Snow approached, then kneeled in one smooth motion and set the tray before me.

"My apologies. It is difficult to be precise where food is concerned."

"Or in the timing of the arrival of your guests," I said. "No apology needed."

The food was for me alone. I considered whether this meant anything or not. An *asobi* might dine and drink with a client but a noblewoman would no sooner eat in front of a man than she would entertain visitors in a privy.

Lady Snow left me again but soon returned bearing a thirteen-string *koto.* "If you like, I will play for you," she said.

"Please."

I already knew Lady Snow was an excellent dancer, but I soon discovered that even this skill was eclipsed by her mastery of the *koto.* For a little while I forgot the simple but extremely well-presented meal before me. When I finally did start to eat, the food, as I expected, was excellent, but I found myself barely tasting it as I listened to Lady Snow play song after song. Some I recognized, some I did not, but her skill was evident in all of them. I was almost sorry to finish the meal because I knew it would bring the concert to a close. Yet the time came and Lady Snow put the long instrument aside. She politely offered me saké, which I politely declined, and then she got down to the matter I knew actually concerned her.

"I regret the necessity of dampening your enjoyment, but I must again ask for your help, Lord Yamada."

"And I regret the necessity of spoiling your hopes. It seems extremely ungrateful of me after such a fine meal and entertainment, for in truth I cannot remember better. Yet, unless matters have changed greatly since our last meeting, I must again refuse."

"Matters have indeed changed, if I might be so bold as to say," she replied. "Are not the obligations that formerly held you in the Emperor's city no longer at issue?"

She obviously knew I was without a patron at the moment, and this was about the politest way of saying so I could imagine. "How did you know that?"

"By asking," Lady Snow said, looking down with a demure expression. "Some men will tell a woman things they would not tell their own brothers. Forgive me, but you do know my interest in this matter."

I was less certain now of which matter we were actually discussing. "While it is true that my obligations have ceased for the moment, my concerns remain unchanged, both in your regard and to that of my former employer."

"You remain discreet about your former patron, and it does you credit. Still, there have been no new attacks for some time."

I should have been surprised Lady Snow knew so much. I was worried, certainly, but not surprised. I imagined there would be little Lady Snow could not uncover, had she a need or wish to do so, a fact which made my reluctance in the matter of my father and Fujiwara no Kiyoshi harder to justify; not impossible, perhaps not even difficult, but harder.

"I'm not convinced the attacks have ceased, and since I don't know their true nature, I can hardly call the matter settled. I do not believe the danger is past."

Lady Snow met my gaze then. "Lord Yamada, you must believe me when I tell you I would like nothing better than to have the matter of the attacks resolved. Taira no Kei . . . I knew her. She was a gentle girl and a cheerful spirit. Perhaps her *karma* was to blame, but I do not think she deserved such an ending."

Well, here was something I had not known before. "May I ask how you knew Kei?"

She shrugged. "An *asobi* is often near to the Court, if never a part of it, and there are many idle young men in Princess Ai's circle who sought my acquaintance. I met Kei-chan on one such occasion. She was kind to me, Lord Yamada. As with Kiyoshi, one learns to appreciate kindness since to some of us it is so rarely bestowed. That matter aside, for the moment you are without hindrance. I recognize this may change, but it is certainly true now, yes?"

"It is so," I said and waited.

She produced a scroll. "This may not be the definitive proof you require Lord Yamada, but I think you will find it interesting. I copied the original, even though I was not able to procure it."

I took the scroll, but I was not sanguine. A mere copy was unlikely to be substantive enough to satisfy me no matter what the original document purported to reveal, leaving aside the Minister of Justice or anyone empowered to act in this matter. At least, I was convinced of that until I read the scroll Lady Snow had given me:

All is prepared. Lord Yamada meets the Emishi prince at the Izawa barrier at noon on _____. I have my men ready. Be sure their king stands aside as promised. His son will not be harmed, but once the foolish prince plays his part, we will play ours.—Sentaro

The salutation of the letter was to Abe no Ginjo, the chief of the Abe clan. The clan which—for that past year—the governor of Mutsu Province had been charged to subdue without much success. Prince Kanemore could say a thing or two about the intensity of the fighting there. Granted, seventeen years ago that branch of the Abe had been simply a border clan, who were granted their lands solely for the purpose of containing the Emishi barbarians in their strongholds north of Izawa and Shiba, where Sakanouye Tamuramarou had first driven them two hundred years before. It was only recently that the Abe Clan had begun to ignore or circumvent the will of the Emperor. It was not in open rebellion yet, but I knew Kanemore and others fully expected the current hostilities to escalate.

Sentaro's close ties to the Abe of the time was questionable but not suspicious. If that had been all there was to the letter, I would have dismissed it out of hand.

Curious.

"Well?" Lady Snow asked.

"Where did you get this?"

"I can't tell you, precisely. Yet it clearly shows that Yamada no Seburo was the victim of a conspiracy."

I grunted. "One could as easily argue my father planned to form an alliance with this 'barbarian prince' mentioned in the letter, and that Lord Sentaro got wind of it and laid a trap for him with the aid of the provincial governor. That reading makes just as much sense as yours. Perhaps more."

To my surprise, she smiled. "I admit you are right in every point. So why are you troubled, Lord Yamada? Why do you hesitate? Shall I tell you? It's because there is something present in that letter that makes no sense to you."

She knew. Of course, she *would* know, if the entire letter was a fabrication. Common sense said as much. Yet, if so, it was a fabrication well-chosen to intrigue me, and I had to admit it had done so; I did not understand why anyone would go to so much trouble.

"Actually, there are two things. The first that does not make sense is the chief of the barbarians would co-operate to reveal a spy in his own enemies' camp."

"What is the second?"

"That my father was taken at Izawa barrier. I had thought he was taken at Chiba, since that is where he was executed."

"I do not know. I only know this letter is an exact copy of one Lord Sentaro wrote. I also know that, just before the incident, he wrote another letter. To your father."

That stopped me. I was in the Imperial University when my father had been executed, and in one of my father's infrequent letters a few weeks prior he had mentioned an important letter from Lord Sentaro, though not the contents. He seemed quite pleased about it, and hinted of good things to come—though I was strictly ordered not to mention it to anyone else, which I had not. I never knew the nature of Sentaro's letter, and had pretty much forgotten about it, until Lady Snow refreshed my memory. Yet this was something she could not possibly know, unless . . .

"Are you saying you've seen a copy of Sentaro's letter?"

"No. I have seen the actual letter. It was part of your father's effects that were seized during his arrest, and these items were kept together. The letter had been resealed so I could not read it. Yet perhaps, if you were with me, we might be bolder?"

"You're speaking of an archive. Any such would be here in the city."

She smiled again. "It may not surprise you to learn that Lord Sentaro kept documentation of his many activities. These are not part of the official record, and they most certainly are *not* in the city."

"How did you find this?"

"From the time I learned Kiyoshi had been murdered I knew who my enemy was, Lord Yamada. I've made it my mission to learn everything about him that could be learned by one such as myself."

That rang true enough, as did the existence of such an archive in the first place. Someone like Sentaro no doubt had many dealings he would want to reference at need but certainly not keep part of the official record. Yet this would be a personal archive, well hidden and secret for obvious reasons. I started to ask how Lady Snow had gained access, but realized she had already told me how, at least in broad strokes. The details didn't really matter.

I've made it my mission.

She looked at me, her face expressionless. "I cannot tell you where the archive is, Lord Yamada. Forgive me, but not unlike Lord Sentaro I, too, have secrets to keep and confidences to protect. However, if you are willing I can take you there."

"I will need some time to think about this."

She covered her smile with her fan. "Certainly no one can accuse you of rashness. Or is there another obligation?"

"I will be making a pilgrimage to Enryaku-ji in the next few days. Even if I were to agree, I cannot possibly accompany you anywhere until I return."

She bowed again. "Would this have anything to do with the delegation from Imperial Court?"

I frowned. "I should ask how you know about that."

"If you consider for a moment, I am sure an answer will present itself," she said. "Still, it is fortunate you have friends in such high circumstances, including one of the heirs to the Imperial Throne. That could prove useful to you in getting justice, once you have the proof you require."

" 'Heirs'? Takahito is crown prince. To whom are you referring?"

She looked puzzled. "Why, Prince Kanemore, of course. He is second in line for the succession. Forgive my impertinence, but your recent association with him is well known."

"Kanemore is not in line for the throne at all, except in the sense that every member of the extended Royal Family could be termed so. If anything, the gods forbid, happened to Prince Takahito, Norihira is next in line, and there are two other Fujiwara princes in the direct line after him."

She bowed low. "Perhaps I am mistaken," she said. "But I had heard His Majesty's intentions were otherwise."

"I am sure that you are," I said.

She bowed again. "Such lofty matters are outside my scope of concern, of course. It was foolish of me to mention what are surely no more than rumors."

"It's nothing. Please consider the matter closed."

I'd have liked to have done the same, but if this was an actual rumor it was one I had not heard. I wondered if Kanemore had. It was something we perhaps should discuss along the road to Enryaku-ji.

"You have not yet told me 'no,' Lord Yamada. May I take that as a sign of hope? Will you seriously consider my proposal?"

"I am considering it," I said. "But that is all I can promise at the present time."

She smiled a little wistfully then and didn't bother covering her mouth. "You must be weary of me, Lord Yamada. This silly woman with all these stories of things that happened long ago and should not matter to anyone now. Still, they do matter to me. I had hoped they would matter to you."

"Nothing can restore my family to what it was," I said again. I was beginning to feel the phrase had become some sort of mantra. "If your evidence was above refutation, I would still refuse to have any illusions in that regard. That is not to say I am uninterested in the idea of justice."

"Whereas justice is *all* that interests me, Lord Yamada. If the blame for this is laid at Lord Sentaro's feet as it should be, Kiyoshi will still be dead. The life I wanted, the life I could have had by his side is less than a dream now. Youth fades, and I cannot be an *asobi* for very much longer; my options will rapidly dwindle. At best I will become the wife of some fat merchant, else I must become a nun and beg my rice at the side of the road. But while I have the means and the strength, poor though either may be, I will continue to seek justice for Kiyoshi. It's foolish, perhaps, but there it is. Refuse me and I will continue."

"Why?"

"To answer that, I must ask you a question first: have you ever been in love, Lord Yamada?"

I answered even before I thought about it. "Yes," I said.

"Who was she, if I may be so impolite?"

"Her name does not matter. Suffice to say she was a woman of higher station than my own, and in most other regards my superior as well. Our lives took different paths."

"Did she love you?"

Such a simple question, the answer to which I expected would crush me like a worn-out cicada shell underfoot. "I thought so at the time. I will probably never know, yet I must face the possibility I was wrong."

"Forgive me, but can you not ask her? Surely she will accept a letter."

"She is deceased."

Lady Snow reached out and touched my hand. It was the first time I had felt the warmth of her, and it had been a much longer time since I felt the warmth of anyone.

"Then you know what it is like, to lose what you hoped to hold forever. Perhaps you can at least understand why I do what I do. We are not so very different, Lord Yamada."

"No."

There followed a silence. Not really awkward, nor one needing to be filled; rather, an expectant silence. A waiting silence.

I got to my feet. Lady Snow did not move. She merely looked up at me patiently as I said foolish and self-evident things. "It is very late, and I have a long way to go tomorrow. I have greatly enjoyed your company, but I must leave now."

She looked at the floor. "It's really not so wise to go out in the city at this hour. The demons would get you. I do not want that on my conscience."

"The demons and I are old friends, Lady Snow."

"Then show pity on me, for I would never forgive

myself should anything befall you before you reached your destination."

Of course this wasn't about demons or ghosts or anything else now stalking through or flitting about the streets of the city. I could be incredibly thick at times and the first to confess it, but even I understood Lady Snow's meaning.

I let out one long, slow breath even as I called myself the worst kind of fool. "I would not wish to cause you any distress."

My common sense told me this was simply another method of barter, offering what she had to give for something she wanted. It was this knowledge that almost allowed me to walk out the door, but in the end I chose to stay. I was not seduced, or beguiled . . . well, perhaps a little. Yet I knew I had a choice just as Lady Snow did, for I was not, like some, a man to use force to get what he wanted. We both chose that I stay. I could not see the good in it, and I was sure I would regret the night's lodging, but my choice did not alter.

"I must be away before dawn," I said.

"Of course. I will see to it," Lady Snow said, and she slowly got to her feet, not looking at me. I followed the elegant Lady Snow to her own chamber, wondering all the while if the face she kept turned from me showed pleasure or disappointment, something else, or anything at all; it was not the last time I wondered, through the dark of that night. All I could do was wonder since, as in so many things, I could never know for certain.

Lady Snow had one peculiarity, if one could call it that—she was very careful with her hair, meticulous to keep it out of her way or out of my hands. She was careful of nothing else, either of herself or of me, and for a while all my wondering ceased.

The false glow before dawn came all too early, but Lady Snow was as good as her word, and I was ready and waiting at the Demon Gate when Prince Kanemore's delegation arrived. It consisted of four *bushi* wearing Taira colors, and two nuns ably handling an oxcart where, I presumed, the offering to Enryaku-ji was stored.

"Walk with me, Lord Yamada."

"As His Highness wishes."

I bowed formally to Kanemore and fell into step beside him as we left the city on the road to the temple. The escort *bushi* were keeping a respectful distance, and I kept my voice soft.

"I left my sword behind as you requested, but you do realize I have a dagger up my sleeve?"

Kanemore grunted. "Certainly, but if you let anyone else see it, I'll chase you back to the city myself. Understood?"

"Completely."

"Besides," he said, "it's really not necessary. You will see."

I almost grinned. "I look forward to it."

Kanemore glanced at me. "Are you well?"

"I feel very well, and thank you for asking. Though I'm curious as to why you felt the need."

Kanemore frowned. "You just seem to be in a rather good humor, for you. No offense intended."

I almost smiled then, remembering the reason for that good humor. Then I remembered some of the matters that needed addressing on this trip and lost most of the good feeling in an instant. I just shrugged.

"No reason. It is a beautiful day, is it not?"

It was. The sky was clear blue with snow-white clouds, without even a hint of rain or darkness. Probably one of the few such days that remained before the haze and smoke of summer asserted itself around the city. I just hoped this haze would not be overly enhanced by the funeral fires of Mount Toribe. Yet the city and its ghosts had been quiet since the night the weaver's wife had been taken.

I did not want to ask the questions I needed to ask, but there would not likely be a better time.

"Prince Kanemore, I realize this is an unpleasant subject, but do you remember where my father was executed?"

He frowned. "Near the barrier at Chiba, I believe."

"Yet wasn't he taken at Izawa?"

"Please recall I wasn't actually present, but yes as I understand it he was. I believe there was another incursion near the barrier at Chiba that had to be dealt with before the formality . . . well, the sentencing of your unfortunate father."

So that part of the letter Lady Snow had shown me was accurate. So far everything that could be verified had been verified. Again, not proof, but there could not have been very many people who knew these details. That left the question I dreaded even more.

"Prince Kanemore, forgive me for asking, but what is your rank in the current order of succession?"

Prince Kanemore broke stride but quickly recovered. At that point I was fairly sure I already had my answer.

"May I ask what prompted this question?" Kanemore asked. He sounded unsteady.

"I have heard a rumor that you have been placed next in line after Takahito. Even before Prince Norihira."

"Palace gossip," he said, and I smiled. One of the things I most respected about Prince Kanemore was he was a very bad liar.

"It's true, isn't it?"

He looked unhappy but did not dissemble further. "Yes. Though how you found out is beyond me. Very few people are supposed to know this. Yourself, no offense intended, not included."

"Who did know?"

"Well . . . His Majesty, of course, since this was his idea. Chancellor Yorimichi and the former Minister of Justice."

"Lord Sentaro? Why was he told rather than the Minister of the Right? He outranks Lord Sentaro."

Kanemore looked grim. "It wasn't his rank that awarded Lord Sentaro that dubious honor. His Majesty wanted to make very sure Lord Sentaro knew, after that . . . business, of my late sister."

"In other words he wanted it clear that, if something 'unforseen' were to happen to Takahito, then Norihira would not ascend?"

"His Majesty was even more blunt: if Prince Takahito should be assassinated, then none of the Fujiwara heirs would ascend, including Norihira."

"What if Takahito, the gods forbid, should die of disease or something other than poison or obvious physical violence?"

"Then the throne goes to Norihira. And yes, as I'm sure you were about to point out, if I *wanted* the throne, the easiest way to take it would be to have my own nephew murdered. And since I do *not* want the throne, any failure to protect my nephew becomes a double blow, because of course I would be suspected. The irony of this situation has not escaped me."

I frowned. "You can be sure I will not speak of this and let any other such rumors lie where they fall. I do think the Emperor was wise to take this course, though I understand his decision has placed you in an uncomfortable position."

"To say the very least, Lord Yamada. It is only part of what I must endure to carry out my sister's wishes."

Neither of us said anything for a time. I did not know Kanemore's thoughts, but mine were racing off in a hundred directions at once. One thing and perhaps one thing only was clear enough—Lady Snow's information had been accurate about the order of succession. Incomplete, certainly, but accurate. Perhaps her information was accurate in other regards as well.

If I had correctly interpreted my father's hints and instructions, Lord Sentaro's letter and its contents were meant to be secret and had remained so for seventeen years. Whatever the nature of the letter might be, how could Lady Snow have even known of the letter's existence if she had not seen it as she claimed?

I still did not fully trust Lady Snow, and yet I realized I wanted to. As much as I had argued with her, and with Kenji and with myself, and for all that I knew was possible and not possible, I wanted what she told me to be the truth. I wanted there to be a possibility of proof, a chance to restore my family's honor; for my own sake and that of my foolish father.

Even for, perhaps one day, a household of my own?

It was not wrong to want those things, I knew. Just foolish. And very, very dangerous.

Our progress was slow, and Mount Hiei did not appear any closer by the time our group stopped for the midday meal. Lady Snow had thoughtfully prepared food for me and packed it in a black lacquer box, and I ate with Prince Kanemore.

I looked up once to find him regarding the box with some curiosity.

"That meal was prepared by a woman, and I do not think that woman was Mistress Tamahara."

"I never claimed to be a monk, Highness."

Kanemore grunted. "You never had to. Honestly, I've known monks who have lived less celibate lives. I confess I've been curious about that."

This was an area I definitely did *not* want Prince Kanemore to be curious about. As for the existence of Lady Snow, she might be just the distraction I needed, and yet I did not want to tell him about her. At least, not yet. Not until I knew more than I did at present.

"We all live as makes sense to us." It was a weak response, I knew, and invited a stronger one.

"I know you were in love with my sister, Lord Yamada. I'm not so thick as all that."

It appeared I wasn't to escape so easily. "I suppose my feelings were fairly obvious, which helped speed my hasty transition from minor Court official to nobleman's proxy. It was a foolish infatuation on my part, Prince Kanemore. Your sister did not share it."

Kanemore smiled a faint smile. "I think perhaps it fairer to say she did not share your priorities. Or mine, for that matter. Still, I'm glad you've found someone, even if only for the moment," Kanemore said. "Whatever her true feelings, I do not think Teiko would wish you to grieve your life away."

Perhaps Kanemore was right about that. Perhaps "grieving my life away" was exactly what I had been doing. If so, the process started long before Princess Teiko jumped off the mountain into Lake Biwa. I had no idea when or if that grieving would end except when I ended.

"I will try to keep that in mind."

"Good. Then we need not speak of it again."

I hoped we did not. Some demons were to be uncovered and destroyed. Other demons were best left to slumber undisturbed. I judged the matter of my relationship with Princess Teiko to be of the latter category.

We reached the rugged slopes of Mount Hiei by nightfall and took lodging in some of the temple buildings maintained for that purpose, near the base of the roadway. The nuns shared one small outbuilding, the Taira another, and Prince Kanemore and I a third.

The barrier to the temple was manned by the same warrior monks whose brothers now patrolled the streets of the city. There was quite a military disposition to the forces around the mountain and its temple complex; however, I knew this situation was not lost on Prince Kanemore and so did not bother to mention the obvious.

The next morning our little procession re-formed and made its way past the barrier, and up the narrow mountain road to the main temple complex. The way was steep but not overly difficult; it was pleasant to make our way up the mountain. In addition to the pines of winter, all trees were now showing green. While the morning sun was still gathering strength, the shade from the maples and pines kept the worst of the heat at bay. As we gained height, the number of maples shrank and the pines increased; the air was fragrant. If I didn't know what awaited us at Enryaku-ji I'd have considered this journey no more than a diverting excursion. But I did know, and I did not let down my guard for one moment.

As we came into full sight of the mountain temple, I began to fully appreciate the power and wealth of Enryaku-ji. It had been the first of the new temples founded at what was then called Heian-kyo that was allowed to create its own path to ordination, thus making a clean break from the power of the monks at the former capital of Nara. Now, generations later, the circle had completed itself. While most of the men trained at Enryaku-ji remained there, many also came to the city to work as officials in the Imperial administration, and the temple's power had been growing for some time now.

To call Enryaku-ji a temple was at once accurate and misleading. In fact, it was now the center of a large administrative complex with meditation gardens, audience and instruction halls, barracks, kitchens, forge, guest housing, and training grounds. It was almost a small state unto itself, with its own concerns, its own army, and its own ruler, Lord Sentaro, former Deputy Minister of the Right and Minister of Justice, now the monk called Master Dai-wu.

While the gate to the main approach now stood open, it could just as easily be closed and defended, and any force moving against it would have a rough task getting past the gate if those on the inside did not wish them to do so.

The monks of Enryaku-ji's private army were nowhere in evidence as we arrived. Several apprentice monks had been sent to see to our housing and to take possession of the silk; the actual formal presentation was set for the next morning in the main hall. We were fed a meatless meal as was the custom there and then left to our own devices for the remainder of the evening; or at least I so presumed.

I had some vague notions of wandering about the grounds but realized that, at least to all appearances, Enryaku-ji was not hiding anything. Both its power and presumed peace were in plain sight. I would not penetrate that particular mystery by wandering around and poking my nose into areas which, one assumed, did not concern me.

I had found a quiet spot in one of the meditation gardens when Prince Kanemore approached. I started to rise, but he merely squatted down next to me.

"I have yet to see a garden you could pass by," Kanemore said. "And this is a particularly fine one."

"I assume that's how you found me?"

"I had a good idea," Kanemore said cheerfully. "But in truth the groundskeeper told me the way you had gone. He seemed pleased that you appreciate his handiwork."

"It is a fine garden," I said. "Sometimes one can see the advantages of becoming a monk."

"You mean other than the chance of Enlightenment?"

"I'm not convinced such a thing is necessarily to be found at such a place as this."

Kanemore grunted. "There are monks who earnestly seek the Way, and there are monks who use the path as means to more prosaic ends. Sometimes it's hard for even the wise to tell the difference. I'm content with my path as it is. For now. Well then, it's getting late. Let's be off."

I blinked. "Off to where, Highness?"

"Oh, did I forget to tell you? We've been granted a private audience with Master Dai-wu."

"This is your doing, yes?"

He grunted. "I said you needed to know what I know, to see what I have seen," Kanemore said. "If you want to catch a deer, first you have to make sure that you're hunting on the right side of the mountain. This may prove important for both our sakes and for the future of Teiko's son. You need to see him."

"I agree, and while I have not yet changed my mind, I am perfectly willing to be convinced. Please lead on."

That was a lie of sorts. I was not "perfectly" willing, or willing at all. I rather expected I would have to be dragged bodily to any such extreme conclusions concerning Lord Sentaro's character and motives. But I did wish to see "Master Dai-wu" for myself, so at least I might at last understand what cloud of confusion had been spun around Prince Kanemore. It was only my knowledge of Kanemore, and my understanding of the depths of the loathing that Kanemore had for Lord Sentaro that allowed me to even ask the question. The best I could hope for was that I might find a way to turn Prince Kanemore from his error.

There are artists at the town of Otsu on the eastern road who sell small, humorous pictures to travelers and other pilgrims. Some showed ogres dressed as mendicant monks in the company of courtesans. Some showed ogres sitting in proper meditation, seeking Enlightenment. So far as I was concerned, any of those painted ogres had far more chance of reaching Enlightenment than Fujiwara no Sentaro had of abandoning either politics or ambition for the peace of Enryaku-ji, or for that matter anywhere or anything else. It was as if one expected a snake to forego slithering and walk upright; the concept was simply nonsense.

To break the Demon Gate, one must first open it.

I wondered at the origins of that saying, as the Demon Gate

had never been breached in a military sense but was a constant avenue for ghosts, demons, *tengu*, and worse. Still, I found myself thinking about the proverb as I followed Prince Kanemore through the inner compound gates and into a large meditation hall.

The hall was empty, save for Lord Sentaro kneeling at the foot of the dais, apparently waiting for us. His head was shaven now, and he wore the proper robes of a temple *hojo* with a string of large wooden prayer beads around his neck, but the face was the one I remembered. That is, until we got close enough to bow formally and kneel before him on the cushions provided. When I gazed into the man's face from a distance of no more than the height of a man, my first thought made me forget to breathe.

That is not Fujiwara no Sentaro.

Certainly, Master Dai-wu bore a remarkable similarity to the former Lord Sentaro. If I pictured the man now kneeling in front of me with hair and formal Court robes, he could certainly pass for Lord Sentaro by feature, but the resemblance was merely at the surface. No matter how my eyes reassured me that this man was, indeed, the former Minister of Justice and Deputy Minister of the Right, my mind refused to believe it. I looked into the kind, gentle eyes of Master Dai-wu of Enryaku-ji and I simply could not see Lord Fujiwara no Sentaro in there anywhere.

I finally took a slow breath. Fortunately, Prince Kanemore took care of the formal greetings; I merely had to bow slightly as Prince Kanemore introduced me. Of course, I needed no introduction to Lord Sentaro, but Master Dai-wu was another matter completely.

In my time I had known many men and women who were adept

at keeping their emotions under control and their faces blank. Others were masters at writing lies upon that blank paper for all to see and believe. I had been fooled before, but never twice by the same person and always because, for whatever reason, I had let my guard down. Yet as guarded and watchful as I was now, I was seldom fooled, because the one thing no one can do face to face is hide their eyes, for the truth is always there if you know how to look. Perhaps intent is hard to see; subtle, but it is always present. I looked into the eyes of the man I had known for years as Fujiwara no Sentaro, and I could find no trace of him. None. The man looking at me now, calling himself Master Dai-wu, *hojo* of Enryaku Temple, had eyes as open and guileless as those of a child. I did see a shadow there, something I could not quite identify, but its nature was not clear, and the hint of whatever it might be did nothing to change my initial impressions. Despite my great respect for Prince Kanemore, my presumption all along was that he had simply been fooled.

If that was the case, then I had just been fooled, too.

Dai-wu was speaking again. I forced myself to listen.

"On behalf of Enryaku-ji, I accept the Emperor's gracious gift. I, too, have a gift for His Majesty. May I entrust this to your protection?"

Prince Kanemore bowed low. "As Your Immanence wishes. Are there any special preparations that must be made?"

Master Dai-wu smiled. "Nothing so delicate as that, Highness. My humble gift is merely a fine new copy of the Lotus Sutra that His Majesty requested for his study and benefit. The two nuns who accompanied you here will see to its conveyance. All you need do is give them safe escort on your return to the Imperial Court."

It was a perfectly reasonable request. While the roads were relatively safe on this side of the capital, there was always the chance of misadventure for women traveling alone, nuns or otherwise.

"It will be done," Prince Kanemore said, bowing again.

The master of Senryaku Temple now turned to me, though he still spoke to Kanemore. "Highness, I think your companion and I have something we need to discuss in private. Would you please indulge me for a few moments?"

Prince Kanemore frowned and glanced at me, but of course I had no basis to object. As Kanemore withdrew I waited and wondered what I would hear from the man I had once known as Lord Sentaro, and now did not think I knew at all. One thing I did know, as now Master Dai-wu and I kneeled facing each other, was the man opposite me now was afraid. Very afraid.

Of me?

No. The fear was there plain to see as Master Dai-wu, so far as all my senses and skills told me, concealed nothing. But I did not think I had triggered it. Now I recognized his fear for what it was, I think it had been there all along; it was a shadow on the man's face I had seen but did not understand.

When Master Dai-wu spoke, it was very carefully and softly, as if he were afraid we would be overheard. I did not see how this could be so since we were the only two people present, and if some other presence should appear, such as a ghost or demon, I was certain that I would know it. At the moment there was nothing.

"Lord Yamada, you were educated at the Imperial University, were you not? I mean, yes, I understand I should know this, but is it so?"

"It is," I said, wondering why it mattered. Most men of noble blood were sent to University at some point, even one as lowly as myself. Since there weren't enough Fujiwara to fill each and every niche in the Imperial administration, such training was considered necessary for the upper classes, though some did manage to avoid it.

"Then I trust you know what the term *inazuma* means, in a poetical context?"

"The flash of lightning, separate from the lightning itself. Since the kanji for the name can also symbolize rice, it's often used as a poetic allusion for harvest time." I was a little satisfied that I still remembered, after so long. I was more puzzled, however, as to why he was asking the question in the first place. Apparently my puzzlement was as obvious as Master Dai-wu's fear.

"Please bear with me, Lord Yamada. I would say it plainly, but then it could not be said."

I frowned. "What could not be said?"

"And there's the problem. I will do my best. It's not my doing. None of it."

"I don't understand."

He sighed. "No. Neither did I for a long time. I think I do now. *Inazuma*. Sometimes people say it means lightning, but you know better. It is the flash, the illumination, not the thing itself. One does not fear the flash. One fears the lightning. Rightly so. Remember that."

I wasn't sure what I was supposed to remember. I was slowly coming to the conclusion that the man was stark raving mad. Then, when I had stopped looking for it, clarity came. Master Dai-wu looked at me.

"What is faster than lightning? The flash of light that precedes it. What the lightning would destroy, it first illuminates, that is its nature. There is almost no time between one and the other, but there is some time. Very little. Yet the wise man, the prepared man, may have time to act."

He was gone. Almost between one breath and the next, Master Dai-wu was gone. In his place sat a man who looked like Master Dai-wu and was dressed as Dai-wu, but no one, and especially not me, would ever confuse the two.

I was now looking into the hatefully familiar face of Lord Fujiwara no Sentaro.

"Lord Yamada," he said, in a voice of pure poison, "We meet again."

PART FIVE

In prayer, you clap
to get the god's attention.
Gods are too flighty.
As is my heart's true desire.
How shall I gain your notice?

The effect was instantaneous; I sensed no transition. If the room seemed a little colder, it was only because of the man before me now. Lord Sentaro, no question, no doubt. The tonsure and the robes meant absolutely nothing.

"I've been expecting you for some time," he said. "Frankly I'm disappointed it took you so long to seek me out."

"It is you now, isn't it? How are you doing that?" I asked.

He smiled. "Do? My dear Lord Yamada, I have done nothing. Yet. Wheels are turning, just like the Wheel of Life and Death and Rebirth that I must harp about when I am Master Dai-wu. But action? That is to come. Yet I am pleased you remember me. The one whose noble purposes you previously thwarted? Yes, I think you should remember."

"Noble?"

He sighed. "One such as yourself would never understand what planning and preparation is required, the time spent nurturing one's vision so that matters will turn out as they should. I cheerfully concede that Princess Teiko bested me once, but she is no longer a consideration. And, while I also concede that I underestimated you once, it is a mistake I will not be repeating. If you believe nothing else I tell you now, please believe that."

I felt the presence of the dagger in my sleeve, hard and reassuring. "What are you going to tell me?"

"Why, I am going to tell you what I am going to do, Lord Yamada. That's what you want to know, is it not? You see, I had some time to think about this while I was at Suma. I have given the matter very careful consideration indeed."

"So this really was about avoiding your banishment, and revenge on me. Nothing more."

Lord Sentaro made a face. "Lord Yamada, this may be a shock to you, but neither my world nor anyone else's is centered on such a wretched creature as you. Oh, I'm going to have my revenge, make no mistake. It's a pettiness on my part, certainly, yet that revenge is merely repayment for what I suffered and a side matter at best. My true purpose has not wavered. Shall I tell you what that is?"

"No need. You want to see Prince Norihira on the throne."

"Want? No, Lord Yamada. I *will* see Prince Norihira on the throne. How? I should think that is obvious: I'm going to kill Prince Takahito."

I almost forgot to breathe again. "You won't."

He smiled then, a smile that was a horrible parody of the serene, benevolent smile of Master Dai-wu. "I will. And there is nothing, I repeat, *nothing* you can do to stop me."

"Prince Kanemore will stop you. *I* will stop you."

He laughed at me, then sighed. "Fools. Kanemore only sees Master Dai-wu, and that is the way I want it. But you are fortunate, Lord Yamada. You have seen the truth. Shall I tell you why? Have you guessed? No? Then I will tell you. See, I seriously considered killing you. That would bring me a moment or two of satisfaction, I admit, but deep down in that pit you call a soul I think you really want to die, and should I serve you as you wish? No. So then I thought of a much better idea."

While I had little doubt he was going to tell me whether I wished to hear it or not, I had to ask the question. "And what is that?"

His expression was pure mad joy. "Princess Teiko's bastard son will never sit on the throne, but to that I add this: you're going to know that Prince Kanemore has failed her, that *you* have failed her. That Princess Teiko's death, which I concede was very well-played, was ultimately for nothing. You are going to live, Lord Yamada, knowing that Teiko has lost and I have won. Bear this knowledge for just as long as you wish. That is my gift to you."

I thought of the dagger in my sleeve. What would follow would only be the work of a moment. I thought.

"Please leave your silly knife where it is, Lord Yamada. I am not unprotected, even like this. Do not make me prove it to you."

I believed him, and tempting as his throat was, I could not take the risk. "I had not thought even you were so great at deception, Lord Sentaro. Your 'Master Dai-wu' guise had me fooled."

"As usual, you think you understand," Lord Sentaro said, "but of course you do not. Good. You do not disappoint me. You may withdraw now. Prince Kanemore is waiting. He will not, of course, believe you."

I did not bow. It was all I could do to rise and walk toward the entrance without staggering or being sick. When I glanced back, I saw nothing but Master Dai-wu, serene before the buddhas on the dais, with eyes concealing nothing, expression kind and gentle. I knew that if I had not seen what I had just seen and heard what I had just heard, I would have left the temple compound of Enryaku-ji as completely fooled as Prince Kanemore still clearly was. I wasn't sure what I could do about that, but at least there was no longer any doubt about Lord Sentaro's intentions. I found myself feeling grateful for that bit of clarity.

An area where some clarity would have been greatly appreciated was the matter of how Lord Sentaro's deception had been accomplished. The transformation was so complete and sudden, it was if Master Dai-wu had been possessed.

Possessed by what? Himself?

Lord Sentaro was wrong about one thing, at least—I did not think I understood, at all. I was no closer to an answer but much closer, I knew, to the point where the answer would no longer matter.

Once out of the immediate presence of Lord Sentaro, the air and my head both began to feel clearer. Prince Kanemore was waiting for me at the door.

"Well?" he asked.

"I have seen what you have seen, in Master Dai-wu," I said carefully. "But you have not seen everything."

Prince Kanemore let out a gusty sigh. "Are you going to start this argument again?"

I wanted to, but I knew a losing battle when I saw one. "No. I know why you feel the way you do. I cannot blame you. I must think about this matter some more, for I am very puzzled. Will you settle for this?"

"I had hoped the matter of Lord Sentaro was at least one concern we could put behind us." Prince Kanemore did look a little disappointed, but he finally spread his hands. "So be it. You are a stubborn man, Lord Yamada."

"True, and this is not always a bad thing. So, how long are we to remain at Enryaku-ji?"

"We'll leave tomorrow morning, assuming Master Dai-wu's gift is ready by then. You may be able to indulge yourself in the fine gardens here for a little longer."

"For that alone it was worth the trip. Thank you, Highness."

Prince Kanemore left me then and I, for want of a better plan, went to the main garden to find a place to think. There were three nuns in meditation by a small bridge crossing a stream, two of whom I recognized as being in our party on the trip out. I withdrew to the relative solitude of a small grove bordering the garden proper and found a tree to lean against; just in time, for suddenly my legs didn't seem to want to support me any longer. Again, and for several moments, I thought I was going to be sick. I knew the signs. This wasn't some passing disease demon; I felt as if I had been exposed to something of extreme power and malevolence, and even with the clear air outside the hall it took a little while for the effect to pass. It didn't take much thought to know what and who had caused it.

Lord Sentaro.

He was something else that did not make sense. Before I met Master Dai-wu, I had never believed that Lord Sentaro was anything other than what he had always been—an agent and vessel of Fujiwara ambition. Then in a moment I had been snatched from believing Lord Sentaro had changed for the better to understanding that, perhaps, he had changed for the far worse.

Fujiwara no Sentaro was callous, ruthless, and ambitious, and I had hated the man almost from the day we met, but even I had never thought of him as evil. Yet Lord Sentaro at his worst was not a match for what I had felt in the temple.

Is it . . . a transformation?

The lore of ghosts and demons was full of such accounts, and while I made no claim to know all the instances—despite my time at University, I was no scholar—I had seen one or two such things myself.

The priests taught that this physical body was not our true nature, and in this regard at least I knew they were right. Sometimes what people felt, or believed, or desired as human beings became too great or too vile for a mere human body to contain. So a woman who had lost her children might transform into an ogress that ate *only* children, trying in the only way she could to regain what she had lost. Alternatively, a priest overcome with lust might transform literally into a cunning rat, or a woman into a devouring snake, to better pursue the objects of their lust.

Yet what had Lord Sentaro become? A monk? Hardly. He looked like Lord Sentaro playing the part of a monk, and that was all. He had not transformed even in that small degree. More, he was no ogre or demon. What I felt made no sense, and while I trusted what I felt far more than what I had seen—and I had seen and heard more than enough as it was—I still had nothing that would convince Prince Kanemore or anyone else of "Master Daiwu's" plainly spoken intention. Teiko's son was in great danger, and I did not know how to protect him.

I will not fail you, princess.

Empty words, empty thoughts. I needed action, a plan, and I had neither. Lord Sentaro was right, unfortunately. I did not know when or how he planned to strike, only that the strike was indeed coming. The nature of the attack had to show some delicacy, but I had no doubt Lord Sentaro would indeed stoop to simple assassination. While it was true that Kanemore was in line for the throne in such a case, there was nothing to say that a dagger used on one could not be used on another. Perhaps Lord Sentaro planned to kill both; direct, uncomplicated, and had the added virtue of completely clearing a path to the throne for Prince Norihira. And, while I would not wish to be the assassin set against Prince Kanemore, at least in theory the plan was simply a problem of execution. Despite what Lord Sentaro had said, there was no need to look for anything more subtle.

Except that I knew there was need to look for something more subtle, because the small voice in my brain that never hesitated to call me an ass when I was being stupid was doing so now, and very loudly.

Would it be too much to ask, Little Man, that you once explain yourself before I have to sort it out for myself?

I wished then Teiko was still alive, and it was not the first time I had done so; mostly for my own selfish reasons, true, but also because she was, no argument, far more perceptive than I would ever be. She would know what to do to protect her son. Yet she was not here with me and never would be again. She had done what she felt she needed to do and left Prince Kanemore and me behind, trusting us to deal with whatever happened next. If Takahito was to live long enough to inherit the throne, it was now up to us. Just then I felt the matter was disproportionately up to me.

嘉

When we returned to the capital the following day, I parted company with Prince Kanemore and the procession at the Demon Gate. I returned to my rooms at the Widow Tamahara's establishment to find a poem from Lady Snow:

> *The cranes fly away,*
> *Writing songs on the cold wind.*
> *In winter they leave,*
> *In spring return. Which season*
> *brings back the sound of your wings?*

I smiled. It was almost . . . sweet. It had been a long time since anyone had bothered to take notice of where I was, even if I knew her reasons were not as I might wish. Still, the poem made me feel even more the bastard for what I was about to do. While, perhaps, it would serve both our interests, I couldn't escape the feeling that my next course of action would require me to deceive Lady Snow. I'd do that and worse besides if it would help save Teiko's son. That did not mean I had to enjoy what I was about to do.

According to Tamahara-san, Nidai had brought the message and promised to return each and every evening to await a reply. When evening came, I was waiting.

"You may tell your mistress that, if it is convenient, I will call upon her tomorrow evening." Nidai hesitated. I raised an eyebrow. "Was there something else?"

"You should write her a poem, too," he said, then added, "She deserves a poem." Nidai looked at me then, fearful but defiant.

I sighed. "Master Nidai, I consider myself properly chastened. If you will wait a bit yet, I shall see what I can do."

I considered the matter for a bit as I made fresh ink, and despite my own fearfulness at attempting the gentlemanly art, I then wrote:

> *Cranes may soar on wings,*
> *but donkeys must plod the earth.*
> *And yet a road brings*
> *both to their destination,*
> *though they must soon start anew.*

I handed the paper to Nidai without bothering to seal it. "Can you read?"

"A little. Lady Snow has been teaching me," he said proudly. He studied the paper for a while and then looked up at me. "I'm not sure I understood it all. Does this mean you've agreed to help my mistress?"

"Yes, Nidai-kun," I said. "That is what it means. I think you and Lady Snow must prepare for a journey."

The following evening I called on Lady Snow as agreed. This time we both sat down for a meal and Nidai served. He was so serious and determined to bring each course in the proper order with no spilling, that I inwardly cheered when he managed two delicate bowls of *miso* soup without spilling a drop.

"I must say you have trained that little monkey very well."

She turned the compliment aside. "I have done little. He is a quick student."

We talked about very little for a while. Then Nidai served a pot of green tea to close the meal, and Lady Snow and I both sat in complete silence for a time, broken only by faint sips as I attempted to match Lady Snow's delicacy of manners. The attempt was not a complete success, though I felt it necessary to try.

"I suppose," she said at last, "that I should not ask you why you changed your mind."

I shrugged. "I have not changed my mind. How could I, since my mind was not resolved one way or another before now?"

She was having none of it. "You were clearly leaning away from me, just as now we seem to be leaning together. While that should be enough, I still find myself wondering how the wind has changed."

I thought I understood Lady Snow's motivations enough to trust her up to a point, but I also did not think now was the time to get careless. "There is no obligation holding me here, as you yourself pointed out at our last meeting. While I tell you bluntly that I do not expect to find what you hope to find at Nara, I'm no longer certain enough of that to take the chance. So to satisfy myself in this matter I will go with you to Nara, and we shall see what we find there."

It wasn't exactly a lie, but it wasn't the entire truth either. Lady Snow's goals and mine were not the same. While I was not averse to avenging my father if possible, my primary concern was Takahito's safety.

If Lady Snow was correct that my father was betrayed and falsely accused by Lord Sentaro, then Lord Sentaro's execution of my father was not an execution—it was murder. If such charges could be substantiated, even to the degree required to launch an inquiry by the Ministry, then Lord Sentaro could be removed as *hojo* of Enryaku-ji at least temporarily, perhaps long enough to interrupt and possibly discover and thwart his plans for Takahito. It was a gamble born of desperation and I did not pretend otherwise. Yet I was a drowning man with no other straws in sight.

"What man would not enjoy placing himself in your company?" I said.

She smiled demurely. "As lies go, that one was gallant enough. No matter. You may keep your reasons to yourself; it is enough for me you have agreed. When can we leave for Nara? Dare I hope for tomorrow?"

"I see no obstacle to that."

She bowed. "I will inform Nidai we will be retiring for the evening."

I hesitated. "As much as that prospect delights me, I must return to my own rooms for now, Lady Snow. Shall we meet tomorrow morning at the Rasha Gate? Since our road lies to the southeast, that seems the most reasonable departure point."

Her expression was as unreadable as a stone's. "If that is your wish."

I was not always the quickest to understand anything, but it occurred to me that Lady Snow might feel insulted. I didn't have any answer to that except the absolute truth.

"It is not my wish, though I do think it is the wisest course."

"If you are worried about my patron, I assure you he is not in the city at present."

It was all I could do to keep from smiling. "Your patron does not concern me now, Lady Snow. You do."

She frowned. "Me? I am harmless."

"No," I said, "you are not harmless, any more than I am."

She smiled a rueful smile. "The passing of an evening in the company of a man is no more than I am accustomed to."

"And as an *asobi* you well know that to many men such opportunities are no more than sport, or the chance at a good meal, quickly enjoyed and quickly forgotten. I have never been able to master that philosophy, Lady Snow, which is perhaps one reason why I spend most of my nights alone. I did not pass that night with you with no thought of the morning, nor will I forget. If you did and will, then you will not mind that I do not remain here tonight. If you did not . . . well, you may at least understand my caution."

There was a tear in the corner of her eye. "Until tomorrow, then, Lord Yamada," was all she said.

Outside all was quiet except for a faint breeze. There was a chill on the wind, despite the season. I looked carefully, but there was no sign of the Dark Cloud or even so much as a moth-demon about, for all I could tell. I almost hoped for a spiritual or physical attack to materialize, to give me something to distract me from my own dark mood, but of course there was nothing. Thanks to the monks of Enryaku-ji, the streets of the city were as serene as a temple hall; even the ghosts were keeping themselves more inconspicuous than usual. At most I saw one or two *onibi* down the alleys off Shijo-dori before reaching the Widow Tamahara's establishment. There was the sound of laughter from the large front room that served as the wine shop as I started to pass through the gate.

I recognized that laughter. It was Kenji.

I stepped away from the gate and hurried past the curtains,

the only barrier to the night air now that the large main door was open. I stepped inside just in time to see Kenji, quite obviously drunk, raise a cup of saké in salute to the Widow Tamahara, who was staring at the monk in open consternation. She saw me enter and hurried up.

"Lord Yamada, thank the gods . . . will you please remove this crazy *baka* before he brings those monks down on my head?"

"This '*baka*' isn't through drinking, *Tamahara-sama*," Kenji said in a voice loud enough to wake a dead ogre. "I am celebrating!"

The other patrons, a few *bushi* in visitation with some lord or other, were openly scowling, and I thought that in a few minutes the monks of Enryaku-ji might be the least of Kenji's problems; and by association, my own. I took the saké jar from the Widow Tamahara.

"Then we shall share a drink in my rooms and you can tell me all about why you are celebrating," I said.

Kenji stared up at me blearily. "Yamada-san! Took you long enough to get here, you ingrate. Or perhaps I should have gone looking at another lady's home, yes?"

I hauled Kenji to his feet. He protested loudly but was too drunk to do much about it.

"Friends share good news. Let's leave these good people in peace and go do so."

The Widow Tamahara slipped up to the side of me, opposite Kenji and whispered, "Must you take the jar, too?"

"If I don't, I won't be taking Kenji anywhere. Consider it the price of getting rid of him."

"Cheap at that," the old woman muttered. "Just hurry."

"I heard that," Kenji said. "I'm drunk, not deaf."

"We'll use the saké to soften the insult," I said. "You'll feel better. Or you won't feel anything."

He laughed then but let me lead him through the curtains, out into the street, then back through the gate to the Widow Tamahara's courtyard.

"You were joking about the saké, weren't you?"

I smiled. "You mean about sharing it? Certainly. It's all yours."

Kenji, appeased, grunted assent and let me half-lead, half-carry him up onto the veranda then into my rooms, where he more fell than sat down. He tried to kneel properly but couldn't quite get his legs to cooperate. He finally gave up and lay on his side with his head propped up none too steadily on one elbow. From there he was able to handle the jar of rice wine well enough to keep drinking. I wasn't as tempted to join him as I thought I might be. I paused to light a lantern.

"Are you *trying* to get your scrawny self hauled off to Enryaku-ji?" I asked.

"I am *trying*," he said, "to drink enough to forget what a sorry state this city has come to. So far I have failed miserably."

"So you weren't actually looking for me."

"No," he said. "With all due respect. I was lying about the celebration, too. There's nothing to celebrate. Not even this saké. It's foul stuff, even by the esteemed hostess's low standards."

" 'Appropriate to the customer' is, I believe, the term she would use. So why are you here?"

"The truth? I got tired of hiding. It gets tiresome very quickly, Yamada-san. Especially when one has done nothing wrong."

I raised an eyebrow. "The day you do nothing wrong is the

day the Sun Goddess dances naked on a table at the Widow Tamahara's, but let that be. You'll stay here tonight."

"I think I would have to be carried anywhere else," Kenji said ruefully. "You're a good friend. I will try not to soil your floor."

"Just do your best. Honestly . . . is this what I look like when I'm drinking?"

Kenji grinned. "Worse. There's a sort of single-mindedness that comes on you. I've seen it in your daily pursuits and . . . " he paused to yawn hugely, "in your drinking. Makes me look like a dabbler by comparison."

I grunted. "I'll have to keep that in mind. Now, as long as you *are* drinking, please drink quietly. I have work to do."

"As my lord commands."

I ignored that and proceeded to do something, which in hindsight I realized I should have done weeks ago. I moved a pile of old clothes and junk covering a small black lacquered box, one of the few personal items I had kept when I'd left Kyoto intending to follow Princess Teiko into exile. There wasn't so very much to look through: a comb and mirror that had belonged to my mother, a set of prayer beads I never used and don't know why I kept, Princess Teiko's last letter, a few more odds and ends. With such a small haystack it did not take long to locate the needle I was looking for: a small bundle of letters from my disgraced father. As with the prayer beads, I wasn't sure why I had kept them, save that when one has lost almost everything one tends to cling tighter to whatever odd and useless bits remain.

My father had traveled a great deal in my early years, usually on minor assignments or postings that greater and better-placed men would shun. Whatever his failures, I could never fault his diligence, even if that meant I seldom saw him. The assignment to Mutsu during that earlier barbarian uprising was of somewhat greater importance than he had been used to; his pride rather came through in the letters he sent, and he wasn't afraid to name places and people. Even so, most of the letters were little more than lectures: that I prepare for the burdens that would one day be mine, that I be diligent in my studies, that I avoid wild company and do nothing to bring dishonor to the family. The irony of that last one almost made me smile.

It was my father's final letter I sought, and after a brief perusal of most other letters in the bundle, I found it. There were no lectures in this one and very little real information. I wasn't expecting any such; I simply wanted to check my memory of my father's letter against the copy of the document that Lady Snow had last produced, purportedly from Lord Sentaro. When I read my father's letter, I found the thing that had been nagging me was not any contradiction between my father's letter and Lady Snow's document, but rather something she had said about Lord Sentaro writing a letter to my father just before the . . . incident.

My father's letter did not say much at all: a report on a triumphal skirmish, the odd-looking swords and hairy appearance of the barbarians. And one last little snippet I had completely forgotten: " . . . Lord Sentaro has changed the time and place of my assigned meeting, so I will not be leaving for the capital tomorrow as planned."

Now I remembered. The reason for the delay or the nature of my father's business in the north had been of less than no concern to me at the time. All I could recall feeling was relief—now I had a little more leeway to repair both my studies and my relations with some of the teachers there at the University, before it would be necessary to report my lack of progress to my father.

Lord Sentaro changed the meeting.

So Lord Sentaro had known about and had been involved in the meeting from the start, assuming this was the same one at which my father had been seized. I could not know for certain, but rather suspected as much since my father had not exactly been discreet about his assignments, his pride perhaps having overruled his sense. Or he merely was lacking in guile, among other faults. Either way, while my father's letter was not proof of anything, it did not contradict the one apparently from Lord Sentaro himself, which Lady Snow had produced in copy, and together their implication was very interesting.

"Kenji-san, exactly how drunk are you?"

"Not as drunk as I might wish, Lord Yamada. I can still see you."

I was a little surprised to be answered immediately; by that point I had honestly expected nothing but a snore. I told Kenji about my audience with "Master Dai-wu" first and the great change that came over the man, and he frowned but confessed himself as baffled as I was.

"You know Lord Sentaro better than I, but I never believed his conversion was anything more than a way out of making salt on a northern seacoast for the rest of his life," Kenji said. "Yet I have no idea exactly what you saw in him that day. Perhaps he is a better dissembler than even you believed."

"Possible, but there's more."

I told Kenji about the three letters, the one from my father in my own hands, the one I had seen in copy, and the private letter from Lord Sentaro to my father, both of the latter which might not even exist.

"Hmmm," was all Kenji said at first.

"There's an obvious conclusion. Will you draw it or shall I?"

Kenji yawned. "Your father was not a traitor. Lord Sentaro himself set up the meeting with the renegade barbarian prince on one pretext or another, and ordered your father to undertake the negotiation. He then seized and executed your father when he did exactly as commanded. It would have been simple enough to confiscate any incriminating documents seized in the name of 'investigating' and remove them as necessary. It would not have been either just or fair, but Lord Sentaro has no reputation for either virtue."

For all I knew, events unfolded exactly as Kenji described. His summary fit the facts as known. Of course, so did the possibility that my father actually was a traitor. Of the two explanations, the latter was simplest; that didn't necessarily mean it was correct.

"I have considered this possibility since my first meeting with Lady Snow, but still it makes no sense to me. Why? What purpose did betraying my father serve? He was no threat."

Kenji shrugged and scratched a delicate area. "Why would it be necessary that he should have been so? If you assume Lady Snow's information is correct, then clearly the betrayal of your father must have served Lord Sentaro's purpose. What purpose? One would need access to the deepest reaches of Lord Sentaro's twisted mind for the answer to that. I'd rather not explore that particular bog."

"Nor does it matter at the present moment. What matters is that Lady Snow's document is not in Lord Sentaro's hand, nor under his seal. Now, if I had both Lady Snow's letter and the alleged 'missing' letter in the original . . . "

Kenji grunted. "Rubbish. Assuming there was such a letter bearing his personal seal, Lord Sentaro would have been a fool not to destroy it once it was back in his hands," Kenji interrupted himself with another yawn, "and a bigger fool if he had trusted your father to do so, as the letter doubtless requested. If I were you, I would not trust in letters. They seldom are about what they seem to be. You should not need me to point out these things."

It wasn't the first time he'd hinted that he knew more of the affair of Princess Teiko's stolen letter than I'd ever told him. How much? I did not care so long as he kept the matter to himself. I smiled.

"Agreed. What I need you for is to accompany myself and Lady Snow to Nara."

Kenji frowned. "Nara? Whatever for?"

"You can read. Three pairs of eyes are better than two, and we will almost certainly be in a hurry. Or would you rather remain here in the capital and wait for the monks to drag you off to Enryaku-ji? There's no wine there, my friend. After my meeting with Master Dai-wu, I looked."

"Well, that being the case . . . "

"We leave at dawn tomorrow," I said.

"Hmmm."

"Do you need anything?"

Apparently not, since this time the only answer was indeed a gentle snore; the priest was fast asleep. I put my father's letters back in the chest and carefully removed the saké jar from Kenji's slack fingers.

I wanted to follow Kenji's example and get some rest, but

the puzzle of it all would not let my thoughts be quiet. While I had no doubt that Lord Sentaro was capable of doing all Lady Snow had said and more, I kept stumbling over the reason. I had known people of the sort who would crush a life for the sheer pleasure of it, but even I had never counted Lord Sentaro among that number. No, he would kill, but only for a purpose; and there simply did not appear to be one.

One would need access to the deepest reaches of Lord Sentaro's twisted mind . . .

Or perhaps not. Maybe one should consider the results and work backward. Yet what had been the result of Kiyoshi's death and my father's disgrace and execution? So far as I could see, it was only that the northern provinces remained in a state of unrest, drawing the resources and the attention of the military families away from the capital. Who did that benefit? Certainly not the Minamoto and Taira, nor even the Emperor, whose own purse was strained and whose attention was thus preoccupied. The answer, when it finally came to me, was both simple and diabolical.

The Fujiwara.

As before, I still had no proof. But now, at least, I did have a reason. After a little while I blew out the lantern and followed Kenji's example.

⛩

The next morning Kenji's condition was no more or less than what one would expect after such a binge. He did manage to crawl out into the courtyard before becoming spectacularly ill. Yet, once that bit of drama was over, he was relatively mobile and alert. I concluded, and not for the first time, that Kenji had the constitution of a much younger man. He was indeed fortunate, else he would have been dead long before now. He even managed to eat a little of the breakfast the Widow Tamahara provided while I finished preparing my travel bundle. After he was finished I tossed two bundles of brown cloth at his feet.

"What's this?"

"A *hakama* and over jacket. Put those on over your robes and keep your hat on otherwise. Once we're out of the city, you can revert to your normal threadbare robes."

"If you think it wise, but I shall feel naked."

Kenji carefully removed the brass cap of jingling rings that marked his priestly staff and converted it into a plain traveler's staff. While no one would mistake him for a prince or even a nobleman in my old clothes, with his priest's robes covered and a straw *boshi* shielding his shaved head, Kenji would pass for a normal traveler easily enough to let us slip past any monks we met before joining Lady Snow at Rashamon, which was all that concerned me on that part of the journey. There would be plenty of other things to be concerned about later.

The disguise turned out to be a very good idea, as we passed several of the monks on Sanjo-dori before we could turn south to the areas of the city where they patrolled less frequently.

"You'll note they do not stray too far from the Demon Gate," I said.

Kenji grunted. "You mean they don't stray too far from the Imperial Compound. Frankly, I trust the Tendai sect as far as I can toss a horse."

I vaguely knew that Enryaku-ji was a different Buddhist

discipline than the one Kenji was trained by, though all such fine distinctions were lost on me.

"If one wanted to improve the condition of the city, surely one would start with the area nearest the Palace and work one's way down."

"So why haven't they? I was at the Rasha Gate for the better part of a month without seeing one of the city's 'protectors.' Frankly the entirety of the itinerant brotherhood could have hidden with me in plain sight."

Kenji was right of course, but I didn't know the answer to that any more than Kenji did. There were several possibilities and all, to my way of thinking, very alarming. I tried to stop thinking about it as we approached the Rasha Gate. Lady Snow and Nidai were there, waiting patiently. Nidai was coping manfully with a large travel bundle and Lady Snow carried a smaller one. She wore simple and practical traveling clothes of dark blue with a hat and veil; there was no hint of the *asobi*'s normal garb, meant to attract attention rather than, as now, avoid it. No one was there to challenge us as we passed through Rashamon and set out on the southeastern road.

"I was beginning to think you had changed your mind," she said. "I am grateful you have not."

"My associate needed some time to, shall we say, compose himself. Lady Snow, this is Adachi no Kenji."

Lady Snow bowed and Kenji managed to return the courtesy with something at least approaching the correct decorum. "My friend is too kind. I was fighting off the effects of saké."

Lady Snow covered her smile with a fan. "I have seen the condition before, Lord Kenji."

"Just 'Kenji,' " the disguised priest said. " 'Lord' belongs to

Yamada-san here. Considering the luck he's had with the title, he's welcome to it."

I didn't know whether to laugh or hit him, but there didn't seem much advantage in either. I just walked in silence, as did everyone else until the city was well out of sight. Then we all, I think, breathed a little easier.

"I think you can remove those clothes now," Lady Snow said when the crest of a small hill finally shielded us from sight of the city gate. She was speaking to Kenji.

Kenji and I both just frowned for a moment, and Lady Snow blushed. "I meant Kenji-san's disguise, of course. I assume he does not mean to travel all the way to Nara like that."

Kenji and I glanced at each other, then I simply shrugged. It was the Enryaku-ji monks we meant to deceive, though obviously Lady Snow was more observant. There was no harm in her knowing that she traveled with a mendicant. It might avoid certain misunderstandings, at least on her side, when Kenji attempted what he was almost certainly going to attempt, somewhere along the road.

Kenji at least had the delicacy to slip behind some trees. When he re-emerged, he was back in his tatty but familiar robes. He presented the loaned clothes to me, neatly arranged, but I made him stuff them into his own small bundle.

"You'll need them when we return," I said.

Kenji grunted. "No doubt. One cannot be too cautious with the monks of Enryaku Temple swarming like ants over the capital."

I frowned. "For my curiosity, Lady Snow, how did you know Kenji was a priest?"

"He walks like a priest," she said immediately. "Left elbow

carried high at his side as if the fold of a robe was draped over his arm."

Kenji grinned. "Old habits," he said. "My more proper ordained name is Daisho, but hardly anyone uses it, and I prefer 'Kenji' in any case. That was very observant of you, Lady Snow."

She brushed the compliment aside demurely. "Simple necessity. A woman, and especially one so disreputable as to travel alone from time to time, must be aware of her surroundings. Not all men are as . . . constrained as your noble selves."

I barely suppressed a laugh, and Kenji shot me a hard look, but said nothing. Nidai glowered.

"You are not alone now, Lady Snow. *I* will protect you," he said, and he shook his travel staff at some invisible aggressor. "I will break the future generations of any man who dares threaten you!"

I almost smiled. I had been thinking of Nidai as a child, but realized he was well into the age when young boys started to become young men and could barely wait for the transformation, with all the confusion and unreliable certainties this entailed. A grown woman not his mother had shown him kindness, and now he was in love with her. Lady Snow. I could not blame him but hoped his inevitable disappointment would be gentler than my own.

Lady Snow simply bowed to her young servant and said, quite politely, "I am grateful for your concern, Nidai-kun, but please do not place yourself in danger on my account."

"It is my duty," Nidai said sternly, or as sternly as one could say anything while also looking extraordinarily happy and pleased with one's self.

Lady Snow simply bowed again, though this time I saw

her smile. There was a touch of sadness in that smile I think I understood. At least, I hoped I did.

While the way going south was somewhat easier than the mountain roads further north, our progress was still slow, and we did not quite reach the village of Uji on that first day. While I would not have been averse to finding some lodging that did not involve using grass for a pillow, I was a bit relieved. The area around the river bridge south of Uji was notorious for its bandits. After each incident the Imperial government always made a fresh attempt at restoring order, but the fact was the less-used southern road to the old capital simply was not a high priority, and for the most part policing the road was left to local officials and the provincial governor, with only limited interest and success. My own suspicion was that at least some of the villagers at Uji were complicit, and the less we did to bring attention to ourselves, the better.

We found a small cleared field just out of sight of the main road. There were the ruins of a home, but clearly no one had lived in the area for some time. We put down our burdens some distance from the abandoned building, and the three male members of the party gathered some wood for a fire. We avoided touching the rotting remains of the house, partially because the wood was wet and of little use, partly to avoid disturbing any sleeping demons or spirits.

"Keep your eyes open," Kenji said to Nidai. "Ghosts favor such places."

"And demons," I added.

Nidai tried to grunt, though it came out as more of a hum. "I once slept rough on the streets of Kyoto. You think a provincial ghost is going to frighten me?"

"Well, then, you gentlemen may consider yourselves properly answered," Lady Snow said, smiling demurely. "Though being alert is always good advice for any traveler. Now then, we have a fire. Nidai-kun, will you fetch me some fresh water? There's a spring on the other side of the field."

I started to ask how she knew, but realized she had been this way before. Kenji and I made ourselves comfortable while Lady Snow started to prepare a meal. When Nidai returned with a full jar of water he was moving a little faster than the situation seemed to warrant.

"There's a ghost," he said, apparently trying to keep his voice level and matter of fact. "It's a girl."

"What did you see?" I asked.

"A *girl*," he repeated, as if I hadn't been paying attention. "I saw her very plainly."

"I think Lord Yamada means you should be more specific, Nidai-kun," Kenji said. "What did she look like?"

He considered. "Maybe a year or so older than I am. Very long wild hair, dressed in white. She had no feet, and sort of floated on the opposite side of the spring, but the rest of her was plain as you are."

"Funeral robes," Kenji said. "It is often thus, poor thing. Perhaps I should send her to the other world . . . "

"No!" The force of Lady Snow's word startled all three of us. She realized we were all staring at her, then repeated in a softer voice, "No, there's no need. She's not dangerous."

"I assumed you'd been here before," I said. "Is this *rei* known to you?"

"I've seen her," Lady Snow admitted. "Here and there. She means no harm, I know."

"She should not linger here," Kenji said, not unkindly. "A false attachment to this world will surely long delay her path to Enlightenment. It's not right."

Lady Snow did not look up from preparing our supper. "What is not right is that so many people must leave the world before they even have a chance to experience it properly, or understand any of it or find the one thing that, perhaps, they had been put here to experience in the first place. All paths must lead to the same place eventually, Master Daisho. Not even the wisest know the best course for everyone."

"Kenji, please," he said.

"You were speaking as a priest," Lady Snow said. "I thought I should address you as such."

Kenji smiled a rueful smile, and it was all I could do not to laugh. If this had been the game of One Hundred Poems, Lady Snow had just taken every card.

"Well then," Kenji said wryly. "I certainly make no claims to either wisdom or great understanding. Unless the ghost attacks us or requests otherwise, I am content to leave her be."

"It is a small matter, but thank you," Lady Snow said.

"Small matter" indeed. Even when she had been trying so earnestly to persuade me to her cause, I had never seen her so passionate or fearful as she was concerning this one lonely ghost.

Lady Snow was heating *miso* soup and water for tea. I rose from the ground and started toward the spring.

"I'd like to wash my face."

She shot me a hard glance and looked as if she wanted to say something but finally turned her attention back to the food without a word.

Kenji shrugged. "If you smell anything like I do, I think you should merely *start* with your face. If you do decide thus, move downstream a bit. We don't want to foul the water. Or frighten the ghost."

"I'll keep this in mind for later," I said. "So will you."

A bath actually wasn't a bad idea, though I felt a little uncomfortable at the idea of bathing in the presence of a strange girl, even if she was a ghost. Perhaps it could wait until Nara.

I found the spring near a bamboo grove on the side of a small hill. It welled out of a rock, flowed into a cracked stone basin, then out again into a small stream that marked the edge of the abandoned field. I looked around, but there was no sign of anyone else, ghost or otherwise. Defying Kenji, I washed my face at the stone basin.

When I looked up again, a glimmer of movement to the left caught my eye, and then in the interval from one blink of the eye to the next, I saw her. She hovered near the edge of the stream, pretty much as Nidai had described. There came a rustling of wind through the bamboo, and a sound that might have been a sigh or simply the voice of the wind. In another moment the ghost was gone. I wanted a better look at the ghost's face, but obviously I was not going to get it. I waited for a few moments, but it did not reappear. I walked back toward our small camp, considering what I had seen. What I thought I had seen—and that was the ghost of Taira no Kei, one of the very first victims of the dark spiritual energy, whatever it was, that had ravaged the city. The girl whose body I had attended at Senrin-ji.

This far from Kyoto? This place would have no meaning to her.

While patterns and colors of the clothing of most young girl's Kei's age were as different as they could make them within the boundaries of taste and refinement, funeral robes were pretty much the same. One young girl prepared for burial looked a great deal like another, to one who did not know either. Doubtless I was mistaken.

Kenji hailed me from the campfire. "About time. I was about to persuade Lady Snow to start without you."

"Kenji-san is, indeed, quite persuasive," Lady Snow said. "But we waited nonetheless."

The meal was simple, as befitted our current circumstances, but good and substantial. Even Kenji ate all of his portion with apparent enjoyment. When we were done, Nidai dared the stream again to wash our bowls, and Lady Snow withdrew to a discreet distance. I assumed this was to make her sleeping arrangements, but instead she reached into her bundle and pulled out a polished bamboo flute. She got to her feet and began to play. The first few mournful notes seemed to fill the air around us like the voice of melancholy itself. Lady Snow walked, her long sleeves trailing, as she played. Kenji settled back to listen, his eyes closed.

Nidai returned from his washing and packed everything away. "She's back," he said, his voice barely above a whisper.

"Who? The ghost?" I asked, also keeping my voice low so as not to disturb the music.

He grunted assent. "Lady Snow started playing, and the next time I looked up, the girl was there again, just across the stream."

"Did she try to talk to you?"

He looked puzzled. "I don't think she noticed me at all. I think she was listening to the flute."

Curious.

What was even more curious was that Lady Snow seemed to

be playing as much to the trees across the field as to us, or anyone in particular. Part of me just wanted to enjoy the music, but when the ghost showed herself on the near side of the field, my mind would not let me.

There was a belief in some quarters that a spirit could not cross running water, but that was rubbish. I'd seen Seita do it numerous times. Mostly any hesitation on the part of a spirit was simple reluctance to stray from a familiar area or path, but now the ghost girl hovered just inside the edge of the field. I had the distinct impression that she wanted to move closer but would not.

I wondered why. Was it the remnants of the house? Perhaps this place had been her home, but something had driven her into the woods to die. Was there a battle? Bandits? Plague? Any one seemed as likely as another. Or maybe it had nothing to do with the house at all. Perhaps it was us.

To test the idea, I moved closer.

The ghost did not react. I kept back far enough not to cross between Lady Snow and the far edge of the field; she was now looking directly at the ghost, and the music did not falter.

I studied the ghost. Before I had merely suspected; now I was certain. I said nothing. Finally, Lady Snow lowered the flute, and the music and the ghost vanished together. I looked at Lady Snow. She was weeping.

"That was the ghost of Taira no Kei, wasn't it?"

"Yes."

"Did she follow you?"

"I have seen her before. We were friends; I told you."

It wasn't exactly an answer, nor was it a denial. "I'm not

accusing you of anything, Lady Snow. I've just never seen a ghost travel so far from the scene of its death before, though of course I've heard of such things."

"I think she liked the music."

"We all did. You are very skilled."

She wiped her tears on her sleeve. "My skills are poor things hardly worth mentioning, but thank you."

"Does she ever speak to you?" I asked.

Her face was unreadable. "I'm sorry, Lord Yamada, but I'm not certain I would know one ghost's voice if I heard it. There are so many."

That wasn't exactly an answer either, though it occurred to me I was delving into matters that, perhaps, were none of my concern. That was the recurring problem when one built one's life around asking and answering questions—sometimes it was very hard to know when to stop. I wished Lady Snow a pleasant night and withdrew. I was a little amused but not surprised when Nidai moved his bedding to lie halfway between where Kenji and I slept and where Lady Snow retired for the evening.

We crossed the river the next morning at the bridge south of Uji. We stopped in the village only long enough to trade for some fresh vegetables and set out immediately, quickly crossing the bridge. The road led into a bamboo forest where bandits were waiting.

I counted no more than five, well but crudely armed. Two had swords, two others clubs, one a thick staff. My *tachi* was clear of its scabbard before they were well out of the forest, but I had foolishly allowed Lady Snow to wander a good four paces ahead of us. An older, toothless brute who was their apparent leader reached her before I could do anything. He held her roughly by one arm as he brandished a rusty sword.

"Throw down your weapons or . . . "

We never did find out what "or" was. What came next happened so fast I almost didn't see it. Lady Snow's free arm withdrew into its sleeve and when it emerged there was a flash of steel. Her captor immediately released both her and his weapon, which fell unheeded to the road. Now both his hands were wrapped around his throat and his face had turned ashen gray.

The bandits were momentarily stunned by the turn of events, but I wasn't fool enough to give them time to recover. I killed the man with the staff while he was too busy watching his former leader pitch face first into the dirt. The other three quickly turned to face me just in time for Kenji to bring his priest's staff down hard on the remaining swordsman's head. He joined his leader and the first swordsman in the dirt, and the last two dropped their clubs and ran off into the bamboo as I rushed up to Lady Snow.

"Are you injured?"

"I have blood on my sleeve," she said ruefully. "I-I think I need to sit down."

We found a maple tree that had somehow endured the encroaching bamboo, and Lady Snow used it to lean against. "I will be fine. Please check on Nidai."

Nidai was fine. He was busy pummeling the one fallen bandit who, I was certain, was not dead.

"Nidai-kun, I believe your opponent has had enough."

There was a light of vengeance in the boy's eyes. "This isn't battle, Lord Yamada. This is punishment," Nidai said.

"I understand, but your mistress needs you now. See to her. Kenji and I will take care of this."

Nidai gasped and then rushed to Lady Snow's side, where she was forced to reassure him over and over that she really was all right and finally gave him the task of cleaning her dagger just to keep him quiet. While they were so occupied, Kenji and I studied our fallen attackers. Shabby clothes, poor weapons, and today, even poorer luck. Kenji had his priestly methods for dealing with ritual impurity, but I could not care less for my own part. The leader's body was face first. I turned it over with my foot. As I suspected, his throat had been cut cleanly, which explained all the blood pooling under him.

"It seems Lady Snow is not the helpless flower she appears," Kenji said.

"If you ever thought she was such a flower, you clearly were not paying attention. Even so, that was impressive."

"An understatement," muttered Kenji who, I was certain, was now re-evaluating any notions he may have held as to the seduction of Lady Snow.

I was not at Kanemore's level of swordsmanship, but even so I was certain my own opponent would not be getting up again. That left the third, whom Kenji had felled.

"He's still alive," Kenji said. "What shall we do with him?"

I knew what it was to be both poor and lacking in options. While I could not be certain it was this that turned the man to banditry and not a violent and brutal nature, my instinct was to spare the man. Common sense and justice both argued against that.

"Wake him up," I said.

Kenji splashed some water in the man's face and, after a few moments, had him kneeling if not standing. I waited until some focus had returned to his eyes.

"My name is Yamada no Goji," I said, "and I have every right to cut your head off. Please explain to me why I should not."

The man gibbered and bowed, and I could not get one coherent sentence out of him; certainly no justification for not treating him as he richly deserved. I methodically cleaned my sword to give him more time to think on the matter, but in the end I simply put the sword back in its scabbard.

"What is your name?" I asked.

"Y-Yoshi."

"Yoshi, as of this moment forward your head belongs to me," I said. "If I ever see you again, I will claim it. Do you understand?"

He stopped gibbering and bowed lower, which I took for assent.

Kenji frowned. "You're going to let him go?"

"I'm going to treat him as we treat the others. Normally I would hang them at the bridge as a warning, but they'd be cut down by nightfall. Throw him in the river."

The bandit found his voice again. "But . . . I cannot swim."

"Now would be an excellent time to better yourself in that regard."

We hauled the man to his feet, and together we dragged him to the river's edge and tossed him in, soon followed by the bodies of his companions. By the time we threw in the last body, he had managed to splash his way to shallower water and crawled out of the river on the far side. If he had so much as shaken his fist at us, I would have not hesitated to take the time to hunt him down and collect my debt, but he just staggered off into the bamboo on the other side of the river as quickly as he could go.

"As a priest, I must of course applaud your mercy and sense of restraint," Kenji said. "But as a traveler who may need to pass this way again, I really think you should have killed him."

I sighed. "There are plenty left to replace him, but for what it may be worth, I agree. Most likely he'll be waiting with even more of his friends upon our return."

"You won't see him again," Lady Snow said very calmly. We had not heard her approach.

Lady Snow had just had her life placed in great danger and then killed a man. While she had been upset and shaking as one might expect, that all seemed to have passed. She seemed perfectly composed now.

"Indeed? Why do you think so?" I asked.

She looked away. "Most men have far less imagination than we might think. I don't believe it had ever occurred to that fool that his prey might one day turn on him. Now he knows that, he will seek another occupation."

I sincerely hoped Lady Snow was correct. While I prided myself as a judge of men, I would certainly admit there were large gaps in some aspects of that understanding. Somehow I doubted if that would be true for Lady Snow.

Nidai accompanied her to the river where she attempted as best she could to remove the bloodstains from her sleeve. Fortunately by then the bodies had been swept downstream, and the water was relatively clean. She tied her wet sleeves up to keep them from touching the dirt, and we resumed our journey on the southern road. I wanted to be well away from Uji as soon as possible in case any of the bandits' friends and family came seeking revenge, but the day passed without further incident or any signs of pursuit. We pretty much had the road to ourselves, as this direction was not well traveled except for certain festival times linked to the temples at Nara, but this was the wrong season for that sort of travel.

That evening we made camp in a maple grove far enough off the road to obscure, if not hide, our campfire. After we were done with our meal, Lady Snow played the flute again. Again, the ghost returned. It did not approach any closer than before but simply hovered at the farthest extent of the firelight, apparently listening. I had already satisfied myself as to the ghost's identity. There was far more that I did not understand. When Lady Snow finally put her flute down, she rejoined us at the fire.

"That was the same song you played the first night. I confess I am unfamiliar with it. What is it called?"

" 'Sunset at Mount Toribe.' It was Kei's favorite. She was a cheerful enough girl, but she did have her melancholy streak."

"It seems you spent a great deal of time with her," I said.

Her face was impassive. "It does not seem like so very much time now that I see it complete. We argued sometimes, but she was a dear girl. She did not deserve such a thing."

"Does she follow you for the music?"

"She follows me," Lady Snow said, "whether I play or do not play. I hope the music gives her some comfort, but I do not know that, or what she wants. Sometimes I think she is trying to tell me something, but I cannot hear her."

"Does she come to you in your dreams?"

"I do not know," Lady Snow said. "I can never remember my dreams."

I'm not sure what moved me to share what I did with Lady Snow, but I think it was the pain in her eyes. "Shortly after her death, I dreamed of her. I do not know why; I never met her while she was alive."

Lady Snow looked at me, suddenly intent. "Did . . . did she say anything? Please, she was my friend."

"Yes. She said that I should take tea with her older sister, and that I should please be kind. Does this mean anything to you?"

Lady Snow did not look at me. "Her older sister was Taira no Hoshiko. If you ever meet that worthless creature, perhaps you can ask her."

"From what you said to me when we first met, I gathered that you were not fond of Lady Hoshiko."

"I had many problems with Lady Hoshiko," Lady Snow said, "though perhaps no more than one of my lowly station should expect. Still, I was fond of Kei."

"The ghost seems to think her sister is in pain."

She didn't look at me. "We are all in pain, Lord Yamada. Since no one knows who killed the poor child or why she haunts me now, I would rather talk of other things."

Kenji grunted. "Who? I rather think the creature that killed your Taira no Kei was more of a 'what' than a 'who,'" he said. "Possibly a demon."

Lady Snow frowned. "You know how Kei died? What killed her?"

I glared at Kenji, but he only shrugged. "Rumor says far more than even you know, Yamada-san. I doubt Lady Snow knows much less than you seem to think is secret."

"My movements at Court are somewhat constrained," Lady Snow said. "Please continue."

"I thought you wanted to speak of other things?" I asked.

"I do. Yet I have an urge to believe that, one day, whoever or whatever killed Kei-chan will be discovered and punished. Foolish of me, perhaps, but there it is. Lord Yamada, I do not ask that you betray confidences or tell secrets to one such as myself, but the nature of my profession does allow me a freedom of travel about the city that many other women do not have. Perhaps I can be of use to you when we return to the capital."

While I still wanted to strangle Kenji for his loose talk, I had to admit Lady Snow had a point. Nor could I see any harm in telling what little we knew. We were far from the only ones who knew it. Lady Snow listened attentively to everything I said, and when I was done, she appeared very thoughtful.

"But there would be no reason," she said aloud. I didn't think she was talking to me.

"What do you mean?"

"Well, Kei was still a child, even by the standards of the Court. She had no lovers, no jealous rivals."

I frowned. "Well, yes, but I don't understand what this has to do with the matter. We already know Kei was not attacked by a human being. Such was impossible. The only common factor is this dark spiritual energy that I mentioned before. Unless we sort out what the thing is, we have no way of fighting it."

"I don't know anything about clouds and such, but of course it's possible. What I'm saying is there was no *reason*. Kei-chan had no enemies," Lady Snow repeated.

Now both Kenji and I were staring at her. Nidai, for his part, merely looked confused as if he had come across three gods discussing one of the finer points of spiritual refinement and karmic debt.

One of us had to ask, so I was the first. "How could a person strike unseen? Are you talking about magic? While I certainly am no expert on Yin Yang or other magical forms, an associate of mine is, and there was nothing about the attacks he recognized." That had been one of my earlier suspicions, especially considering the persistent rumors about a link between Lord Sentaro and Chinese magic. While I admitted the possibility that Yu had lied to me, there didn't seem much point to doing so. Especially since Kanemore would have richly rewarded him for solving the murders.

"I certainly was *not* speaking of magic. Who would need such a thing anyway? If someone wished Kei ill, they would more likely strike the same way the Lady of Rokuji did."

Now we were all staring at her, even Nidai. Kenji and I exchanged glances, but I simply shrugged and let Kenji be the one to ask the obvious question.

"Who is the Lady of Rokuji?" Kenji asked. "The Sixth Ward of the city contains quite a few noblewomen. A few are of my personal acquaintance."

Now it was Lady Snow's turn to stare at us as if Kenji and I had grown an extra head each. Then she suddenly bowed low and started to shake uncontrollably. Nidai rushed to her side, apparently thinking my first thought that Lady Snow had been seized with some sort of fit and needed help. The truth, once it finally revealed itself, was a little more puzzling. She was laughing.

At us.

Nidai sat back on his heels, frowning. I merely waited for Lady Snow to compose herself. I was not used to being laughed at and could not say that I cared for it, but at the moment I was far more curious about what had caused Lady Snow's uncharacteristic merriment.

"We said something humorous?" I said, as if it were an actual question.

Lady Snow finally managed to raise herself off the grass. There were tears in her eyes and her nose was running. All in all, she did not look her best. Even so, the laughter made her look years younger. Nidai produced a cloth that could not have been any too clean, but Lady Snow did not question. She merely blew her nose and wiped the tears away.

"Forgive . . . forgive me, gentlemen, I just realized." Whatever she just realized set off another laughing fit—of shorter duration this time. The cloth was scarcely needed. When she looked up again, she managed to keep her composure. "Again I must apologize. It's just that it never occurred to me you didn't know, didn't recognize . . . "

"The Lady of Rokuji? As Kenji pointed out, there are many such."

"No, sirs, there is only one. A person," she said, "from *Genji Monogatari*."

For a few moments all I could do was blink like an owl surprised in daylight. Of course I had heard of the story of Genji; it had been written about fifty years earlier by a lady of the Court known as Murasaki. As it was the height of bad manners to record a lady's name directly, lest it be linked to rumor and gossip, her actual name was obscure. Doubtless there were one or two souls still on the earth who knew her true identity. Still, *The Tale of Genji* was just one of several yarns of romance and courtly intrigue much favored by the women—and some men—of the Court and upper classes, though in my opinion it had the added disadvantage of being the longest.

Lady Snow glanced from one of us to the other. "Neither of you has read it?"

"Such things aren't generally available in a temple," Kenji said, "and would be frowned upon in any case."

While I certainly couldn't claim Kenji's excuse, I didn't feel I needed one. "I tried to read it, once, before I left the Court," I said. "A . . . friend recommended it to me."

A part truth; Princess Teiko had recommended it to me. I had quit after the early chapters, unable to understand why anyone could possibly find enough of interest to keep them going page after page of little but Genji's shining attributes and romantic adventures. It was the one and only occasion I had reason to question either Teiko's judgment or taste. She had simply smiled when I told her, as if my failure in this matter was a foregone conclusion. While from that moment forward I had rather suspected that perhaps I had missed something in the tale, I was never so curious as to try the scrolls again and doubt I would have done so even had they fallen into my lap.

"The Lady of Rokuji was one of Genji's lovers," Lady Snow said.

"Most of the women in that book were Genji's lovers, from what little I know. Or, if not, it was not for lack of his trying," I said dryly.

Lady Snow merely sighed at the interruption and continued.

"The Lady of Rokuji was different. Unable to reconcile herself to Genji's eventual disinterest, she turned her jealousy and her vengeful spirit on two of Genji's other women: his official wife Aoi and one of his mistresses, Lady Yugao—especially after an insult in which the Lady of Rokuji's carriage was forced from its spot by a procession in favor of one of the other women. She killed both of her rivals."

"Killed? How?"

"As I said: her vengeful spirit. This apparition was spotted on at least one occasion by Genji himself, who mistook the creature for someone else."

Kenji frowned. "You're saying the lady's spirit attacked these other two women even though she was still alive?"

"Certainly," said Lady Snow. "The details of the matter are all there. Though in fairness to the Lady of Rokuji, she didn't actually mean to harm anyone. Part of the tragedy was that she struck without intent and without realizing what she was doing; her emotions simply got out of her control. So when an unseen attacker killed Taira no Kei, I assumed it was something similar. Yet there was no Lady of Rokuji, at least so far as Kei-chan was concerned; she didn't have an enemy in the world. That's why the idea makes no sense."

"Not to be difficult, Lady Snow, but does it make no sense because it's just a story?" I asked. "It didn't actually happen."

Lady Snow frowned at me. "Are you so certain? The story was written nearly fifty years ago. How do you know Lady Murasaki was not describing an actual incident? It's not as if the concept of the *ikiryo* did not exist before she wrote of it."

That was true enough, and in fairness now that she mentioned the word I had heard of such a thing as an *ikiryo*, though I had no personal experience with one and didn't know anyone who had. Also, I had never in all my time, before or after Court, come across any incident where this was alleged to have actually occurred, and if Lady Snow was correct, Kei had no enemies anyway. There was no reason for an *ikiryo* to have attacked her.

No reason at all. At least, not for Kei . . .

For several long moments I don't think I took a breath, and when I did it came out as a sort of hard gasp that made everyone look at me. I had often said there was a little voice inside my head that told me when I was being an ass, though I didn't always listen or understand. I listened to that little voice now and understood what it told me, and knew it for truth. I was an ass, and one of truly epic proportion. I hoped it was not too late to stop being so.

"Everyone please get some sleep. Tomorrow we're going to get an early start."

At first Lady Snow misunderstood. "At most it will take a half day tomorrow to reach Nara. I'll arrange rooms for us, and we can proceed with our business the day after. There's no need for haste."

"On the contrary, there is a need for a great deal of haste, Lady Snow. We're not going on to Nara tomorrow. We're going back to the capital."

I hated the stricken look in Lady Snow's eyes and the desperation I saw there. I hated even more that I was the one to put those things there. But I had no choice.

"But . . . you *promised*," she said, in a small voice like a child's.

"I promised to go with you to Nara, and I still intend to do so," I said. "But right now I must return to Kyoto. It is, unfortunately, imperative. I would let you continue to Nara and meet you there later, but Kenji will be returning as well, and despite your obvious skills, I cannot allow you to travel unescorted."

"It would not be the first time," Lady Snow said, resigned. "But no matter, I will return with you. But can you at least tell me why we are going back *now*?"

I wanted to embrace her and tell her she may have just given me the key to solving her friend's death and preventing worse, but I could not do that, not before I knew. I did tell her the truth, so far as I understood it.

"I cannot tell you why, because I am sure of nothing as of yet, and I will not slander where I have no proof. Yet if I am correct, there is not a day to lose."

A single tear glistened on her left cheek, but others did not join it. She met my gaze squarely. "Well then. I will ask no more. Good night, gentlemen. Nidai, please walk with me for a moment."

We did not hear whatever she had to tell Nidai, but he listened very solemnly as they walked together. When they were out of earshot, Kenji turned to me.

"What is this all about? That *ikiryo* business?"

"I think it might be," I said.

"Are you saying all those people were murdered by the spirit of a spiteful woman? That *this* is what the dark cloud is?"

"Of course not."

"Then I don't understand why we're going back now."

"We're going back now because any later may be too late. It may already be too late. But maybe there's a chance."

"To do what?"

"To stop it. To stop the killing, the monks, Lord Sentaro,

everything. But first I need to ask you something: how many of your brother priests remain in the city?"

Kenji pretended to yawn. "A few."

"I suspect there are more than a few. Can you make contact with them?"

Now Kenji's eyes narrowed. "Perhaps so, given enough time and reason. Why?"

"Because we need their help."

Kenji grunted. "After what they've been through? I'm not sure they'd be willing."

"Then you must persuade them. Use some of that charm of yours I hear so many rumors about, but never see. Unless you and your brother priests want to remain in hiding from Enryaku-ji for the rest of your lives?"

"Since you put it in those terms, I'll see—Yamada, look out!"

The last bit came out in a shout. I had never been subject to the military discipline of someone like Kanemore, but let it never be said that I could not obey an order, especially from someone obviously fearful for my life. I threw myself forward and heard the whisper of a blade through the air inches from my right ear. There was a whooshing sound and the thud of wood on flesh. I heard Kenji howl and then curse, and then the whoosh and thud came again.

Thought failed me. I did not remember I had laid my sword to my left, but apparently my body did, and on such things a person's entire world may turn. I rolled left and came up with the blade just as Lady Snow slashed at me again. I barely blocked the blow with the scabbard, and before she could press her attack I had my blade drawn. She stepped back, her eyes wild and her hair streaming out in a sudden breeze like the flow of a dark river.

"Kenji?"

"Here, Yamada-san."

Kenji came limping back into my field of vision, holding Nidai's staff in one hand and a squirming Nidai in the other. The boy tried to strike Kenji again with his bare fists and the priest shook him hard.

"Try that again and I'll have your scrotum for a purse!"

I pointed my sword squarely at Lady Snow. She turned the dagger in her hand to trail the blade down her forearm, and turned to the side to present the least amount of target. Whoever had taught her to fight had done it well; it was classic defense for dagger against a sword. Of course, the best defense was not to put oneself in that situation in the first place.

"Kiyoshi taught you that, didn't he? He sought the *bushi* path, as did Kanemore. I think they trained together at times. Did you watch them?" She just glared at me, and I continued, "Lady Snow, I've seen your handiwork before. If you attack me again, I'll have to kill you. Please believe I will do so."

Lady Snow abandoned her stance and faced me squarely. My blade was inches from her breast. For a moment I believed she was actually considering impaling herself on my sword. Then the moment passed, and sighing she threw the dagger aside and kneeled in front of me, head bowed.

I glanced at Kenji again. He was favoring his left leg and arm. "Are you hurt?"

"Quite," Kenji said ruefully. "Much is bruised but nothing's broken. Not that young Master Nidai here wasn't doing his best."

"We'll attend to him later. There's some rope in my bundle. Tie him up for now."

"Please don't hurt him," Lady Snow said. "He was only following my instructions. I'm responsible."

"Are you?"

I kept my voice hard, my face cold. I wanted to scream, but oh, no, I couldn't react and do all the stupid things I wanted to do now. I had to keep my head clear, no matter what happened next. I understood that, and I kept my screams silent.

Lady Snow glanced up at me, then back down at the ground. She was weeping, but whether in frustration, sadness or rage I did not want to guess. She bared her neck as if awaiting execution.

"Do it," she said. "I am ready. But please, let Nidai go."

"Perhaps you are ready," I said, "but I am not. And for now Master Nidai remains where he is. What happens to him rather depends on you now. Please explain yourself."

"It was all a lie," she said. "Everything. There are no documents at Nara. I made a fool of you, and then I tried to kill you. That is all you need to know."

I put my sword away, but not before I had secured Lady Snow's dagger and subjected her to the indignity of a search. When I was certain she was carrying no other weapons, I took another length of rope from Kenji.

"Lady Snow, it is for me to decide what I need to know. Prepare yourself for a very uncomfortable night. Tomorrow we're turning back to the capital as I said we would."

When I had her secured, I took a closer look at Kenji's injuries. They were obviously painful enough but not, as he correctly judged, serious.

"The little demon was aiming at my head," he muttered. "The

only reason he missed was I was dodging at the time. He got several good whacks before I got the staff away from him."

"I appreciate your restraint. Lady Snow is correct in one regard—he was simply doing what she told him to do."

"My sense of justice tells *me* he should be beaten half to death. Or maybe the rest of the way."

"Mercy, Kenji. He's just a boy."

Kenji scowled. "Yamada, sometimes I think you're more a priest than I am."

"Lady Snow is more of a priest than you are. Even so, we're going to need your priest's training when we get back to Kyoto."

Kenji tried to ease himself into a more comfortable position. Lady Snow's tears had dried. She merely kneeled there, bound, her expression resigned. Later I would adjust the ropes so she could lean against a tree, but for now she could stay as she was.

Kenji sighed. "Do you have any idea why she attacked us?"

"She's refusing to say at present, but I believe it was because we were turning back."

"Why would she care whether or not we went to Nara if there was nothing there?"

I grunted. "Obviously because someone wanted us out of the capital. Or rather, they wanted me out."

"Why?"

"I don't know," I said, which was the truth. I did not know. But I suspected a great deal.

PART SIX

The inazuma
at harvest breaks the dark sky.
In a heartbeat shows
What was hidden and secret.
Awaiting now the lightning.

Kenji was wearing my spare clothes again when our little procession passed back through the Demon Gate. We took that route rather than the much closer Rasha Gate to avoid a lengthy progress through the city, which would attract far more attention than I wanted. As it was, Lady Snow and Nidai's hands were bound, and we got several stares and some muttering but no interference. That was fortunate, for I was in not in a gentle mood.

We took the closest street to the eastern gate of the Imperial Compound, where five Taira stood watch.

I was addressed as "Lord Yamada" more out of courtesy than fact, but when I marched up to the gate detachment I played the part to the hilt and in full voice of command. I recognized one man as the *bushi* in charge, and handed the end of the rope attached to Lady Snow's wrists to him. For a moment he could only stare at it.

"From this moment forward, you will consider this person Prince Kanemore's prisoner. You will choose two men to escort her and her servant to her home, as this gentleman," I said, nodding at Kenji, "will direct you. She is not to leave or have any visitors save me or Prince Kanemore until the guards receive further instruction. Do you understand?"

"*Hai!*"

The effect was instantaneous. In short order Lady Snow departed, closely escorted by Kenji, Nidai, and two armed *bushi* of the Taira Clan. I did my best Lord Yamada scowl.

"I require an audience with Prince Kanemore. Now."

The remaining guards bowed, and their leader spoke: "Prince Kanemore has been searching for you, Lord Yamada. He did not realize you had left the city."

"Please take me to him."

They sent a runner ahead as one of the remaining *bushi* escorted me to the former home of Princess Teiko. We had just reached the gardens when Prince Kanemore himself came hurrying up. He dismissed the guard.

"Lord Yamada! Praise Buddha you are here."

"Takahito?" I asked, afraid at what the answer might be.

"He is well. But there have been more deaths, last night and again the night before. A servant to His Majesty himself and an officer of the guard of the Minamoto Clan were both taken."

"What says Enryaku-ji?"

"That we need to round up more itinerant priests. Master Dai-wu insists there are many such still within the city."

"I pray he is right. I've asked Kenji to bring them together."

Kanemore frowned. "The priest will work against his own?"

"To the contrary—the priest and his lay brothers will help us save Prince Takahito's life, if it is not already too late."

"You know who our enemy is? Who is responsible for these attacks?"

"I do. It is Lord Sentaro."

Kanemore glared at me. "Lord Yamada, are you going to start this again? I know that Master Dai-wu is not responsible! He could not be!"

"He isn't. I said Lord Sentaro. I said nothing about Master Dai-wu."

Now Prince Kanemore stared at me as if I had just started barking like a dog. "Lord Yamada, please stop speaking nonsense. Lord Sentaro *is* Master Dai-wu! They are the same man!"

"I once thought that. Now I know better. Thanks to Lady Snow."

"Lady Snow? The messenger mentioned a prisoner. Has she some part in this?"

"A very major part, Prince Kanemore, the precise nature of which I have yet to sort out. I will need to speak to her again and soon, after I've had a little time to consider. But you can be certain she was acting on Lord Sentaro's orders when she tried to kill me. Reluctantly, at least in Lord Sentaro's regard, I am sure. He doesn't want me dead. Yet."

"And what proof do you have for any of this?"

"None," I said. "Not one scrap. Except for the attempted assassination. I have a witness for that. Kenji."

"Who is under threat of arrest as soon as he shows himself," Prince Kanemore said. "Honestly, Lord Yamada, I want to believe you . . ."

I smiled at my friend. "I am not asking you to believe me, Kanemore-sama. I am asking you to trust me."

Prince Kanemore stood silent for several long moments, staring at nothing. I felt every one of those moments like a dying heartbeat. He finally grunted.

"What do you need me to do?"

I started to breathe again, and then I told him. "You will let it be known that, in two days' time, Prince Takahito and his immediate household will be removed from the Imperial Compound and relocated to the Mansion of the Southwest Ward."

Kanemore frowned. "The Sixth Ward mansion? That place is only used in times of sickness. Takahito is healthy as a bull."

"I'm pleased to hear it. But you will say Prince Takahito has fallen ill and that, in the meantime, priests will be brought in to recite prayers for his recovery. One of Enryaku-ji's best spies is currently in your custody, but she will be far from the only one. Word will reach the temple by nightfall."

"Speaking of the woman you call Lady Snow, I would like to question her," Kanemore said.

I sighed. "I know, and there will be a time when all your questions will be answered. Again, you must trust me when I tell you this time I speak of is not now. Let me question her first."

"Very well. Use whatever methods you deem necessary. But just to be clear on this point: if anything happens to Prince Takahito, it is my honor . . . and your head."

I almost smiled. Not because I thought he was joking, because I knew he was not. Rather, what I found humorous was the idea that, in such an event, my head would still matter to either of us.

"For the sake of both let us hope I am right. If I am wrong . . . well, the disposition of my head will be the least of our troubles."

Kanemore conceded the point. "Is there anything else?"

"Two things. When I was at Court in my youth, Princess Ai had a young attendant, no more than ten years old at the time. Her name, if I recall right, was Maiya. Is she still at Court?"

"Yes, and still in attendance on Princess Ai . . . which is frankly astounding, given Ai's temper. She's married now to one of the Taira *bushi* under my command."

"That complicates matters . . . oh, wait. Request that her husband be sent to relieve one of the guards we stationed at Lady Snow's house, and that his wife accompany him. Say the prisoner needs a temporary attendant during his watch. There's nothing improper in a married woman flitting about the city with her own husband as escort."

"True enough, but you're sending a noblewoman to wait attendance on an *asobi*? It's an insult!"

"I do not believe the lady in question will find it so," I said, and Kanemore scowled.

"Is Lady Maiya involved in this too?"

"Not at all. Yet I believe she may have some knowledge that will prove helpful to me if I am to get at the truth. As for the second matter . . . " I reached into my sleeve and pulled out a small scroll. "Will you have this message delivered to the boy named Nidai at Lady Snow's place of confinement?"

"Easily arranged."

Kanemore took the scroll and, after I explained what would be required of Nidai, he left to start his preparations. It was past time that I saw to my own.

Logically I had every right to find satisfaction in what I was about to do, but I did not. In fact, I found myself dreading the whole sordid business. I think Lady Snow had fully expected me to kill her there on the road to Nara. I thought, perhaps, in time she would come to wish I had done exactly that, for if my suspicions were correct, what I was about to do to her was much worse.

I made contact with Kenji at several points during the day. He was still traveling as "Kenji-san," not as a priest, and using one more set of spare clothes I had managed to scrounge in order to slip his brother priests into the now-shuttered hostel south of the Demon Gate.

He paused in the fragrant shade of a *sugi*, its evergreen fronds whispering in the breeze. I passed him a wine bottle.

He spat and then swore. "There is water in this wine bottle!"

"And that is all you're going to drink until this matter is settled. If you behave yourself, next time I will bring tea. I need us both sober, Kenji-san."

"Tyrant."

"When necessary. How many mendicants have you located so far?"

"Twelve. How many do we need?"

"Sixteen at the least, and better more than fewer. Don't make me go calling at any of the other temples to fill out the number. While many of them are no friends of Enryaku-ji, that's still a risk I'd rather not take. How much time do you need?"

"As much as you can give me. Kintaro tells me of two more hiding in the Sixth Ward, and Gen claims there is one hiding in the Gion Shrine itself. I'll see if I can find them. They may know of others."

"It wouldn't surprise me if the priests of Gion felt the urge to break wind in the direction of Enryaku Temple," I said. "No matter. Since all must be in readiness by tomorrow night, you must be done by tomorrow noon at the latest. You know as well as I that some of your brothers will need instruction in the proper execution of their duties beforehand. Your lives and ours will depend on it."

"They will be ready," Kenji said grimly.

"I'll leave it to you then."

"Right now I'm more concerned with my failing legs than my brother priests' neglected spiritual practices."

Kenji was free to grumble so far as I was concerned, just as long as he did what he was supposed to do. After a brief rest he was off his rear and on his feet again. I didn't want to tell him I'd have traded assignments with him in a heartbeat if it were possible.

My next goal was the shop of the illustrious Chang Yu. I was afraid the recent crackdowns may have spread to the old Daoist as well, but I found him in his shop, looking like a fat angry spider.

"I'll speculate," I said, "Enryaku-ji has left customers both frightened and scarce?"

"Those infernal monks say I am a bad influence," Chang Yu said, scowling. "Chinese magic and foreign ideas, that I am no better than those unsavory homeless priests who used to wander the city. I suppose I am next, Lord Yamada. Really, now, should an honest tradesman be subject to such abuse?"

"Suppose I were to tell you there may be a way that we can help each other?"

"I would assume in such a case it involves personal danger."

"A bit," I admitted. "But no more dangerous than sitting

around here waiting for the monks to surrender to the impulse to pull your shop down around your ears."

"Point taken," the old man said. "I've lived a long while, that doesn't mean I am quite finished with this old body just yet. What do you want of me?"

"When you trapped that spirit in the alley behind your shop some weeks ago, your barrier prevented the ghost from moving in one direction only. Its own spiritual compulsions would not allow it to move in any other direction. Can you confine a spirit who has no such compulsions? Say, in a house?"

"I suppose," Chang Yu said, frowning. "The barriers extend through the earth and upwards on the same curve. It would be a tricky affair, mind. Three barriers would have to be in place before the creature entered, and the fourth barrier put in place to complete the sphere the moment the spirit is inside. Contact with any of the other barriers already in place might give warning."

"So you're saying we would first have to know by which direction the spirit will be entering, yes?" The old magician indicated this was so, and I went on, "Do not fear. We know."

Chang Yu scratched his scraggly beard. "Is this a powerful spirit?"

"I have never seen one more so," I said. "Are your barriers up to the task?"

At first Chang Yu appeared affronted, but it did not last. He scratched his beard again. "You must realize, Lord Yamada, that the spirit in the alleyway was a small, pitiful thing."

"You were listening when I addressed it the first time, yes?"

Chang Yu didn't answer me directly, but then he didn't need to. I considered his eavesdropping a foregone conclusion.

"I honestly cannot say what will happen, Yamada-sama," he said finally. "While I have yet to meet the spirit that could defy my barriers, I do not claim such spirits do not exist."

"We must risk it, Master Chang Yu. For the future of many people, including what's left of your own."

"I will need an assistant," Chang Yu said. "Some of this must be done quickly, and I am not so young as I once was."

"If you will direct the placements, I will see to it. If you do your best and the barriers fail, you have my permission to run as fast as those scrawny old legs can carry you."

Chang Yu grinned, showing what few teeth he had left. "You might be surprised," he said, "at just how quickly an old man can run, properly motivated."

There was little more to do until evening. I returned to the Widow Tamahara's establishment. I felt somewhat better after some tea and rice. I was considering taking a nap when Nidai appeared on the veranda.

"Nidai-kun. I was beginning to wonder if you were coming."

"The guard didn't want to let me go," he said sullenly, "but then I showed him what you had written. Is it true? Will you help her?"

"I must tell you the truth, Nidai-kun, and I expect the same from you. You are almost a man now, and these are grave matters indeed. Do you understand?"

"*Hai*, Yamada-sama."

"Very well. The truth is that Lady Snow's life is no longer in my hands. When we returned to the capital I had to place her in the custody of Prince Kanemore, as I did not have the authority to hold her."

"You could have let her go," Nidai said.

"I could have cut her head off on the road to Nara, too," I said. "But I did not. So, there we have two paths not taken. How much time shall we waste discussing what is no longer possible?"

He bowed. "I am sorry. I am . . . concerned."

"Rightly so. You are in trouble, your mistress is in a great deal of trouble and likely to be in more before long. I want to help you both."

Nidai started to say something but hesitated. "What is it, Nidai?" I asked.

"It's just that . . . well, you said you wanted the truth. Lady Snow tried to kill you. I did as she commanded *because* she commanded. I bear neither you nor Kenji-san any ill will, but my one regret is that I did not serve her better. Why would you wish to help either of us?"

I grunted. "Spoken like a man and a sensible one at that. Your question deserves an answer, Nidai-kun. It's true I am very angry with Lady Snow, but I want to help your mistress because I believe it will be to my ultimate advantage to do so. Now, whatever follows next, I cannot guarantee her life. As I said, that is beyond my power. Yet what we will ask of you in the days ahead will require bravery, as it involves a great deal of danger. If you serve us well, that fact will weigh on the scale in your favor and in more eyes than my own. I assume you showed my letter to Lady Snow?"

He reddened slightly then. "Yes. Was that wrong?"

"It was expected. What did she tell you? Again, I want the truth."

"She instructed I do as you command and that I not attempt anything foolish on her behalf."

"Very well. Report to the eastern gate of the Imperial Compound and take this," I produced a second letter, "to Prince Kanemore. He is expecting you. It is my command that you obey him in every detail, though I'm certain he'll expect no less with or without my word."

"A real prince?" Nidai looked a little pale.

I kept my smile hidden. "None more so. Now off with you. Time is short."

Nidai hurried away, and I heard the closing of the compound gate. I thought of where he had come from, what he had known growing up on the streets of the capital. One would consider himself a fool if he did not immediately flee his captors now that he had the chance, and get as far away as possible. That is, one would do so if he had been allowed to remain as he was, but I knew Lady Snow had permitted no such thing. Nidai had changed. I was about to place the boy in great peril for my own selfish reasons, but I knew he would not run and take joy in so refusing. There had been a time when I assumed one such as Nidai was unworthy to be Lady Snow's servant. Now it was my fervent hope she might still prove worthy of *him*.

The sun was soon to set. I indulged in a long, hot bath and for the first time in a while, saw to my neglected sword. There was a proper way to care for a blade, especially one as fine as my own. I polished it carefully, tapping it at the end with a small mallet to shake loose any metal filings or abrasives from the final polish. When I was satisfied, I placed the sword in its scabbard and stuck it through my sash. I had avoided my next duty as long as possible, but the day was nearly done and I could not wait any longer. I went to see Lady Snow.

The guard stepped aside as I approached the gate. I found Lady Snow calmly having tea with a slightly younger woman whom I finally recognized as Lady Maiya, though the last time I had seen her she was a mere girl.

"Welcome, Lord Yamada," Lady Snow said, as the women bowed low in unison. "Lady Maiya, this pot is empty. Some tea for our guest?"

Maiya bowed again, then rose with the practiced deftness that never ceased to astonish me, no matter how many times I had seen it. The clothing of women at Court was not designed for quick movement, and formal dress for Court functions sometimes required a *kimono* of no fewer than twelve separate layers. Frankly, I was amazed they could move at all. Granted, Lady Maiya's current attire was far more practical, but the principle still held.

I turned my attention back to Lady Snow. I had already seen part of what I had expected to see, but still expected one more bit of evidence to present itself, if I was patient. I resolved to be so.

Lady Maiya returned shortly with a steaming pot decorated with plum blossoms. In more formal surroundings the powdered tea would be mixed and prepared before me, but this was simple refreshment. She poured a cup for me and a fresh cup for Lady Snow, then retired to a position behind Lady Snow, to the left. The cup that Maiya herself had been drinking from earlier was nowhere in evidence, and I realized now that she had taken it with her when she cleared away the formerly empty teapot.

Ah.

I really needed little else, but matters were at a crisis and I had to be certain beyond any doubt. I sipped my tea as the silence lengthened. Lady Snow for her part saw no need to attempt to fill that void, and she matched me silence for silence. That was no more or less than what I expected, but my attention was not on Lady Snow. In time my patience was rewarded.

It was no more than a glance, really, from Lady Maiya to the woman whom I had always known as Lady Snow. Lady Maiya was afraid, but not of Lady Snow. She was afraid *for* Lady Snow.

I heard the muffled sound of a challenge from outside, then a response. I grunted.

"Lady Maiya, that will be your husband's relief. You are free to go, and thank you. Lady Snow and I have some matters to discuss in private."

That worried look again, but Lady Snow was reassuring. "Yes, thank you, Lady Maiya. You have been most kind."

Maiya bowed and withdrew, leaving Lady Snow and me back in our silence. Lady Maiya had told me what I needed to know, without saying a word. I did not think this was the correct time to confront Lady Snow on this one particular point; the fact I knew who she really was, was an advantage. I didn't have nearly so many as I needed.

"Do you normally take tea with your attempted assassins?" Lady Snow asked finally.

"You're no assassin. You've taken it upon yourself to learn certain skills, but that's not why Lord Sentaro sent you. Unless I am quite mistaken, your instructions were to get me out of the city and keep me there for some days, thus the matter of the letters and conspiracies of my father. You attacked me only when it was clear I meant to return to the capital prematurely. I rather believe your attempt on my life was an act of desperation, perhaps unfortunate but in your judgment, necessary."

I still wanted to think of her as simply Lady Snow, even when I knew better. As for Lady Snow, she merely sipped her tea. Of course, the easy part was confirming her true identity; I had not really expected the rest of my answers to come so easily.

"One way or another, Lady Snow, you will tell me what I want to know."

"You would do terrible things," she said finally, "to me or anyone else if you thought it necessary. Are you so much better than I?"

"No, I am far worse," I said. "You merely tried to take my life. I must take something from you that is far more precious."

She raised an eyebrow. "And what would that be?"

"Your ignorance."

She sighed. "*My* ignorance? Nonsense. Lord Yamada, I lied and misled you. I tried to kill you. I am guilty of these things and far more besides. It is not unusual for an *asobi* to work as both spy and assassin. We need not dwell on these unpleasant things. If your sword is ready, so am I."

"My sword?"

"You're not the only one who notices things," she said calmly. "There was a loose cord on the hilt of your sword at our last meeting. Now it has been repaired. I rather suspect the blade has been sharpened as well. For that courtesy, I thank you."

"Do not thank me yet, Lady Snow."

She shuddered delicately. "Please. I have admitted my guilt, and I will accept the consequences. What more needs be said?"

"Many things, Lady Snow. I do not think you fully understand these 'consequences' you speak of. There is still the matter of your patron."

She looked at the wooden floor, and at a vase of little white flowers carefully arranged; anywhere but at me. "You say it is Lord Sentaro. I have said nothing on the matter. This will not change no matter what you do. I am stronger than I look."

No doubt, but it was time to see just how strong Lady Snow was.

"I am content to refer to this person as your patron for the time being. At the moment I am not seeking information. I am giving it."

That got her attention. "Lord Yamada, what are you talking about?"

"Your patron's true agenda and the actions he's taken to achieve his ends. Aren't you even the least bit curious?"

"That is none of my concern."

"Taira no Kei was not your concern? She was your friend, was she not?"

Lady Snow gasped. "Her death had nothing to do with this!"

She quickly recovered from her outburst, but pretending indifference was no longer possible.

"No? Then why is her ghost following you, and why won't you listen to her? What are you afraid she will say?"

"That I wasn't there when she needed me," Lady Snow said softly. "I was her friend, and I wasn't there to protect her."

"No, Lady Snow. She was trying to tell you that you serve the man who killed her."

I've seen open-eyed stares on dead men that were less fixed and unmoving as the expression on Lady Snow's face then. "You are trying to trick me. It will not work."

"Why should I? As I said, my current intent is to give information, not receive it. I do not need your confirmation as to the identity of your patron, Lady Snow. I already know. The documents, remember?"

"They were nothing. Lies. I told you that."

"That's what Lord Sentaro wanted you to think. He knew I would pounce on anything that did not fit the facts as known. I'll give him this much—he knew his victim. So why should he not just tell the truth? There's a proper piece of bait for a reluctant fish."

"Nonsense. Even assuming what you say is true, why take the risk?"

"What risk would there be? None of the documents actually existed, and so nothing he told you could be proven."

She frowned. "You just said . . . "

"That the information in the letters was true. It was, all of it. Dictated to you by Lord Sentaro from memory. I daresay he has a very good memory. He knew about my father's meeting with the barbarian prince before it happened. My father was aware that Lord Sentaro knew, but met at the appointed time. Why? Because Lord Sentaro ordered him to arrange the meeting in the first place. Lord Sentaro did betray and murder my father."

"You could not possibly know that!"

"I can and do, because my father told me. In a letter I doubt even Lord Sentaro knew about. Granted, it took me seventeen years and Lord Sentaro's transcribed letters to finally understand what my father was telling me, and then there's the matter of Fujiwara no Kiyoshi. One thing to murder my father, who was nothing to him, but he murdered his own nephew. When you said that, it was also the truth."

"Lord Yamada, please . . . "

There would be no pretended indifference here. I almost relented. Perhaps if it had been only my neck under the sword I might have. Yet this was far beyond either me or Lady Snow now.

"I said all of it, and I meant all. The story he gave you about the death of Kiyoshi? That was true, too."

"But . . . there was no *reason*," she repeated, as if we were back on the road to Nara, listening to events from *Genji Monogatari* once more.

"There was a very good reason, Lady Snow. I should have told you about a letter I once read, now in the archives of the Minister of Justice. It was from Kiyoshi. It mentions my father and speaks of a mistake his uncle made that Kiyoshi hopes to correct. Whatever that mistake was, he was killed before he could do anything about it. If you had known of this . . . well, perhaps you would have realized what was happening even before I did."

She glared at me. "That proves nothing. Lord Sentaro's nephew could have been referring to almost anything."

"Taken alone, yes. But remember that Prince Kanemore was also on that expedition. He confirmed to me Kiyoshi was killed with an arrow in the back. All of the enemy forces were in front. Plus, the barbarians have weaker bows for which they compensate by poisoning their arrows. This arrow was not poisoned. It was not made by a barbarian. Yes, I know such things happen in war. They tend to happen more often when someone has something to hide. Kiyoshi learned my father had been unjustly accused. I don't know how; he was Sentaro's nephew so it's easy enough to imagine. I knew Kiyoshi. So did you, Lady Snow. That part wasn't a lie, was it?"

She didn't answer me. She didn't have to.

"If he knew a man had been falsely accused of a crime, any crime, what would he do?" I asked.

Her voice was barely above a whisper. "He would try to set it right."

I grunted. "Just so. I believe he confronted Sentaro, because he would do what it was his nature to do. I believe Lord Sentaro did the same."

Lady Snow was battered, but not beaten. She had one more weapon up her sleeve and she used it. "A very interesting tale, Lord Yamada. You should write it down, and perhaps, one day it will stand beside the great romantic stories of the past. But it is nonsense."

"I'd like to think so myself. Can you tell me why?"

"Because there is no *reason*," she repeated. "For any of it. Why kill Kiyoshi and your father? Why extend hostilities with the barbarians?"

"That puzzled me for some time as well, but then I forced myself to think like Lord Sentaro and it occurred to me that if the great military families are occupied and weakened with unending strife in the north, they would be unable to turn their attention to Court matters. The Fujiwara would have and keep free reign at the Court. That was the purpose, Lady Snow—to ensure the position of the Fujiwara would remain unchallenged for generations."

Lady Snow looked at me. "No one could be so callous."

"You think not? It is in the Fujiwaras' interest there be no peace in the north or anywhere else, and the Emperor's current troubles with the Abe Clan are a direct result. It was a long-term strategy, Lady Snow. I despise the waste and brutality of it. Still, one must admit it has been effective. As for my father and Kiyoshi, compared to Lord Sentaro's vision they were nothing. Used and discarded without a second thought, and your future and mine along with them."

She didn't want to believe me. She was trying hard not to believe me. But the facts drew her along the same path they had drawn me, and to the same place. Yet that place was much worse for her.

"Of course, without Lord Sentaro's original letters, I can prove none of this. But I know it is true. And so do you."

She took a deep breath. Tears were streaming down her cheeks. "I didn't know . . . Lord Yamada, you must believe that."

"I do. You had nothing to do with the deaths. Except the one that was almost mine."

I was somewhat gratified to note that Lady Snow looked at least a little ashamed. "I panicked," she said. "There is no excuse I can offer you; I behaved foolishly. When you turned back . . . I don't know why my patron wanted you out of the city. I did not care why, only that I be paid in the manner we had agreed."

She still would not say his name, nor did I demand it.

"It's all right, Lady Snow. I know you're telling me the truth."

There were more tears. She didn't bother to hide them. "But *how*? Events have proven me to be a worthless, lying creature. There's no reason to believe me."

I smiled. "Oh, but there is. There is an esteemed person of high rank who personally attests to the truth of what you say."

She frowned. "Who?"

"Prince Genji."

She frowned. "The romance? What has that to do with this?"

"You told me how the people in the capital were being killed. It was almost cut in stone *who* was responsible. 'How' was eluding me. One cannot assemble a broken bowl without all the pieces. You gave me the missing piece."

"I do not understand. Prince Genji is not real, nor is the Lady of Rokuji or any of the people in that story. What has the jealous spirit of a woman who never existed to do with this?"

I grunted. "More than you know, which I must count in your favor. If you did know and were truly privy to your patron's intent, you would never have spoken of Genji on the road to Nara in the first place. That is how I know you're telling the truth now."

"I don't understand," she said again.

"You will. Yet I have told you quite enough. Now it is time you tell me something I wish to know."

"I cannot . . . "

" . . . Betray your patron? After he betrayed you?"

"He has done all he has promised and kept his word. I must keep mine. Even . . . even if everything you have told me is true."

On another day I might have found that admirable. "I'm not asking you to break faith. Do not name your patron, do not confirm anything I have told you. Nor should you reveal the full extent of your patron's plans, even if you do know them. I do not ask you to betray him or anyone, Lady Snow. Simply answer a question of mine on a separate matter."

"A separate matter? What is it?"

"As an *asobi*, you are well accustomed to journeys. If one were planning a trip to the old capital, how long should such a journey take, if one did not remain there?"

She hesitated, then looked away. "Four days. No less."

One last piece of the bowl. "Thank you. I must go now, Lady Snow. If I do not return, chances are you will be released as it is likely no one living will remember why you are here. If that happens, may you be contented with the price of your freedom."

I was a little ashamed of myself for that last, but under the circumstances I thought my restraint more than adequate. I also had reason to believe that when Lady Snow had a little more time to digest what I had told her, especially when she made the connection to Taira no Kei, likely her own thoughts would be even less kind.

Before I left, I had a few words with the guard at the gate: "At some point during the next day or so, your prisoner is probably going to try to kill herself. Please make certain that she lacks the means."

Four days.

We had already used three. I made my way from Lady Snow's house to the Demon Gate, but all was quiet. I knew I should have been grateful for that, but it was hard to do so when I knew what lay ahead, whatever our preparations might be. My attempted subterfuge concerning Prince Takahito was likely moot—the spiritual darkness was on its way to kill Teiko's son. Yet Lord Sentaro was wrong about at least a few things: I did know when, and I had a reasonably good idea of where. Yet I wasn't certain how much difference this would make when it came to his final pronouncement; that there was nothing I could do. All we had to bring against the coming darkness was my best guess,

Kanemore's sword, a mostly charlatan Yin-Yang magician, and a scruffy band of poorly trained, disreputable priests.

I considered our chances no better than terrible.

⛩

It was obvious there were serious flaws in my plan, not least of which was how we were going to smuggle nineteen mendicant priests into the Imperial Compound. Even with the Captain of the Palace Guard, Kanemore, on our side, the real trick was to get them inside the walls and in position without sending the Court into a flurry of speculation and gossip that would surely leak like a fisherman's net.

Once we had them inside, Princess Teiko's former mansion—now Takahito's quarters—was isolated enough from the rest of the Compound that we could probably maneuver as necessary. But first we had to get them inside.

When I reached the hostel the following noon, I found Prince Kanemore, Kenji, and two of the mendicants whom I remembered from the night the weaver's wife was taken, in hushed but spirited conversation on that very topic. Nidai kneeled some distance away, off Kanemore's left side.

Prince Kanemore nodded at me as I entered the dim room but didn't drop his sentence. "I can secure enough monk's robes to clothe everyone here as members of the Tendai sect," he said. "But I do not think this would work."

"Why not?" Kenji asked. "Enryaku-ji is Tendai. You've already let it be known that Prince Takahito is ill. Say that the priests were sent to pray for his recovery."

"Enryaku-ji wouldn't send this many if the Emperor himself

was ill," Kanemore said. "It will arouse suspicion, and suspicion is something we cannot afford unless we waited until the last moment. I do not think waiting until the last moment is wise."

"I'm afraid I must agree with Prince Kanemore," I said. "It is best if get into position well in advance. Now, simple enough to get Master Chang inside . . . "

"Already done," Prince Kanemore said.

I smiled. "As I said. Still, nineteen?"

"You asked for as many as possible," Kenji said dryly.

"And I meant it, and I am grateful to you all," I said, loud enough at least for my voice to carry through the room. "And the wise course would be to get into position far ahead of time. But I'm afraid the situation requires we wait until the last possible moment, so matters may unfold quickly enough that a suspicion— on anyone's part—will be too late to change what happens."

"That is very risky," Kenji said. "I'll do what I can, but without preparation . . . "

"I don't like this," Kanemore said. "Yet what other option is there?"

"Ano . . . ?"

The voice was small and hesitant. It took me a moment to realize it was Nidai who had spoken. He bowed low and Kanemore scowled.

"Yes?" I asked, "What is it, Nidai-kun?"

"Well . . . " he said, "I realize it is not my place to speak here, but would it solve the immediate problem if the priests could enter the Imperial Compound unseen?"

Kanemore and I exchanged glances; then everyone, ourselves included, had their attention fixed on the boy.

"Of course," I said. "Yet how could this be accomplished? The

Compound is walled and all the gates are guarded. Even Prince Kanemore cannot remove a detachment from any of the gates without attracting unwanted attention."

"There is another way. The north gate of the Compound is seldom used and borders a wooded area. There's a large *sugi* whose branches slightly overhang the wall there. It would be a simple matter to lower oneself from the branch."

"How do you know this, if I might ask?"

"I've seen it before," he said, bowing even lower.

I smiled. "Nidai-kun? The truth, remember?"

I heard him sigh. "Very well. I used that avenue, once or twice."

"Thief," Kanemore muttered, but Nidai denied this vigorously.

"No, Your Highness. I took nothing, I swear. It was just . . . well, she was so pretty. I had never seen anyone like her before."

Kanemore frowned. "She? Who?"

Nidai was blushing furiously. "I do not know her name. Her home was not far from the wall. I could see her from the tree sometimes, taking the air on her veranda with her servants. At other times I came closer just to see her. I swear, nothing more."

"By the north wall . . . " Prince Kanemore looked confused for a moment, and then his eyes went wide. "Princess Ai?" Kanemore's eyes glistened, and I knew it was taking every scrap of restraint he possessed not to burst into laughter.

"Is that her name?" Nidai asked. "It's a pretty name . . . "

"If she ever finds out you've been spying on her, you'd rue the day you ever heard it," Prince Kanemore said sternly.

"You . . . you won't tell her, will you?" Nidai pleaded. "I swear I meant no harm."

Prince Kanemore kept his voice gruff with obvious effort, and now I was trying not to laugh myself. Well enough to appreciate Princess Ai's beauty from a distance for she was, by any measure, a handsome woman, but the closer one got the less enthralled one might be. She remained one of the Emperor's principal wives, but even he did not visit her more than once a month or so; an arrangement apparently agreeable to both of them.

I turned to Kanemore. "I assume he's telling the truth about that tree. Were you aware of this?"

"Certainly. I tried to get the branches pruned more than once, but Princess Ai wouldn't hear of it. Said it would spoil her view." He turned to Nidai. "That area is heavily patrolled. How did you manage to do this without getting caught?"

Now Nidai smiled. "The guards keep a consistent pace. All one need do is count ten fingers ten times from the last patrol to the next. They never vary more than the time you can count one hand."

Kanemore grunted and I could tell he was impressed despite himself. "I'll make a note to vary those patrols . . . tomorrow."

"Even so," Kenji said, "we're talking about the difference between one boy and nineteen men. Even if we all get in, I doubt any of us are as nimble as our young Nidai-san here. We'll never be able to climb back out."

"If we succeed, it will not be an issue," I said. "If we fail . . . well, it will not be an issue either."

Kanemore rose. "Tonight two of the guards will be ill. Furitake and I will take the northern patrol ourselves. There's no moon tonight, so it's unlikely Princess Ai will be outside. If she is, well, the gods have not smiled on us."

"It's not much time," Kenji said. "We won't be able to move until after nightfall."

I shrugged. "Some time is better than none. Besides, we'll probably need the interval between sunset and dark to get everyone to the north wall in the first place. We still have the patrols from Enryaku-ji to deal with, unless Master Nidai has a solution for that as well?"

Nidai blushed again but kept silent. Kenji shrugged and went to a stack of plain wooden chests and opened the topmost. He pulled out a set of clothes.

"So many of my brothers have seen the worst for so long that they've come to expect it." He held up a fine silk *hakama* and jacket. "I've always wanted to try being a lord for a day."

I turned to the gathered priests, who had watched all this with expressions varying from fear to amusement. "So, gentlemen," I said, "does everyone remember how to climb a tree?"

When their preparations were well under way, Prince Kanemore and I departed separately from the hostel, and met again in the southwestern corner of the city where Takahito's new quarters were announced to be. For the first time, we saw monks from Enryaku-ji on the streets there.

"I suppose it was mere coincidence," Prince Kanemore said, "that now they've shown an interest here?"

"Say rather that certain people may have given them reason to think so," I said, "though the command would not have come from the monks. Surely you will concede that?"

"I hadn't thought it was a subject for argument," Prince Kanemore said.

I bowed. "Just so. Forgive me."

He sighed. "There will either be nothing *to* forgive," he said, "or far too much. I'm not enough of a seer to know which, so I guess we must both wait."

Since Prince Kanemore was supervising Takahito's move to this part of the city, it made sense he come personally to check on the preparations. All appeared in good order and proceeding well; the mansion would be ready for the crown prince by the following evening, on schedule, Kanemore was assured. The workmen and servants were told to expect Prince Takahito and his household before sunset the following day.

On our way back up Karasuma, Prince Kanemore said, "I assume you've already spoken to Lady Snow."

"Yes," I said. "What she's told me confirms what I already suspected."

He looked at me. "We're all taking a terrible risk, Lord Yamada. Can she be trusted?"

I smiled. "No, she almost certainly cannot be trusted," I said, "but that's all right. The crux of the matter is whether or not I clearly understand *why* she cannot be trusted. And I believe I finally do."

"I knew better than to ask," Prince Kanemore said. "And yet I did it anyway. I'm praying that you're far less a fool than I am."

I had no answer to that which would not either insult my friend or worry him any more than he already was. I decided to change the subject. "I'm just picturing all those reprobate priests scaling the wall of the Imperial Compound. One should laugh. I think the alternative is madness."

Prince Kanemore checked the position of the sun. "We'll know soon enough who laughs and who does not."

There would be no answer to that save time. I left Prince

Kanemore at the east gate to make his final arrangements for the coming evening.

For my part, I had done all I could do for the moment. I found a nice shaded spot in the grove north of the Imperial Compound, and to the degree I could force myself to do so I rested and waited. I may have dozed, but only just.

The shadows were lengthening when the first of the priests slipped furtively into the grove. One by one they joined me there and spread out among the trees and bushes so as to be less conspicuous. I moved toward the edge of the grove where it bordered on Karasuma, and kept watch for patrols.

The priests crossed Karasuma in ones and twos, no group larger than three. Kenji himself arrived with the last group and we gathered by the wall. The sun was well set, and the shadows were turning into night. We didn't dare wait any longer. I made certain my sword was secure and led the way up the tree.

I would have preferred that Nidai had been present to lead this part of the operation, but he had other duties. I slipped only once, and froze on the branch like a lizard until I was certain my fumbling had not been noticed within the Compound. When I finally pulled myself on the large branch that crossed the wall, I got my first good look into the area we were trying to reach. The guards were immediately evident, but as one of them was Kanemore, I took no more notice of them. To the right the veranda of Princess Ai's mansion was in clear view.

There was someone standing there.

I almost swore or something else equally foolish before I realized it was only one person, a servant, and she was merely finishing a hastily arranged meal outside. I waited until she had finished and gone back into the house. When the screen slid shut, I inched forward on the branch.

I heard a scraping sound behind me and knew that Kenji had followed. He eyed the branch with some suspicion.

"And how shall we deal with this portion of the plan?" he asked.

"Watch me and have those that follow do as I do," I said.

"Suppose you break your neck?"

I sighed. "Then have them do something else. I'll leave that part up to you."

The descent looked simple enough: one hand to grip the branch, the other to swing forward to a handhold further down, then at the lowest part of the swing, push off on the center of the wall's tiled roof and use that momentum to catch one more handhold an arm's length further down. At that point, we simply had to hold on and let our weight lower the branch as far as it would yield, and then let go. There would certainly be some sound as the branch snapped back into place, but there was a breeze off the western mountains freshening the air; with luck the sound of a swaying branch would be just one among many. I took one last breath and put the plan into effect.

To my utter amazement, it worked.

I dropped farther than I wanted to and rolled, but when I came up nothing was broken or sprained. Kanemore and his companion halted in their circuit to assist the priests who, one by one, dropped into the Imperial Compound like overripe fruit as Kenji herded them up the tree and over the branch. One plump fellow bent the branch a little farther than we expected and shattered a tile on the wall. We cringed as we heard the pieces drop.

"Into the bushes. Quickly!" Kanemore hissed, and the rest of us took cover just in time before two other guards appeared; Minamoto, by the look of them. They were so close I could hear every word they said.

"Princess Ai's household reported a disturbance here," the larger of the two said.

"No wonder," Kanemore answered. "That branch she won't let us cut has just broken a roof tile."

"I didn't think the breeze was that strong," said the other.

"Not behind the wall, as we are. Look up and see how the branches are swaying." It was true, at least for the *sugi*. The main branch was still waving from when the portly priest had released his grip, and it had set some of the others in motion, aided by the wind.

The two *bushi* noted this and, after a few more words were exchanged, withdrew.

Kenji and the last priest quickly made their way down the branch.

"Now what?" Kenji asked.

"It will seem strange if I leave right now," Kanemore said. "Lord Yamada, lead them to Takahito."

I knew the way well enough. I steered the priests through the gardens by the most obscure paths I knew or could remember. We had to dodge only one pair of clandestine lovers, who fortunately were paying far more attention to each other than anyone near them. The priests were about as stealthy as a herd of wild pigs rooting among dead leaves, but we reached the area surrounding Prince Takahito's mansion without further incident. There were guards, of course, but they were all trusted men briefed by

Prince Kanemore. Master Chang Yu and a young Taira page were waiting for us there as well.

"Have you finished?" I asked.

"All in place save the last piece, as you requested. Are you certain the spirit will enter by the eastern door?"

"Almost certainly, as that is the only way it should be able to get in."

Master Chang sighed. "I did warn you about anything touching the other barriers before the trap is sprung. It will be warned."

"On the contrary—it will be reassured. Just be prepared to insert the final piece at our signal."

Master Chang looked dubious but promised to do as we directed. The hole before the threshold was already dug. It would be the work of a few seconds to set the object and complete the circle, though a few seconds might prove far too long.

The priests, without a word spoken, quickly divested themselves of the clothes covering their robes. They looked like tardy butterflies shedding themselves of their cocoons in late summer, to emerge already tattered and careworn. Kenji quickly set to work arranging the priests: four each at the north side, west side, and south. At the east wall by the door only two priests were posted, carefully chosen by Kenji, while four more were held in reserve. When all was in readiness, he reported back.

"My brothers are in meditation now, preparing themselves. How long?" he asked.

"As long as it takes. You hear anyone snoring, kick him."

Kenji smiled. "Count upon it."

I left him there and went inside. A lone figure in rich robes sat, forlorn, on a stool on the dais where once Teiko had kneeled in state.

"Is it happening?" he asked.

"Soon, prince. Be ready."

"I am ready, and I hate waiting," he said.

I could not blame him for that. I wasn't entirely fond of waiting, myself. I was somewhat relieved when Kanemore appeared, but only a little. While there was no one else I'd choose to be beside me in a fight, this was one instance when Kanemore's sword would not be of much use.

"Have you agreed with Kenji-san and Master Chang on a signal?"

Prince Kanemore grunted and tapped the shaft of a bamboo flute tucked into his robe.

I frowned. "I didn't know you played the flute."

"My late mother despaired of my ever becoming a poet like my famous namesake," he said, "but she was somewhat mollified to know I had an aptitude for the flute. I seldom have time to play, though. I thought I would seize the opportunity, as it may be my last."

"I look forward to hearing you play many times," I said, not knowing whether this could be.

Kanemore turned to the Prince. "You understand what is expected?"

"I will not fail," the boy said.

Pray that none of us do.

I went to the door and signaled to the guards. One by one the lanterns around the veranda and on the path were extinguished and the *bushi* withdrew to a discreet distance. I had told them it was to thwart any physical attack that might be mounted, but the truth was there was little more they could do now save be underfoot at the wrong time. Their distance was for our protection, not theirs.

It was, as expected, a moonless night. Without the glow of the lanterns a deep darkness settled around us, and for a time I could not even make out my hand in front of my face. Yet without the lanterns, the stars above shone unimpeded, and my eyes soon adjusted to the darkness. I stood in the doorway, and Prince Kanemore joined me there.

"I know there are men surrounding this house," he said, "and yet I can see no one."

"Perfect. If we cannot see them, then neither can anyone else."

"I'd prefer at least one lantern inside," he said. "It's pitch black in there."

"And if something happened to that lantern, we would be even blinder than we are now."

Kanemore sighed. "As a tactician, I know you are right. Yet I would still like more light." His hand was clenched around his flute.

"So would I, truth be told. Yet I think we will be able to see what we need to see." I hoped that was true, but if darkness was part of the nature of what we faced, there was no lantern we could depend on.

We waited. After a while Kanemore withdrew to keep close to the prince. Soon after, two of the priests fell asleep. I heard a harmony of gentle snoring, then a curse and less harmonious yelps as Kenji persuaded each back to wakefulness. One of the priests in front of the door began to shiver in fear and Kenji was there to calm him. I wasn't sure how long our ragged lines of defense could be maintained, but I suspected it would not be long, even with Kenji's best efforts. I sighed and looked to the northeast.

The stars were going out.

I could see little save that for a moment a star hung there, twinkling in the sky and in another moment, it winked out. I knew that a large black cloud was rolling over the mountains to the northeast, extinguishing the stars as it went. I could not see it, but I could see its effect.

"Our enemy is coming," I said.

I heard Kenji hiss and curse again and his quick footsteps around the veranda as he made one last check on his brother priests. Kanemore heard my warning and joined me in the doorway.

"Oh, my . . . "

I had forgotten Prince Kanemore had not seen the cloud before. I had, and even so I was having trouble grasping the full extent of its magnitude. I also knew it would grow even stronger once it reached the city where the ghosts were waiting. I knew there was no way our simple barriers could contain anything that size. We would almost certainly be overwhelmed. That is, we would be if the size and power of the dark energy were all that mattered.

"We're not going to be able to contain that thing!" Kanemore said. "It's larger than mountains!"

"And yet only one person at a time died," I reminded him. "There is both more and less to it. Trust me."

"With my life," Kanemore said. "I was mad to think this would work, but there's no turning back now."

He was certainly right about the latter. If he was also right about the first, well, we would all soon know. The stars went out overhead, and an even deeper darkness settled down on us. It wasn't simply an absence of light. I felt as if a blanket woven of fear and hatred had settled itself around me. Someone whimpered. It might have been me. I was afraid if I didn't speak now, I might never speak again.

"K-Kenji . . . "

I heard his shouted command; somewhat wavering, but clear. In another moment the two priests positioned at the doorway began to chant a sutra against evil influences. It was, beyond a doubt, the worst, most grating, and inharmonious vocalization of a sacred text it had ever been my misfortune to hear. Yet still the darkness shuddered like a living thing. My head was somewhat clearer.

"Kanemore, to the prince," I said, but it was unnecessary. I heard his slow footsteps as he backed away into the main room, and I followed as best I could.

There were two anguished cries, almost in unison, and then the greater darkness filled the room.

PATHETIC.

I did not hear the voice, I felt it; rather, I fancied, like the head of a drum feels the stick. It was time to speak again. I gathered strength and made certain my voice was fully under my command. I would rather have consigned myself to a festival fire than let our enemy bathe in my fear.

"Welcome, Lord Sentaro."

For a few long moments, time seemed frozen. Then the darkness was a little less diffuse. I knew it blanketed Princess

283

Teiko's former home completely like a black fog, but as it filled the room the darkness concentrated itself and two great staring eyes opened.

"So," I said, "the darkness is no longer content to be blind."

The thing laughed then, and the room shook. I heard cries of fear and dismay from outside and could only pray that Kenji could keep matters under control, for inside all was in the hands of darkness.

LORD YAMADA. I SUPPOSE I SHOULD BE SURPRISED, BUT YOU DO HAVE AN UNNATURAL TALENT FOR APPEARING WHERE YOU ARE NOT WANTED. SO, WHAT DO YOU THINK YOU ARE GOING TO DO?

"I am going to stop you."

The thing laughed again, and again the building shook. From somewhere deeper in the building I heard crockery shatter.

I would continue to address it as Lord Sentaro for want of a better name, but I knew matters were not quite so simple as that.

AT MOST YOU ARE GOING TO SPOIL MY FUN BY MAKING ME KILL YOU, TOO. IT'S A SACRIFICE I AM PREPARED TO MAKE. I WILL NOT WASTE MY TIME OR YOURS GLOATING, HOWEVER. THERE'S A TIME FOR ALL THINGS.

What I had seen in Master Dai-wu's face that day at Enryaku Temple was now all around me. I was neither scholar nor mystic; I did not pretend to understand what separated pure evil from the baser human emotions. The limit of my understanding was that I was in the presence of malice, hatred, and greed, and in a particularly twisted fashion, ambition—not the expression of the things, but rather the things themselves. They flowed around and through me, unimpeded. I felt what Lord Sentaro felt. In some fashion I was what Lord Sentaro was. What he had become. I knew Kanemore was feeling the same, and for a moment I was afraid he had been overcome, as I almost was and would be, if the attack lasted much longer. I prayed to anyone listening: the Buddha, the gods of the city, the spirit of my father, anyone, to give me enough strength.

"Indeed. Prince Kanemore, if you please?"

It was taking everything I had just to get the words out, and I was deathly afraid that Kanemore had already been swept away on the tide of emotions contained in that darkness. In another moment I heard the first piercing notes of Kanemore's flute, and a quick scrabbling sound outside.

MUSIC?

"You said it yourself, Lord Sentaro. A time for all things. Please consider yourself our prisoner."

If I thought the thing had laughed before, I was quite mistaken. The darkness *roared*. In the time that its attention was off me, I could think a little clearer. I knew it would not last. There was a murmur from outside, cries of fear. I knew at least some of the priests were trying to flee.

Get them back together, Kenji, I can't hold him much longer.

I FELT YOUR PUNY BARRIER, LORD YAMADA. IT CAN NEITHER KEEP ME OUT NOR HOLD ME HERE FOR LONG. I HAD ASSUMED IT WAS SOME BIT OF TAT AS PRECAUTION FOR THIS BRAT, BUT WHAT DO I FIND? YOU! MY FAULT, SINCE I DID TELL YOU WHAT I INTENDED. I SUPPOSE IT WAS INEVITABLE YOU WOULD TRY SOMETHING FUTILE

AND FOOLISH. YOU SHOULD HAVE BEEN CONTENT WITH MY VICTORY. ARE YOU READY TO DIE NOW?

"I suppose I must be. Yet, for my own curiosity, will you answer a question of mine, first?"

YOU'RE TRYING TO DELAY ME. IT WON'T HELP.

"Of course I am. I'm going to die, remember? I am resigned. That does not mean I am eager."

WELL, WHAT IS IT?

"When did it start? With my father? Kiyoshi? Yes, I think it must have been him. I doubt my father would have provoked a second thought. Kiyoshi? That hurt you, didn't it? A little?"

Silence. Then, more softly, MY NEPHEW WAS A FOOL.

"Of course he was. Sacrificed to the greater vision. Necessary. You did all that was necessary, did you not? For the glory of the Fujiwara? After Kiyoshi, I imagine things were much easier. Your soul could be no blacker than it already was. A useful attribute."

DO NOT JUDGE ME, LORD YAMADA.

I spread my hands. "That is not for me to do. Did you understand what was happening at first? The first time your angry soul left its body? Who died the first time? Was it Taira no Kei, or another? I think your rage was rather unfocused at first. So many to be angry at. Princess Teiko, certainly, but she was dead. The Emperor, of course, for banishing you. Me, for helping to cause it. I rather think you were like a cat among a flock of birds, striking and killing at random. But that did not last. Whose death served best?"

TAKAHITO'S, OF COURSE.

"But you couldn't simply kill him then. It would look too suspicious if he was one of the very few to die. More and more had to die, so that when the crown prince's inevitable end came, no one would think it was anything more than some unknown god of disease striking at random."

YOU'RE NOT DOING THE BOY ANY FAVORS, YOU KNOW. I SENSE HIS FEAR. I WILL NOW PUT AN END TO IT. HE DIES FIRST, LORD YAMADA. YOU'RE GOING TO WATCH.

"If you insist, but there is one more thing I think you should know—that's not Takahito."

Kanemore and I were both nearly knocked off our feet as the dark spirit that was and was not Lord Sentaro rushed forward. I heard the boy cry out, and then the booming curse as the spirit learned of our deception. "Prince Takahito" whimpered once before the darkness swatted him. He flew through the air and crashed through the back wall.

FOOLS! THIS DELAYS ME NO MORE. NOW I WILL KILL YOU *AND* PRINCE KANEMORE. THEN I WILL SHATTER THIS FLIMSY BARRIER AND FIND TAKAHITO. THE EMPEROR WILL HAVE NO CHOICE BUT TO NAME NORIHIRA AS CROWN PRINCE!

"The warrior monks are your guarantee of this? I must say you have thought of everything," I said. Then I turned to Kanemore. "Now, if you please."

The flute sounded for the second time, then the eerie notes faded into a silence that lengthened through one heartbeat, then another. Then another.

We've lost. They've all fled . . .

"No!"

I heard Prince Kanemore put his flute away and draw his sword.

I clearly heard the whisper of the steel as it left its sheath. Prince Kanemore was a man of his word, in matters both great and small. I knew if Lord Sentaro did not kill me in the next few seconds, Prince Kanemore was going to save him the trouble. I did not move. I had done all I knew to do, gambled and lost. Time to pay my debts.

The drone was so low-pitched that I did not hear it at first, and for another moment did not fully understand what I was hearing. Time seemed to hang in the balance as the sound rose like a tide in an inlet. Deep-pitched, rumbling like slow thunder, the chant rose around us and filled the room, which before then I had thought could contain only darkness.

"Ohmedaohm . . . "

Prince Kanemore did not sheathe his blade, but neither did he strike. He stood beside me, immobile as a statue.

MORE CHANTING? YOUR PUNY RITE OF PROTECTION DID NOT WORK WITH TWO PRIESTS. IT WILL NOT WORK WITH A HUNDRED.

"If you were truly the Master of Enryaku-ji, you would know better," I said. "That is not the rite of protection, Lord Sentaro. That is the rite of exorcism."

Fear was always present in the darkness, but suddenly now I was not feeling it. Lord Sentaro was. I felt his withdrawal like someone had just removed a spike from my knee that I hadn't realized was there. There was a flash of pain, then relief. I felt the walls shudder as the dark spirit that once was a human man threw itself against them. Did the barrier give, a little? How long would it hold?

YOU FORGET I AM LARGER THAN THIS ROOM, LORD YAMADA. THIS SILLY CHANTING WILL CEASE!

The chanting did not cease. It grew stronger, steadier as I heard Kenji's voice, encouraging his brother priests and adding his spiritual power to the wall that Lord Sentaro was battering. The darkness pulled back.

"Your malicious spirit may cover this entire area," I said, "but it is not you. You are here, in this room, *because I called you here* and you were foolish enough to answer. Can a snake's tail strike without a head?"

I could see the power of the chant closing in. It would have taken the entire power of several temples of priests and monks to attack the full extent of the spiritual energy that Lord Sentaro commanded, but unfortunately for him the bulk of that energy was not present. It was outside the barrier.

We, as Lord Sentaro had correctly pointed out, were not.

There was a sudden shudder, but this time it was not in the walls of the house or the barrier. The shaking seemed to be coming from beneath our feet. A barrier was failing, but it was not ours. I felt Lord Sentaro's spiritual energy concentrating as if for one last push, but whether against us or the weakening barrier, I did not know. I decided to tip the scale.

"I said I could not judge you, and that is true. You are about to meet the one who can. I've heard him called Emma-o, and Lord Yama, but he's better known as the King of Hell. Bring him my compliments."

YOU . . .

"Yes. Me. All along. Not Prince Kanemore, not even Teiko. It's my doing, Lord Sentaro. You've lost!"

He struck. I felt the darkness closing in on me, smothering me. I struggled against it, but the power was too strong. I understood then what poor Kei and the others felt as Lord Sentaro choked the life out of them with their own hands. I felt my own two hands close around my throat, and however hard I struggled—there was nothing I could do against it. Even the darkness seemed to fade to something else, something beyond light and dark. For a moment I could see nothing, and then beneath my feet I saw the Gates of Hell.

The true Demon Gate broke asunder and cracked wide, and I saw . . . I saw what no living man or woman should ever have to see. My brain could not contain it, and for an instant I went mad. I saw all the hells, branching one off the other, and knew beyond any doubt or question that one of them was waiting for me.

I heard a howl of fear. I thought it was mine, or perhaps it was Lord Sentaro. I did not know. I did not think I would ever know. My hands were now free, but I felt Lord Sentaro's true grip hard on me. I did not know if I was breathing or past needing to ever again. I only knew what I saw beneath me was rising to meet us.

LET US GREET HIM TOGETHER!

Lord Sentaro was being pulled down through the true Demon Gate, and I was going with him, and there wasn't anything I could do about it.

Teiko . . .

I felt a blow to my side as if I'd been gored by a bull, and any breath I had left was gone. I felt myself falling, spinning into the darkness as—far below me and falling fast—a shadow in the shape of a man vanished into the pit. Then I landed hard and waited for the true pain to begin.

Nothing happened.

After what seemed an eternity, I opened my eyes and took a gasping breath.

Kanemore scowled. "Still among the living, I see. He got away!"

I closed my eyes again. "What did you see?"

"A very strange thing. I saw you, choking yourself, and I could not break your grip. I slammed you to the floor in an attempt to knock the wind out of you long enough to stop it. When I got up, Lord Sentaro was gone!"

"He *is* gone," I said, "definitely. But he did not escape. It's over, Prince Kanemore. We did it."

The fog of hate and confusion that Lord Sentaro had brought with him was lifting by the moment. Prince Kanemore helped me to stand, then dashed out to order one of the guards to check on the real Prince Takahito who currently resided unwillingly in Princess Ai's quarters. Kanemore came back inside and went to check on our decoy.

I finally managed to stand up and then staggered after him, and we found Nidai lying in a heap in the next room, groaning among the tangle of robes that had been too large for him in the first place.

"That hurt . . . "

Kanemore checked the boy over thoroughly, but found nothing broken. "You'll be bruised all over," he said, finally satisfied, "but you'll live."

Master Chang Yu and Kenji rushed through the door. "What happened?" asked the Daoist. "The barrier has collapsed!"

"It held long enough, Master Yang, and thank you. Kenji-san, you did it, you and your disreputable priests. The evil is gone."

Kenji looked at me. "Lord Yamada, are you all right?"

I thought about it and answered truthfully. "No. Perhaps one day I will be, but no. I am not all right."

The guard returned soon with the crown prince, and everyone bowed low while Kanemore whispered to him. I was still looking at the floor when I realized that Princess Teiko's son was now standing in front of me.

"Lord Yamada, my uncle informs me I have you to thank for the passing of this threat."

I bowed lower. "There were many valiant gentlemen here who did as much as I, or more."

Takahito put his hands on my shoulders, and I looked up. It had been some time since I had seen him last. He had grown into a handsome youth, almost a man. He smiled at me.

"Be sure that all will be rewarded with more than our thanks."

Spoken like a true prince. He said other things, too, and I tried to listen, but the room was not as steady as I would have liked and I was having trouble concentrating. I withdrew with the others as soon as it was politely possible to do so.

Prince Kanemore joined us on the veranda.

"Please," I said, "see that Kenji and his brother priests are safely housed for the night. There is much still unsettled in the capital."

"Of course," Kanemore said, then looked at me intently. "Lord Yamada, what can I do for you? Is there anything you need?"

Saké. By the barrel.

Yet I knew nothing would ever be enough. Especially not drink, though that would not stop me from trying.

I smiled. "Nothing, thank you."

I took deep breaths of the cleansing night air. Overhead, the stars had returned to shine as if nothing at all had happened and already my visions of hell were starting to fade like a bad dream. They would never go away, I knew, but I hoped that in time they would be no more than one scar among many.

Now as my senses and understanding began to slowly return, I found myself thinking mostly of Prince Takahito, the young man who would one day be emperor; especially his eyes. How gentle and kind they were and yet how sharp, taking in all, missing nothing.

His mother's eyes.

SHIMO-NO-KU

Two days later, the Emperor sent a swift messenger to the Master of Enryaku-ji with a "request" that the warrior monks be withdrawn.

That wish was obeyed immediately. The patrols ceased and by the fourth day all the warrior monks had left the city, and were on the road to Mount Hiea and Enryaku-ji. Some people were sorry to see them go.

Master Chang Yu was not one of those. He politely refused our offer to accompany us on our coming journey to the temple.

"Such places are not for such as me," he said. "It is enough that those infernal monks are gone. If there are greater matters to settle, for my reward I ask only that you please leave me out of them."

It occurred to me Master Yang was far wiser than he sometimes appeared. "So be it," I said. "And thank you."

"Feh. It was strictly for the sake of my business, you understand. I'm too old to find a new trade."

"Of course."

Most who had served to thwart Lord Sentaro that night were of the same mind. Kenji's brother monks were more than content with the absence of the Enryaku-ji monks, and the gifts of rice and fine new robes that Prince Kanemore bestowed on them on

Prince Takahito's behalf. Kenji was the only one who chose to go with us.

"Honestly, Lord Yamada. I would not miss this for all the snow in Hokkaido."

"I do not believe it will be quite as satisfying as you might think," I said. "But there are matters that still must be settled, so you have the right."

At the appointed time, our procession filed out through the Demon Gate: Kenji, myself, Prince Kanemore, and Lady Snow, heavily veiled. Prince Kanemore had gathered as many *bushi* as he reasonably could, including several detachments borrowed from visiting lords, plus two groups of mounted bowmen from the Minamoto Clan. Lady Snow was surrounded by a very large guard of scowling warriors and was accompanied also by an equally scowling Nidai, who gripped his staff as if he would bash the first man to raise a hand against her to within an inch of the wretch's life and beyond.

"Really, Highness," I said, "she's more a danger to herself now than anyone else."

"That she feels her guilt is only just," Kanemore said, "but does not mean I will take any chances. You know my intent with regard to Lady Snow."

I sighed. I did indeed. I think Nidai did, too, and that was one reason he gripped his staff so tightly. What was to follow wasn't going to be pleasant for anyone, myself included. Yet an accounting had to be made.

Prince Kanemore walked beside me. He kept looking straight ahead as he spoke. "Now what's this nonsense about solving the riddle of these attacks by reading *The Tale of Genji*?"

"Actually, I *hadn't* read the tale. That was the problem. No ordinary ghost could do what Lord Sentaro was doing. A true ghost is usually a faded thing, inspiring terror or pity, but not actually dangerous except in special cases. An *ikiryo* is different."

"How so?"

"An *ikiryo* is a living spirit unshackled from its flesh and thus far more powerful. Unlike myself, Lord Sentaro knew about the Lady of Rokuji in the romance, and thus understood what was happening to him when this . . . tendency first appeared. He learned to control it, or so he thought. Yet his spirit-form was powerful enough that he could absorb the spiritual energy of any ghost he encountered and temporarily add it to his own. That is also why most of the attacks were in the areas closest to the Demon Gate."

"Ah. So when he learned we planned to move Takahito . . . "

"Precisely. As you heard him say, Takahito was always his true target, and in the southwest Takahito would be safe indefinitely; even as an *ikiryo*, Lord Sentaro could not muster enough power so far from the Demon Gate with so many fewer ghosts to feed it. Yet when I learned Lady Snow had been directed to keep me away from the capital for four days, and nothing had happened for three, I knew the attack had to come when it did. He had already waited as long as he dared."

"Again, we see what Lady Snow must answer for."

Clearly he wasn't going to be swayed easily. I sighed. "You once asked me if there was anything you could do for me."

Prince Kanemore smiled a grim smile. "And I meant it. Ask me for anything . . . except Lady Snow's life."

"I merely ask I be given a chance to speak before you take her head."

"If you wish, but you know I won't change my mind."

"I also know you are not a fool, and only fools never change their minds. Besides, once you do take Lady Snow's head, there is no giving it back. You may find that is more of an inconvenience than you now believe."

Kanemore grunted but otherwise kept his opinion to himself. We arrived at the temple complex to find the great halls, outbuildings, and barracks all deserted. Enryaku-ji looked like a temple of ghosts.

Kanemore almost growled. "The monster! He's fled!"

The voice answering sounded both weary and resigned. "No, Highness. The monster is here."

Master Dai-wu stood in the doorway to the main hall. He appeared to be waiting for us. I rather imagined he would be. Two of Kanemore's *bushi* remained with Lady Snow. The rest spread out at a command from Prince Kanemore and secured the area around the temple. Master Dai-wu regarded this as placidly as an ox in summer grass.

"Where are your warriors?" Kanemore asked.

"I have sent them into the mountains to meditate. All of them, along with the lay brothers. The nuns are in seclusion at my command, reading a *sutra* for the health of the Emperor. Do not worry, Highness. They will not be done until well after our business here is concluded. I thought this might be more agreeable for everyone."

Calmly and with great dignity he walked down the steps to meet us there on the broad path before the main temple wall. "I assume you will wish to be outside the temple precinct proper before proceeding," he said. "For all its involvement in this unfortunate matter, I think Enryaku-ji deserves at least that much courtesy."

Prince Kanemore looked more and more puzzled by the moment. I was trying not to smile, but at the same time I knew the folly of allowing this particular pot to simmer for too long.

"Then let us get started," I said, before Prince Kanemore could get it into his head to act summarily which, so far as he was concerned, would settle all debts and answer all questions. I wondered if there had ever been a time when I believed that anything—anything at all—could be settled in as simple an act as cutting off a head—not excluding a head that deserved to be cut off.

"Even the Chief Priest of the greatest temple in the land is answerable for a charge of murder," Prince Kanemore said. "As I have been authorized by the Emperor to act on behalf of the Minister of Justice, let us proceed."

Authorized, no doubt, because the new Minister of Justice didn't have a clue about anything that had happened in the last few weeks, and the Chancellor knew better than to interfere. The Emperor, I suspected, had only a vague understanding himself but trusted Kanemore and depended on him to deal with the matter. I intended to help Prince Kanemore do that very thing, though convincing him of what needed doing might be difficult. I produced two cushions from my bundle and placed them side-by-side.

"If Your Immanence and Lady Snow would be so kind as to kneel here on the path?" I asked.

One of the *bushi* reached for Lady Snow's arm, but I glared at him and he stepped back. Lady Snow came forward alone and kneeled with great dignity. Master Dai-wu joined her there.

"Lady Snow," Prince Kanemore said. "You are guilty of assisting this man in the murder of several people, including the noblewoman Taira no Kei. Do you have anything to say?"

She bowed. She was weeping now, and her voice was so soft we did not hear her at first. Kanemore asked her to repeat what she had said and she answered again, louder, clearer: "I want to die."

No doubt.

Master Dai-wu looked unhappy. "Prince Kanemore, may I speak now?"

"You will be allowed to speak in your turn, Immanence. Lady Snow is my first concern," he said.

He bowed. "I understand. It is on her behalf I wish to speak."

Prince Kanemore looked puzzled. "Very well."

Master Dai-wu smiled at the veiled woman beside him. "She did no more than I demanded of her. I held power over this woman and I abused it. Do with me as you will, but spare her. She has harmed no one."

"True enough, but she is guilty nonetheless," I said. "In many ways more so than yourself, Immanence. She made bad decisions, whereas I don't think you ever had that chance."

Prince Kanemore frowned. "Lord Yamada, what are you talking about?"

"You promised me permission to speak before Lady Snow's head was taken," I said. "As that is where this delightful conversation is proceeding, I wish to speak now."

"Very well, but please stop joking. This is a serious matter," Kanemore said.

"And I am being very serious. It is your intent to execute the pair of them, is it not?" Kanemore only scowled, but that was answer enough. "Just so. I wish to speak on behalf of both of them."

There was a shadow on Prince Kanemore's face that was growing higher by the moment. "You just said Lady Snow was guilty!"

"She is, of many things. But, strangely enough, very little of what she is accused of. *The Tale of Genji*, remember? I must point out again she was the one who reminded me of it. If Lady Snow was intent on helping Lord Sentaro commit murder, she would hardly reveal his method."

"So you said before. I consider that idea no more than an interesting speculation," Prince Kanemore said.

"There's more, Highness. I was also searching all this time for the reason Kei and the rest were slain. Lady Snow made me understand there was no reason, or at least their deaths were not for any fault or flaw. Not for Kei, nor any of the other victims. This fact was important in light of what I had just learned. None of them, as individuals, were such that anyone would wish them harm. Not even Lord Sentaro."

Kanemore frowned. "If the attacks were the general displeasure of the gods of the city, then there would be no other reason. I thought that explanation quite sensible, even when I didn't believe it."

"It covered the facts as known," I said, "but there was a fact you didn't acknowledge—by then Lord Sentaro had already revealed his intent to me. Now, perhaps it was merely a coincidence those people were dying and Master Dai-wu had named the cause, but I do not believe in coincidences, Highness. So I knew there *had* to be a reason."

Prince Kanemore looked unhappy. "Lord Yamada . . . "

I smiled. "Peace, Highness. I understand why you did not believe me. I only wanted to point out that, once I understood the *method* thanks to Lady Snow, the *reason* why Taira no Kei and the others died was obvious—Lord Sentaro used their collective deaths to mask his true intent. He said as much when he tried to attack Takahito, remember?"

"I do remember," Prince Kanemore said grimly.

"His plan was almost elegant. If he had killed Takahito earlier in the process, the Emperor might have made good his threat to name *you* his heir. By the time Takahito's death finally was to occur, it would just be seen as one of many attributed to the wrath of the gods, thanks to Master Dai-wu's pronouncement, and no more than Takahito's tragic fate. Prince Norihira would be named heir with no further dissent."

I could almost hear the thoughts gathering in Prince Kanemore's mind, rearranging themselves, judging. I knew he was starting to see what I had seen, at least metaphorically speaking.

"One more crime to be laid on these two," Kanemore said finally.

He doesn't like to give up. A useful trait, but sometimes it leads one to places one should not go.

"Please," Lady Snow said. "Kill me."

"No!" Nidai shouted and would have rushed to her side, but I had warned Kenji beforehand and he was ready. He grabbed the boy in a bear hug and held him against his struggles.

"I am willing and ready to answer for what I have done," Lady Snow said calmly. "I only ask you not allow Nidai to witness this. This is no place for him."

"I disagree," I said. "Choices have consequences, and Nidai has been on this particular journey almost as long as any of us. I think he has the right to see how it turns out. Prince Kanemore, please excuse me for a moment."

Nidai was struggling like a cat in a bag and Kenji was just beginning to lose patience.

"Enough!" I said.

Startled, Nidai stopped struggling and I leaned close. "Nidai-kun, one way or another you're going to have to say goodbye to Lady Snow. That is the way of things and nothing you or I do is going to change it. Now, then, you may control yourself like a man and not cost Lady Snow her dignity, or you can be hauled out of here like the child you're pretending to be. What is your decision?"

Nidai glared but finally said, "I will not embarrass my mistress . . . any further."

"Well then. Kenji-san, let him go."

Kenji hesitated but obeyed, and Nidai kept his place, trembling with fear and rage, but firm. I walked back to where Lady Snow kneeled.

"Prince Kanemore requires more reason to alter his decision. I think that is fair. Lady Snow, please remove your *boshi*."

"I can move the veil off my neck," she said, "it will not interfere with the sword."

"That is beside the point. Do as I command."

Reluctantly, Lady Snow untied the strings from under her chin. Her hair had been coiled up within the crown of the hat and was now released to fall down her back, tied with the usual two ribbons she always wore. Her cheeks were streaked with tears but she looked at me now with a face as impassive as a *gigaku* mask.

"Prince Kanemore, you've been listening to her voice for some time now, so I imagine you've begun to wonder about this woman. Does she seem at all familiar to you?"

Kanemore frowned, and then stepped closer. His eyes went wide. "This is Lady Hoshiko!"

"Yes, prince. Taira no Hoshiko, former Lady of the Court and minor wife to the late Emperor. Elder sister of the unfortunate Taira no Kei. I did not know this for certain until we returned from Nara."

"Lady Maiya . . . ?" the woman I still thought of as Lady Snow sounded bitter.

I smiled. "No, she did not betray you. Yet she was taking tea with you when I arrived that day, neither serving nor being served. I suspected you were a noblewoman from the day I met you, and your reaction to Kei's death was a further hint. It was obvious that Lady Maiya knew you as an equal, and that was all the confirmation I needed."

Every word seemed to stab Hoshiko directly in the heart. Her mask crumbled and she began to weep again.

I sighed. "And that's the real reason she wishes to die, prince. Not because she is guilty of murder or even attempted murder, in my case. Rather it's because of Taira no Kei and Fujiwara no Kiyoshi. Because she now understands she let her desire to escape her family's will cozen her into unknowingly aiding and serving the very man who had murdered the two people she held the most dear in this world."

"Lord Sentaro?" Prince Kanemore asked. "What hold did he have over her?"

"He threatened to tell her family where she was," Master Dai-wu said. "At least, we think he did . . . "

"I assume Lord Sentaro was also responsible for the exorcism of the spirit known as Seita?" I asked.

Master Dai-wu answered. "Of course. Lord Sentaro recognized the ghost as someone who might reveal his intent. He had a monk from this temple perform the rite. This woman was not involved in that."

That relieved me for reasons I could not quite express, yet now Prince Kanemore looked more confused than ever.

"The matter of Seita aside, why are you referring to Lord Sentaro as if he were another person? And what did Lady Hoshiko's whereabouts at the time have to do with this?"

"I think the first question will be answered shortly. As for the rest, I was not certain at first," I said. "I was able to discover the Lord of Hizen had died and Lady Hoshiko disappeared soon after. I assume she fled."

"But *why*?" Kanemore asked. "Are you saying she murdered her husband?"

"You know as well as I that the Lord of Hizen died of a fall from a horse almost two years ago. He was not murdered."

"It's true enough I wished him dead," Lady Hoshiko said then. "My late husband had no interest in women and was a brute besides. Yet no sooner was his body cold than my family had another arranged dynastic match in mind. I am still young enough. A man would still want me," she glanced at me then and smiled a bitter smile. "I'd lost the man I loved and just become free of one I despised. When I was told I would remarry, I decided I would not. Add family disloyalty to my sins."

"But how did Lord Sentaro find you?" Kanemore asked.

"He recognized her," Master Dai-wu said helpfully, "when he first came to the temple."

Kanemore's frown smoothed away. "Ah. She was lodging at the temple."

"No, prince. She lived here," said Master Dai-wu.

"She . . . ?"

It was my considered opinion that Prince Kanemore's confusion had lasted far too long and was quickly approaching dangerous ground.

"Prince, while it's true Lady Hoshiko deceived me, I must emphasize that all she is guilty of under the law is attempted murder. *I* am the one she tried to kill. I think her life belongs to me. Is that justice or not?"

Kanemore scowled. "I am not entirely certain of the law, but I do know beyond question I owe you a great debt, Lord Yamada. As is within my power, I assign her fate to you. Do with her as you will, with the understanding I expect her punishment to be appropriate."

"I think you will find it so." I drew my sword. I thought I heard Nidai gasp behind me, but I ignored that.

Lady Hoshiko bowed her head. "Please end it."

"That is my intention."

Lady Hoshiko still wore her customary pair of hair ribbons, one near her neck and the conventional one lower down. I cut the topmost ribbon with the edge of my sword, and I cut nothing else. Then, before anyone—especially Lady Hoshiko—realized what I was doing, I reached down and took a strong grip on her beautiful long black hair and I pulled.

As I did, I whispered in her ear, "I knew there was a reason you would not let me touch your hair."

A very long section of Lady Hoshiko's hair came off in my hand. What hair was left on her head barely reached the bottom of her neck. Lady Hoshiko just sat there for several moments, blinking, without comprehension. Then she threw herself on the ground and began to sob uncontrollably. This time Nidai did rush to her side and tried to comfort her. No one interfered.

"As you can see, prince, her hair is cut so it doesn't even reach her shoulders. There is one reason and one reason only that a noblewoman will cut her hair. Lady Hoshiko took the tonsure," I said, "soon after her husband died."

"Lady Hoshiko is a nun?"

"Just so. I believe she renounced the world without her family's permission. Such requests are usually granted without question, but not it seems in an ambitious branch of the Taira family with a shortage of marriageable daughters. That is how Lord Sentaro found Lady Hoshiko. That is how he forced her to do as he wanted. She is already dead, so far as this world is concerned. Cutting her head off as well would be wretched excess, in my opinion."

Prince Kanemore finally grunted assent. "Well then," he said, "that still leaves Lord Sentaro."

"No, Highness. That leaves Master Dai-wu."

Kanemore scowled. "Lord Yamada, please do not say what I think you are going to say. I have already admitted I was mistaken. You were right all along. This is Lord Sentaro and he is a murderer."

"Again, Highness, I must respectfully—and reluctantly—disagree. I was right that Lord Sentaro was responsible for these murders and more besides. I was wrong that this man and Lord Sentaro are one and the same. Look into his eyes, prince, and tell me what you see that you did not see before."

Master Dai-wu merely kneeled obediently where we had placed him, looking at the sobbing Lady Hoshiko with compassion.

"Please, my lords, take her to where she can be attended," he said.

I nodded at Kenji, who came forward and helped Nidai half-carry, half-lead Lady Hoshiko into the temple. I turned back to Prince Kanemore.

"Well, Highness?"

"I see exactly what I saw before," he said.

"Yes, and you do not see what *I* saw before, and never will again. Prince Kanemore, I said once that an *ikiryo* is the living soul of a person. That is true, but incomplete. It is also a manifestation of that person's darker emotions: jealousy and envy, in the case of the Lady of the Sixth Ward in the Genji tale. In Lord Sentaro's case, it was all that and more: hatred, rage, avarice, unbridled ambition. All went into the creation of the *ikiryo*."

"He would have used that power to slay my nephew!"

"Indeed. Lord Sentaro thought he controlled these things, but I believe they controlled him by the end. Still, once he discovered this ability, he poured every dark emotion he had within him to create that evil creature we fought and defeated in Princess Teiko's palace. Thanks to Master Wu, Kenji and his fellow reprobates we trapped it there, and what did we do with it then?"

Kanemore looked grimly satisfied. "We sent it to hell."

"Precisely so," I said, and pleased though I was at the result, the memory sent shards of ice through my veins. "It was no more or less than what he deserved. Yet we must now ask ourselves: if we sent Lord Sentaro to hell, then who is Master Dai-wu?"

Kanemore's scowl deepened. "Lord Yamada, I don't like riddles," he said.

" 'What the lightning destroys, it must first illuminate.' That was what Master Dai-wu said to me, that time at Enryaku-ji. Lord Sentaro was the lightning, Highness. Lady Snow, the lightning's flash, the *inazuma*. Even under the control and influence of his dark self that was Lord Sentaro, Master Dai-wu was trying to warn me. Alas, I was too thick to understand what he was saying."

Prince Kanemore thought about that for several long moments. I think Master Dai-wu was the calmest of us all during that time.

"I was ready to take a head, you know," Kanemore said finally. "After my sister's death, and all my worry and fear for Prince Takahito. All this time forced to do little but wait. I was looking forward to it."

"You still can do so. You have the right," I said. "If you want to risk the sight of Kwannon the Merciful herself descending with all the gods of the heavens in attendance to take this now blameless man's soul to the Mountain of the Blest. Personally, I would not invite that particular embarrassment."

Kanemore sighed. "Lord Yamada, sometimes it is wretchedly inconvenient being your friend."

⛩

The next day we were preparing to return to the city when Nidai came to me and bowed low. "Thank you for sparing Lady Snow's life."

I grunted. "I do not think she is as grateful as you are. What will you do now?"

"I do not know. Prince Kanemore has offered to take me into his service. Yet . . . "

"I know. Whatever she may be: nun, *asobi*, or Lady of the Court, you do not wish to leave Lady Snow. Understand this, Nidai-kun—she is leaving *you*. Where she is going now, you cannot follow. You may visit from time to time. If you continue your education as Prince Kanemore will arrange, and if Lady Snow would approve, then you may learn to write letters to her with proper poems included. I think you should. I think she would like that. But that is all you can do. I think you will serve her best now by doing well and not disgracing her instruction."

He smiled. "Yet now I must serve her in at least one more matter—she wishes to see you before you leave, Lord Yamada," he said. "Will you come?"

I thought about it. "I do not think I should. But I will."

Nidai led me to the main hall and then withdrew. I found the woman I had known as Lady Snow kneeling in prayer there in the plain garb of a nun. She turned as she heard me approach and lowered the hood of her robe.

"I really was an *asobi*, for a time," she said. "I had the skills, and I did not mind the duties. Yet there was too much chance of meeting someone I knew or who knew me. I thought I would be safe under the veil, even so near as Enryaku-ji. Foolish, wasn't it?"

"You wished to see me?" I said.

Her smile was hesitant, like a flower uncertain of its blossom. "No, but I did not think I could let you go without an apology.

Though any apology seems inadequate considering what I tried to do to you . . . and for what I succeeded in doing."

"You told me the truth, believing it was a lie. Now you know that truth, and I know my father's honor was falsely taken yet can never be restored. I think it's fair to say Lord Sentaro has had a measure of revenge on us both."

"And what of your revenge on me, Lord Yamada? I behaved foolishly. First I broke my vows with you, and then I betrayed you. I thought my reasons were good, that I understood what I was doing . . . clearly, this was not the case. Why did you let me live?"

"Because once I had a dream of a young girl who died too soon. She offered me tea and then asked me to be kind to her sister, who was in pain. As there was little else I could do for her, I did not want to refuse."

She did not look at me. "And that is the only reason?" she asked.

It wasn't and I think she knew it, but nothing would or could be said of that now. "It is reason enough. I took your ignorance, as I said I would. I have no need of your life, Lady Snow, but I think you might still have some use for it."

The tears had returned to her eyes. "Why?"

"So that you can still have what you say you wanted. A choice." I nodded at her shaved head. "Does this mean you've made that choice?"

She smiled a wan smile. "As you said, 'choices have consequences.' I have made too many bad ones. I must pray for my poor sister for as long as I can, as well as for Kiyoshi. I have failed them both, and yet I must try to live so I may yet atone for what I have done. I do not know if I have the strength."

"Then I think you've chosen more wisely now than you have in the past. May you find that strength, Lady Snow. And if you have any left over . . . "

"Yes?"

Distracted by a sudden memory, I did not answer right away.

Death is easy, Lord Yamada. What comes after is the difficult part.

Seita's words came back to me and for a moment I was once more staring into Hell. I looked away.

"I once had a rather unusual associate. His name was Seita, and he sacrificed a great deal on my behalf. If you have any reason to think well of me in the years to come, please pray for him as well."

I wanted to add "pray for me, too" but I think Lady Snow had more than enough of a burden to carry as things were. We left Kenji and Nidai behind to see that Master Dai-wu and Lady Snow were cared for until they were strong enough to decide for themselves what paths to take. Perhaps Lady Hoshiko would come to terms with herself. Perhaps Master Dai-wu would become, arguably, the greatest caretaker Enryaku-ji had ever known; or perhaps one or both of them would still choose suicide. I did not know.

I tried not to care.

Nidai had a place with Prince Kanemore, if he chose to take it. I rather thought he would, though for a while and perhaps for the rest of his life part of his mind and heart would be at Enryaku-ji.

For my part, as soon as we returned to the city I took my leave of Prince Kanemore and returned to my rooms at the Widow Tamahara's. From there I went directly to the wine shop in the front, and I proceeded to drink; one jar after another, just as in times past. The Widow Tamahara approached me at one point and I simply smiled.

"The rent, Tamahara-san. I have not forgotten. Soon, I promise."

But not that night, nor for many others after it. For a time I tried to forget everything: Princess Teiko, Lady Snow, Lord Sentaro, Hell. When that didn't work, I used the drink instead to help convince myself that all the things I desperately needed to believe were actually true.

I tried to believe Princess Teiko had been right to do as she did, that Prince Kanemore and myself had fought in a righteous cause and helped her accomplish a fine thing, a noble thing, and history would prove it so. First, in the continued decline of the power and influence of the Fujiwara, and second in the glory to come in the reign of Crown Prince Takahito, one day to be known to generations now unborn as his Imperial Majesty, Sanjo II.

My son.

GLOSSARY OF TERMS

asobi: A female entertainer, often also a courtesan.

baka: A general insult. Usually translated as "idiot," but with connotations of being uncouth and wild, like an animal.

eejean: Literally, "beautiful person," usually applied to a female.

boshi: A hat.

bushi: A warrior. Later this would refer to *samurai* specifically.

emishi: An indigenous people usually identified with the modern Ainu.

gaijin: Literally "outside person," a foreigner.

Genji Monogatari: *The Tale of Genji*. Written by a court lady in the tenth century. Widely considered to be the first novel.

geta: A type of wooden sandal.

gigaku: A type of dance/drama performance, believed to have been imported from Korea in the seventh century, but now extinct.

hakama: Loose-fitting trousers.

hashi: Chopsticks.

-hime: Honorific for a high-ranking female, usually a princess.

hojo: The abbot or chief priest of a Buddhist temple.

ikiryo: A "living ghost," essentially an aspect of an individual that detaches itself from that person to attack a romantic rival or enemy. Mentioned in *The Tale of Genji* by Murasaki Shikibu.

inazuma: A flash of lightning.

junihitoe: Literally, "twelve-layer robe." A formal style of clothing worn by ladies of the court.

kami: A divine spirit, roughly equivalent to a god.

kami-no-ku: The "upper phrase," or first three lines, of a *tanka*.

kampai: Equivalent to "cheers!" before a drink.

kana: A native script for informal use, as opposed to the more formal Chinese *kanji*.

kanji: Chinese logographic characters, used for formal documents in the Heian period.

kesa: A priest's mantle.

kimono: Literally "wear thing." Clothes.

koi: A type of carp prized for their beautiful coloring.

koto: A traditional Japanese stringed instrument, similar to the Chinese *zheng*.

matsu: Refers both to a type of cup and the wood used to make it, the pine tree.

miso: Fermented soybeans.

mon: A family crest or symbol.

neko-rei: Literally, "cat ghost."

ohayo: Informal, "good morning." A greeting.

oneesama: Formal, one's elder sister.

oni: A specific type of dangerous monster, equivalent to the Western ogre.

onibi: Ghost lights. Small will-o'-wisp-type flames that signify the presence of ghosts.

rei: Ghost/spirit.

sakura: Cherry blossom.

-sama: Honorific, usually reserved for someone of high social status.

samurai: The warrior class of Japan. It became dominant after the Heian period.

-san: Honorific, showing respect to the person addressed.

shide: A paper streamer used in Shinto rituals. It can also refer to a priest.

shikigami: Artificial creatures created by magic to do the magician's will.

shimo-no-ku: The "lower phrase," or last two lines of a *tanka*.

shoji: A screen made of wooden lattice covered with rice paper.

sugi: Cryptomeria, a kind of evergreen tree.

tachi: A long, thin sword originally designed for use on horseback.

tanka: Classic Japanese poetic form of thirty-one syllables. A longer version of what eventually became the *haiku*.

tengu: A goblin, often depicted with a long nose or beak and crow's wings.

yin-yang: A philosophy rooted in both the balance between and interconnectedness of all things: light/dark, male/female, life/death, etc. Probably derived from Daoism via China.

youkai: Generic term for a monster, or pretty much any supernatural creature.

yukata: A lightweight summer *kimono*.

SUGGESTED READING

As I Crossed a Bridge of Dreams: Recollections of a Woman in 11th Century Japan, translated by Sarashina and Ivan Morris (Penguin Classics, 1989).

The Confessions of Lady Nijo, translated by Karen Brazell (Stanford University Press, 1973).

The Diary of Lady Murasaki, translated by Richard Bowring (Penguin Classics, 1996).

The Gossamer Years: The Diary of a Noblewoman in Heian Japan, translated by Edward Seidensticker (Tuttle Classics, 1989).

The Pillow Book of Sei Shonagon, translated by Ivan Morris (Columbia University Press, 1991).

The Tale of Genji by Murasaki Shikibu, translated by Edward Seidensticker (Knopf, 1978).

The Tale of the Heike, translated by Helen McCullough (Stanford University Press, 1990).

An Introduction to Japanese Court Poetry by Earl Miner (Stanford University Press, 1968).

A History of Japan to 1334 by George Sansom (Stanford University Press, 1958).

The World of the Shining Prince: Court Life in Ancient Japan by Ivan Morris (Kodansha USA, 1994).

Hyakunin Isshu edited by Fujiwara no Teika, translated by Larry Hammer (Cholla Bear Press, 2011).

ABOUT THE AUTHOR

Richard Parks has been writing and publishing science fiction and fantasy longer than he cares to remember . . . or probably *can* remember. His work has appeared in *Asimov's*, *Realms of Fantasy*, *Beneath Ceaseless Skies*, *Lady Churchill's Rosebud Wristlet*, and several "year's best" anthologies. Other adventures featuring Yamada no Goji were collected in *Yamada Monogatari: Demon Hunter* (Prime Books, 2013). A second novel concerning Lord Yamada, *The War God's Son*, will be published by Prime in late 2015. Parks blogs at "Den of Ego and Iniquity Annex #3," also known as richard-parks.com.